Brid was staring straight into a giant almond-shaped eye. The eye wasn't moving, nor was it blinking. It was simply there, behind the wall of CJ's room, where a radiator should have been. Brid wanted to scream because, really, the eye had been spying on them through the grille. She even thought it had winked. Concentrating on the fact that her brothers were watching her and she had to act brave in front of them, Brid put out a shivering hand to touch the eye.

"Ahhh!" she screamed, making contact.

There was a pause.

"Cobwebs," Brid said quietly, filling the heavy silence in the air. She grinned. "I'm screaming because of cobwebs." She giggled, and CJ couldn't help himself; he joined her. Finally, when both kids had regained their ability to breathe, CJ went back to the grille and touched what now appeared to be a very large and realistic painting, extending far down an inside wall that seemed to be behind the wall on that side of his bedroom.

"What in the world . . ." began CJ.

"Who in the world?" Brid answered.

They looked at each other, enjoying the moment, and CJ shook his head. Things were getting more interesting in this old apartment—their new home.

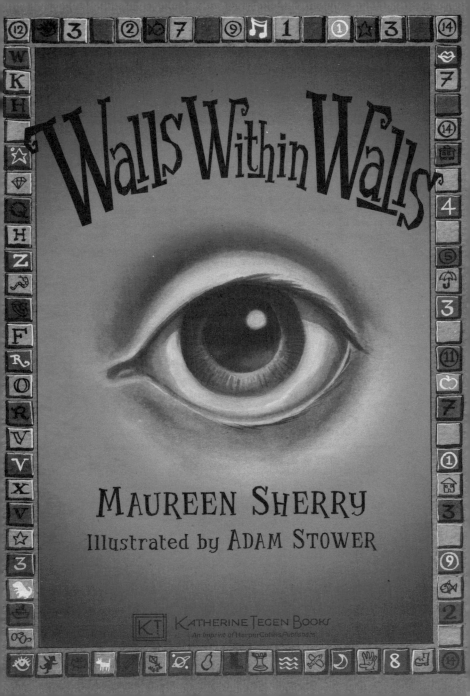

Walls Within Walls

MAUREEN SHERRY

Illustrated by ADAM STOWER

KATHERINE TEGEN BOOKS
An Imprint of HarperCollinsPublishers

Katherine Tegen Books is an imprint of HarperCollins Publishers.

Walls Within Walls
Copyright © 2010 by Maureen Sherry
Jacket/Interior art © 2010 by Adam Stower
All rights reserved. Printed in the United States of America.
No part of this book may be used or reproduced in any manner whatsoever without
written permission except in the case of brief quotations embodied in critical articles
and reviews. For information address HarperCollins Children's Books, a division of
HarperCollins Publishers, 10 East 53rd Street, New York, NY 10022.
www.harpercollinschildrens.com

"The Weary Blues" from *The Collected Poems of Langston Hughes* by Langston Hughes,
edited by Arnold Rampersad with David Roessel, Associate Editor © 1994 by the
Estate of Langston Hughes. Used by permission of Alfred A. Knopf, a division of
Random House, Inc.

Library of Congress Cataloging-in-Publication Data
Sherry, Maureen.
    Walls within walls / Maureen Sherry ; illustrated by Adam Stower. —
1st ed.
        p.   cm.
    Summary: When the Smithfork family moves into a lavish Manhattan apart-
ment building, they discover clues to a decades-old mystery hidden behind the walls
of their new home.
    ISBN 978-0-06-176703-6
    [1. Mystery and detective stories. 2. Brothers and sisters—Fiction. 3. New
York (N.Y.)—Fiction.] I. Stower, Adam, ill. II. Title.
PZ7.S5494Wal 2010   2010009494
[Fic]—dc22   CIP
                                                AC

Typography by Joel Tippie
20 21 22 23   BRR   13 12 11 10 9

First paperback edition, 2012

This book is dedicated to my Poet-in-Residence,
Steve Klinsky

Walls Within Walls

CHAPTER 1

Thump!

The Smithfork kids were sitting on boxes, hanging their legs off the sides and sweating. It was a late August day in Manhattan, the kind their dad said you can taste, when the smells of the city linger in the mouth and nose. It was a day when the heat couldn't seem to find the energy to shove off and go somewhere else. In the window, an air conditioner grumbled fitfully, doing little to cool the bedroom.

Thump!

Brid lobbed another tennis ball at her stack of boxes. They were moving boxes, all different sizes, with the words *Moovin Magic* written on the sides. The kids were supposed to be unpacking, but instead they were seeing who could topple over their stack first.

Nine-year-old Brid was determined to win. Her brothers, twelve-year-old CJ and six-year-old Patrick, were tossing balls at their own stacks, and their boxes were tipping just a little bit more than hers. This made Brid anxious. She hated to lose at anything.

Patrick let one fly and completely missed, knocking over a plastic robot instead. The robot fell off the desk and onto its side, making a big clatter on the wooden floor.

Smash!

Their two-year-old little sister, Carron, was napping in the next room. As the oldest, CJ was not about to be held responsible for waking her up early. "If you're going to miss so badly, dork, don't bother throwing," CJ said. He pushed his wavy brown hair out of his face.

Brid thought about answering with something sharp and mean about how CJ had just gotten cut at tryouts for the soccer team at his new school, but she thought better of it and said nothing. There was such a bad mood hanging in the air. Their new home felt strange, and everyone was anxious about starting at a new school. Brid knew that antagonizing her older brother would end badly.

Brid was a willowy, wiry blond girl; she looked like a strong wind could push her over. Inside, she knew she was tough; she just hadn't been tested yet.

Moving into this neighborhood was supposed to have been a great thing for the Smithforks. It was one of the fanciest neighborhoods in Manhattan, across the street from Central Park and surrounded by private schools. At least, that was what their parents said. In fact, it was the worst thing that had ever happened to CJ. He had a lot of friends in Brooklyn, and he loved his old school. He had pitched for the middle school baseball team, and now he wasn't even on any team. He had given up his wonderful old life for a Fifth Avenue existence he felt only his dad really wanted.

"I mean it. Keep it quiet," CJ said. His voice trailed off.

It was Patrick's turn again. He raised his tennis ball and let loose, taking out the top box of his pile, which was filled with Lego pieces. They tumbled out of the box with a great crash.

Even though he was only six, Pat was tall, still in that in-between place where he sometimes looked babyish and sometimes like a real kid. "Nice, Shortstop," said CJ. Rolling his eyes at Pat was all the encouragement Pat needed to lunge at his brother in an almost serious wrestling move.

Only one year ago the Smithforks were like families in East New York, Brooklyn. They lived in a brownstone house, built in 1880, that, except for plumbing and electricity, had not had much done to it since then. Their mom, Anne, loved architectural history, and she couldn't bear to modernize old buildings. To her, adding conveniences to a building meant losing its original character. "Think of the family that built this house," she would say. "Think how proud they were of this paneled wall, even if it has termites in it." She had painted the old oak floors of their Brooklyn house green, and that's how they had stayed—warped and green—the entire time the Smithforks lived there.

Maybe the best thing about their Brooklyn home was that they had a yard. It wasn't much of a yard, so small their mom said she could mow the lawn with her tweezers. Still, it was a piece of the earth that was theirs, and they could go outside whenever they wanted.

Now they were Manhattanites. It seemed everyone lived in apartments here, stacked one on top of another just like the moving boxes. Worst of all, their mom was too busy to spend her days with them the way she always had. She was meeting with interior decorators and shopping for furniture, and she had hired Maricel, a stern woman from the Philippines, to be their nanny. Maricel was efficient and professional and used to working with families more structured than their own.

Their father wasn't strict at all. Mr. Smithfork used to be poor and now he was rich. After college, when his friends went to work for investment banks on Wall Street, Bruce Smithfork couldn't pull himself away from games—specifically, video games. Not only was he good at playing them, he liked to invent them. He started a company in their Brooklyn basement called LeCube, and his game, the PeeWee, was a big seller.

Then something happened that changed everything. Bruce Smithfork sent the PeeWee to one of his friends for his fortieth birthday. His friend, who worked on Wall Street, liked it so much, he told Mr. Smithfork that his game was better than any game he had ever played, and Mr. Smithfork should take his company public. What he meant was for Mr. Smithfork to sell half of the LeCube company to the public, giving the family a lot of cash and allowing the company to be traded on the New York Stock Exchange.

Within weeks, their Brooklyn living room filled with men in suits. They spread long rolls of paper on the scuffed-up coffee table and punched numbers into calculators. They drank a lot of coffee.

Finally the day came when the men in suits left, and Mr. Smithfork rang the bell at the New York Stock Exchange. The kids couldn't believe it when he came home and said, "Hey, we're millionaires!" He swung their mom, Anne, around, and they all went out to eat at a diner. They ordered whatever they wanted and didn't take home the leftovers. After that, Bruce Smithfork went to work every day in a Manhattan office and wore a suit. He had real employees, rather than his own kids, to test his games on. He had shareholders who insisted his company grow and make more and more money.

Anne Smithfork spent most of her time getting ready to move the family out of Brooklyn. She searched Manhattan for the perfect apartment; she shopped for furniture and curtains and schools for the children. She was rarely around during the day anymore.

Still, until moving day, they were all sort of happy. On that day, Brid lost her appetite and Patrick cried. CJ just kept reading books and said little. Together, they watched as every item they owned was boxed and piled into a moving truck and driven away from their house with its tiny fenced-in yard and the security bars on the windows.

The day after their stuff left, it showed up again in their new home, a Fifth Avenue apartment on the top floor of a historic building. The apartment had gotten tangled in an inheritance battle and remained empty for many years. For the better part of seventy years it had been sitting silent and abandoned, as if waiting for something to happen. It was a huge space, and even though it had been cleaned, it seemed dusty and old. It had bedrooms for all the kids and their parents, a home office for Mr. Smithfork, high ceilings, and mahogany paneling and other fancy woodwork. There were words written on some of the walls in fancy script. Their mom said in the 1920s and 1930s it had belonged to one of the richest families in New York, and there were some rules saying the walls couldn't ever be removed.

All this change was too much for the Smithfork family. It made them anxious, and when they got anxious, they fought.

After the Lego crash, Brid and CJ pummeled Patrick with tennis balls. Patrick fired back, hitting Brid in the face. Brid lunged at CJ, and they both toppled over onto the floor, slamming into a metal grille that covered the room's heating unit. A painful cracking noise came from the wall.

The grille had been framed in wood, and when it was hit, the frame splintered all over the place. For one long moment, the three kids held their breath and watched as the grille rocked back and forth. Then it tipped and smashed dramatically downward, clattering onto the rosewood floor.

"Nice," said Brid to her brothers, in the moment when everyone was trying to figure out how much damage there was and how much trouble they all would be in. She got off the floor and, with difficulty, lifted the heavy metal grille. Neither brother stood to help her. As soon as she had the grille back upright, it slipped from her fingers and banged on the floor once again. She gasped.

"What?" the boys said together.

Brid just pointed. "What is that thing?" she said, covering her mouth with her hands.

Their baby sister started to cry in the room next door.

CHAPTER 2

Brid was staring straight into a giant almond-shaped eye. The eye wasn't moving, nor was it blinking. It was simply there, behind the wall of CJ's room, where a radiator should have been. Brid wanted to scream because, really, the eye had been spying on them through the grille. She even thought it had winked. Concentrating on the fact that her brothers were watching her and she had to act brave in front of them, Brid put out a shivering hand to touch the eye.

"Ahhh!" she screamed, making contact.

In a flash of chivalry, CJ pulled her hand back and examined it for bite marks or amputation, while Patrick ran from the room as if his pants were on fire, waving his hands and screaming.

There was a pause.

"Cobwebs," Brid said quietly, filling the heavy silence in the air. She grinned. "I'm screaming because of cobwebs." She giggled, and CJ couldn't help himself; he joined her. Finally, when both kids had regained their ability to breathe, CJ went back to the grille and touched what now appeared to be a very large and realistic painting, extending far down an inside wall that seemed to be behind the wall on that side of his bedroom.

"What in the world . . ." began CJ.

"Who in the world?" Brid answered.

They looked at each other, enjoying the moment, and CJ shook his head. Things were getting more interesting in this old apartment—their new home.

In the next room, Carron continued bawling, and they could hear Maricel trying to soothe her. Their noise had put an end to nap time. CJ locked the bedroom door, while Brid went over to the eye and touched it again.

"It's part of a painting," she said. "I can see that it goes down a long way, and at the bottom there is some sort of light." She pulled her head back to let CJ look through the narrow space.

CJ pulled a flashlight from a box and pointed it downward. There was silence in the apartment, except for the fussy noise coming from their sister. "The light is actually . . ." His voice trailed off. "The light is on a small hallway or a big shelf. It's coming from the apartment below us."

As luck would have it, Maricel banged on the door just then. "What's going on in there?" she asked.

Brid leaned against the grille, forcing it back into place and quickly swept up the pieces of the shattered wooden frame. CJ swung back the door and looked at Maricel innocently.

"Nothing," he said in his sweetest voice, widening his eyes.

Maricel was a short, round woman. She and CJ were about the same height: five feet tall. Already, CJ knew how to shrink himself down and appear smaller and more deferential when he needed to gain favor with her.

"Um, really nothing," CJ said.

Maricel's face softened. "Watch your sister," she said. "I have to make dinner." Maricel put two-year-old Carron on the bare floor with a loud exhale, before turning and leaving the room. Carron, her brown hair standing on end, looked relieved to be with her siblings. Patrick picked that moment to tiptoe back into the room, his blue eyes transfixed on the grille, the place where the eye was. The older kids could tell that Pat hadn't told Maricel anything about the eye. Patrick just knew about these things.

"Pat, here's the deal," said CJ. "The eye is part of a painting on a big wall behind our wall. There is nothing to be afraid of. There is also a shelf, or hall, far below us with some kind of light coming from it, but it's nothing to freak about."

Patrick just stood there with his eyes wide. He didn't say a word.

"Patrick . . ." said Brid, "we need you to keep quiet about this while we investigate. If Maricel finds out, she'll think she needs to tell Mom and Dad. They'll either take over the investigation or make us promise to mind our own business. Can we have your word?"

Patrick nodded. In the past, CJ and Brid would never have included him in a top-secret investigation. This was his chance to act big, and so that was what he did.

CHAPTER 3

"Urgh!" Patrick was hanging upside down alongside CJ's bed, his feet sticking up into the air, while Brid and CJ each held a leg. His face had turned an unusual hue of purple.

"Let's get him up." CJ huffed from the strain of Pat's weight.

He and Brid hoisted Patrick right side up and helped him to sit on the bed. Slowly his breathing calmed down. "Cool," he said finally.

It was the next morning after breakfast, and Brid and CJ were rehearsing Pat's descent into the space behind the wall. They had been practicing raising and lowering him, to make certain they had enough strength to hold on to him. It was CJ's idea to do a test run.

Patrick was light and lean for a six-year-old, and the fact that he was on the tall side made him more likely to be able to reach the hallway behind the wall. He acted fearless about his mission.

Brid was growing impatient, wanting to try the trick for real. "Are you ready, Pat?" she asked, flicking her hair out of her eyes.

CJ seemed more cautious. "Remember, you don't have to do this if you don't want to."

"C'mon," Brid said. "There's nothing to this—stop worrying him."

Patrick nodded solemnly. "Ready," he said, but inside he was trembling. The opening was very narrow and very dark. He had only agreed to do this to score points with his big brother and sister and show he wasn't a little kid like Carron.

The three children stood at the opening of the grille. CJ reached forward and tore off the construction paper Brid had taped over the eye last night, to keep herself from imagining it was winking at her. "Good, the light down there is off," CJ said. "That means the people below us aren't around. Now is the time."

"You're sure you'll have my ankles?" asked Patrick.

"We will, Pat," said Brid. "Go ahead."

Pat looked straight ahead of him, right into the eye. "Why is she crying words?" he asked.

"What do you mean?" CJ responded.

"This lady's face," Pat said. "She has these funny words in her tears."

"Hey," snapped Brid, "we don't have time for your delaying tactics. Are you scared? If that's what it is, just say so. I can do this for you, too, you know."

"Shush," said CJ. "Patrick, what exactly are you talking about?"

"Nothing," Pat said, embarrassed. "It's just the words she has coming out of her eye. I can't read them." He pointed his index finger at the eye.

"Pat, where do you see words? Because we can't see anything," CJ said.

"In her tears," Pat said.

Patrick had begun to read last year in kindergarten, but it wasn't as easy for him as for the other kids. He jumbled things; he forgot letters. His teachers thought he was lazy. But their mom insisted something was different about Patrick. He noticed more than most people. He had a great memory and an unusual way of learning. Their mom always made Pat feel special about himself, even when the school gave her the official word that he was dyslexic. She taught him to speak up when he noticed things other people didn't, even if he was embarrassed to. This was one of those times.

Though Brid and CJ had shone a flashlight on the eye last night, neither had noticed the fact that the lines around it were filled with tiny letters. To Patrick, they looked like a small stream of tears; to the older children, they looked like wrinkles. But upon close examination, there were, in fact, tiny words.

CJ pulled a magnifying glass from his desk drawer. He thrust a paper and pencil into Brid's hands. "It does say something, but I can't read it. Brid, I'll recite the letters to you, and you write them down."

"Okay," Brid said solemnly. She looked at Pat's face, and his eyes were all twinkly. She felt a twinge of jealousy.

"Here goes," said CJ. "LXOXG space VENXL space HG space LXOXG space LMKNVMKMXL period. ZQM space PTMXE space YKHF space TUHOX space MH space KNIMNKX period."

Patrick peered over Brid's shoulder, trying to figure out what the words meant, thinking it was writing that he just couldn't read. "What's it say?" he asked.

"It's a secret message," Brid said. "Like maybe a word jumble."

CJ was already moving the letters around. He loved puzzles, crime shows on TV, and mystery books, and he knew a lot about clues. "I don't think this is a word jumble, but I do think these are words. Look at the erratic spacing. Maybe it's some sort of skip writing," he said, thinking out loud.

"What's that?" asked Pat.

"It's when you take your message and shift a fixed

amount of letter spaces in the alphabet to conceal the real message."

"I don't get it," Patrick said.

Brid answered. "Say you wanted to write the letter *A*, and you were doing a one-skip message. Instead of just writing *A*, you would write a *B*, or one letter further into the alphabet than you mean. The reader needs to know how many letters you shifted in order to get the message."

Pat scratched his elbow. "Why would someone do that? Why wouldn't they just write an *A* if they wanted to say *A*?"

"Because they were trying to hide the message from . . ."

"From who?"

"Good question. Could be from anyone," CJ said. "Or maybe they just liked puzzles and jumbles."

"So, should we try and read it first?" asked Pat, secretly relieved to not be heading into the wall just yet. "What if it says 'Danger Keep Out'? We'd want to know that, right?"

Nobody answered him. CJ was trying to shift the alphabet one, then two, then three spaces, to no avail. Then he tried it backward, where A=Z, B=Y, etc., and that didn't work either.

Brid was restless. "Let's have Pat look around down

below. We can figure this code out anytime, but who knows when we'll have another chance to be alone here when the people below have their lights off?"

CJ looked up from his scribbling to meet Pat's gaze. "You don't have to do this, Patrick," he said again.

"Brid's right," Patrick said bravely. "It's time."

They all stood in front of the opening in the wall. Brid and CJ each grabbed hold of one of Pat's legs. Ever so gently, they helped him ease himself from a squatting position into a slow-motion dive, face forward, down into the dark hole.

A full ten seconds passed, and Patrick's body started to feel a little heavy to CJ and very heavy to Brid. Finally, they heard, "Mhhh mhit."

"What?" Brid inquired.

"Mhhh mhit," came out again, while Pat's legs seemed to kick.

"Pull, Brid!" CJ said.

"I can't understand him!" Brid said.

"Who cares, just get him up!" said CJ, a hint of panic in his voice.

Together they lifted him up, groaning and straining. As he rose to the surface, Patrick banged his face on the edge of the opening. His arms were tucked in front of him, tightly clutching something. CJ helped him back in through the opening and brushed a bit of debris off his face. Pat spat some cobwebs out of his mouth and began sweeping the dirt off the flat thing he was carrying. He had sawdust in his hair, but his big blue eyes were shining with pride.

"You did it, Pat!" said CJ, hugging his brother, surprised both by Patrick's success and his own relief.

Brid was more interested in the thing Patrick was carrying. It was a dusty, yellowed book, covered with cobwebs.

"What is this?" Brid said, taking it from his hands and opening the front cover. A piece of paper fell out and fluttered to the floor. The edges of the paper were discolored and slightly torn.

"Hey," said CJ, noting the spine of the book. "This was taken out of the New York Public Library. I wonder if whoever took it out is still getting fined."

Brid picked up the paper from the floor, and there, in a large scribble, were the words *Please return*. "Please return?" she said. "Guess someone forgot to do their chores way back then."

"Way back when, exactly?" said CJ, looking in the back of the book. "See, they had no scanners then. The due dates are all handwritten on a card. This book was due April twenty-ninth, 1937."

"Seems like someone was very naughty and does not deserve their allowance," Brid said in a singsong voice.

"Or maybe they thought they could get out of their chores by sticking it on a high shelf where nobody looked?"

Pat said, thinking this was something he would do.

Then CJ said, "I'm not sure the kids who lived here really had chores. Those little rooms in the back of the apartment are servants' rooms. They probably had servants, and returning a library book seems like one of those jobs you would have a servant do."

Patrick and Brid looked at each other before Brid said, "He's right. What's the title of the book?"

"It's *Treasure Island* by Robert Louis Stevenson. Great book," CJ said.

"There are probably a hundred copies of this at the library. They might never have missed it. I wouldn't be too worried about getting it back to them anytime soon."

"But look at this heavy leather cover," said CJ. "Most library books aren't so ornate. It's probably valuable. I mean, it's a pretty early printing."

"We should probably return it," said Pat.

"Return it?" said Brid. "Like, 'Hello, here is our library book and sorry it took us seventy-three years to get it back to you'?"

"Yes," said CJ, "but isn't it sort of like stealing when you find something that belongs to someone else, if you know how to get it back to them but you choose not to?"

"No," Brid said. "Because it's going to look like either we or our ancestors just never got around to returning it. I mean, why bother?"

"I guess I see your point, especially because we'd be giving them back a defaced book," CJ said as he gingerly turned the pages.

"What do you mean?"

"Someone wrote the words *The Seven Keys to* right above the title of the book, *Treasure Island*," said CJ.

"I don't get it," said Pat.

"Someone wrote in pen above the title of the book so that it reads all together, *The Seven Keys to Treasure Island.*" The kids sat in silence, each contemplating what this meant.

"Hey, CJ?" Pat said. "Did you try seven skips?"

"What?"

"To break the skip code, you know, from the lady's eye? Did you try skipping seven places? The borrower of the overdue book seems to have liked the number seven."

"No, not yet."

"Well, maybe you should," Patrick said. "I kind of like the number seven, too."

CJ rolled his eyes. Then he glanced again at the text from the painting. Slowly he skipped seven places for the first word. "LXOXG would become, umm, well SEVEN. Geez, Pat! You're right!"

"Keep going," said Brid impatiently. "Keep skipping seven places."

"Okay, um, VENXL becomes CLUES."

"So it says 'seven clues'; what else?" Brid insisted.

Quickly, CJ went through the other words, scribbling down, "Seven clues on seven structures get water from above to rupture."

"What does that mean?" asked Pat.

"Excellent question, little man," said CJ. "Excellent question."

"Hey, guys," said Brid, "I think we should do as this little piece of paper says. I think we should return this library book."

"It's the right thing to do," CJ said.

"Yes, definitely the right thing," said Pat, happy to agree.

"It's also the only thing I can think to do next," replied Brid, covering up the eye again with construction paper.

CHAPTER 4

Just as the Smithforks were about to leave for the library, a loud buzz sounded from the front of the apartment.

"What's that?" asked Patrick.

"I think it's the front door," said Brid.

"Front door? How can there be a front doorbell ringing when nobody can even get to our front door?" said CJ, suddenly furious. "When anyone wants to visit this apartment, they have to go through a doorman, who then calls upstairs, who then waits for someone to say it's okay to have that person visit. Then that person has to get in the elevator with the elevator man, who takes them to our front door. Nobody just walks in and rings the front doorbell like they did in our old life. Nobody."

Patrick and Brid stared at CJ as the doorbell sounded again.

"I'm going to answer the front door," Brid said simply. She crossed the mahogany-paneled hallway, unlatched the heavy brass dead bolt, turned the elaborate brass handle, and let the enormous, heavy door groan open to reveal . . .

Children.

They weren't ordinary children, the sort who might have come by to watch television or throw a ball around. They were a boy and a girl—about CJ's and Brid's exact ages. They were wearing church clothes, even though it was Wednesday. On their feet they had blue surgical booties, the kind a doctor wears in the operating room. Brid felt rather underdressed in her T-shirt and leggings.

"Hi," she said.

"Hullo. We're so pleased that you have moved in," said the boy. "I'm Lukas Williamson. We're from the other elevator bank in the building, the south side. We live in the apartment on the other side of your living room wall, so we thought we'd come and introduce ourselves."

CJ came up behind Brid, not saying a word, as the girl said, "Hullo. I'm Lily Williamson. So pleased that people our own age finally live in this building. Once we heard you had moved in, we just had to meet you. This has been home for us since we were born, but we aren't around much."

These children had an unusual accent and seemed to

talk a lot, thought CJ. He wondered if they were from England. "Come in," he said. Their guests padded into the apartment, the *swish-swish* of the surgical booties marking their every step.

"Why the footwear?" Brid asked.

"Excuse me?" said Lily.

"Why do you wear those booties on your feet?"

"Well, we don't wear shoes in the home," said Lily, "as Sonia, our housekeeper, likes things extra sanitary. We weren't sure what your house rules were, so we brought our own booties."

"Do you go to Saint James's School?" CJ asked Lukas.

"The local private school?" asked Lukas with a hint of snobbery.

"Yes," CJ said.

"Oh, no, we both go to boarding school in England. Our parents mostly travel, so they think it preferable that we should go to the best schools in the world, no matter where they are." Lukas said this with great enthusiasm.

CJ, Pat, and Brid exchanged knowing glances as they led the way into CJ's room. They all thought the same thing: do not tell these kids about the eye behind the wall.

"Do you know the history of this apartment?" asked Lukas, brushing back his blond hair and hiking up his pants a bit before he sat down on a moving box. Brid thought he acted like a thirty-year-old man instead of a boy of about twelve.

"Not really," said Brid. "Our mom liked it because it was built at an interesting time in New York City—when things were really thriving and changing."

"That's right," said Lily. "Grand buildings were going up everywhere." She ran her hand along the intricate woodwork of CJ's bookcase. "Our parents say it's hard to find places like this anymore."

For a girl of about ten, Lily had an uncanny ability to speak like an adult. She had red-framed glasses and dark red hair held in place by a neat headband. Brid felt squirmy and uncomfortable.

"Our apartments used to be connected, you know," said Lukas. "They were owned by a family, the Posts, of the packaged food empire. They merged with the Huttons, a family that had a banking empire."

"What do you mean, they merged?" Pat interrupted. He had said nothing the entire time the Williamsons were present, which Brid thought was admirable and unlike him.

"A young man from a rich banking family married a lady from the food industry, a family that pretty much invented packaged food for supermarkets," Lily said. "Before that, you had to go to the bakery to buy bread, the butcher to buy meat, and so on."

"Anyway," Lukas continued, "they were married, and at first they lived in a fantastic town house around the corner from here. When the Posts constructed this building, they demolished their old house and rebuilt the entire town house on the top two floors here. They could enjoy views of the skyline and Central Park, while living in one of the grandest apartments in New York City. They were fabulous entertainers and had many grand fêtes here."

Even CJ felt like he needed a dictionary to talk to this boy. "So then years later, when they wanted to sell it, they split their big apartment in two?"

"Four," interjected Lily. "Two apartments on both the twelfth and thirteenth floors. Our living rooms used to be one giant ballroom. When they created our separate apartments, they split it down the middle. That's why your living room is so enormous."

"But we're on the fourteenth floor, not the thirteenth," Patrick piped in.

"Well, they call our apartments fourteen north and fourteen south, but really we're on the thirteenth floor. Nobody would live on a thirteenth floor; people thought it unlucky, so this building goes from twelve to fourteen," Lukas said with a strange gleam in his eyes.

"What do these poems on the moldings mean?" Brid asked as she pointed to the intricate writing far above their heads.

"The Posts adored collecting art and literature," said Lukas. "It was a culturally rich apartment. I'd imagine the poems were just decoration, though we don't have the same sort of detail on our side. You know, a lot of their fortune went missing soon after Mr. Post died in

1937. Because Mr. Post insisted that walls be built in front of the original walls, the search was always focused on them. But everything was searched after his death and before the apartment was split up, and nothing's ever been found."

"Yes," said Lily. "Obviously the fortune was hidden somewhere else."

"Kind of strange it was never found," CJ said.

"Well, the rumor was that someone did find it and kept it," Lily said. "Though much of it would have been difficult to hide: enormous jewels, famous paintings, things like that."

"Oh," said CJ. "Too bad."

"It's really quite a mess in here," said Lily, looking around the room. "Can we help you fix it up?"

CJ hadn't picked anything up after yesterday's wrestling match. Boxes were everywhere, and the room appeared ransacked. Still, Brid thought, what sort of kid was bothered by a mess?

"No, that's all right," said CJ.

"Well," said Lily, "our nanny is taking us to the Metropolitan Museum of Art later this morning. We'd love for you to join us in an hour if you're available. It doesn't open until nine thirty AM."

"That's okay." Brid came to the rescue. "As you can see, we have a lot of unpacking to do."

CJ looked at his sister with relief. Who goes for an

outing with friends to the museum? he wondered. Who dresses up to go to a museum, unless they always dress like that? And why does every kid around here seem to have a nanny? The thought made him shudder.

"One more thing," said Lukas. "Our two apartments share a storage room in the basement. It used to be servants' quarters, but we don't need the space. You can use it as you wish. Our servants have bedrooms in our apartment."

"The what?" asked CJ and Brid together. They remembered their mom saying something about a storage area, but they hadn't paid attention at the time.

"The servants' quarters," Lukas said, obviously having no clue that the Smithfork family didn't have live-in servants. "Most buildings from the twenties had them."

"So what exactly happened in servants' quarters?" Brid asked, pulling out a pink spiral notebook. Brid liked to write things down, and this habit often helped keep the Smithfork family organized.

"Servants' quarters were small bedrooms for staff to live in," said Lukas. "Now people use them to store things. They're in the basement level—no view, or anything. Hard to believe people would let their staff live in such dismal conditions."

"So you say we can use that space?" Patrick asked.

"What I meant is that should you need space to store things, you can use it. You would need to clean it up a bit, as the previous owners, the Post family, left some belongings there."

"Maybe you can show it to us sometime?" CJ asked.

"Yes, with pleasure. Well, good-bye, then," Lukas said abruptly, stretching out his arm to shake hands, while simultaneously swinging his blue blazer over his shoulder. "Until next time."

The kids all shook hands, the Smithforks feeling uncomfortable and formal, the Williamsons looking smooth and used to this.

Two hours later, CJ and Brid were riding the M1 bus down Fifth Avenue to the library. They had told Maricel they had an orientation afternoon at their schools, and their mother had left earlier to meet with a decorator. Without their parents around, Maricel had nobody to check their story with. They felt badly about leaving Patrick behind, but they knew that Maricel could never be convinced to leave Pat in CJ's care.

On the bus, CJ read a book, covered up with a magazine. He was always reading—manuals, mysteries, technology magazines, sports guides, anything. He got embarrassed when other people commented on what he read, so he had learned to never let people see such titles as *How Does Aspirin Find a Headache?* Brid understood why he read in secret, but she still hated that he did it. She liked to know everything that was going on with her family, including what book CJ was reading. She peeked over his *Mad* magazine and thought she saw a poetry book inside. Hmm.

New York City's main library was a huge marble structure that stretched for two whole city blocks and had enormous lion statues out front. "It opened in 1911 and has fifteen miles of shelves," CJ said as the kids stood in front of the massive building, feeling small. "During the Great Depression, the mayor named those lions Patience and Fortitude."

"Why the fancy names?" Brid asked.

"Those were the traits he thought people needed in order to get through that difficult time," CJ said.

As they swept through the revolving doors into the grandest lobby they had ever seen, they had to open their bags to be checked by a security guard. It was then that Brid saw the real title of CJ's book: *Poetry for Dummies*.

"Whatcha reading?" she said innocently.

"Just trying to understand something in my room," CJ said. "You know those poems on my moldings? I'm wondering why they are there."

"You mean, like, what's their story?"

"Like what story the poem is trying to tell the reader," he said simply.

"You don't even like poetry."

"I know, but the guy who used to live in our apartment did."

"That's weird that you care."

"A little weird," CJ admitted. "I mean, he probably just did it for decoration, but still, I like when people can say a lot with the least amount of words. That's one good thing about a poem."

"What do you mean?"

"Like maybe you could say more by talking less," CJ snapped.

Brid just rolled her eyes at CJ as they waited in line to be checked in. People with backpacks, tourists, a lady in a wheelchair—all seemed to move with purpose, knowing exactly where to go. When the security guard took Brid's backpack, she asked him, "Where are the returns?" The guard was tall and big-bellied; his shirt buttons looked as if they might pop.

"Return of what?" he said.

"An overdue book."

"Overdue? Honey, that book must be from somewhere else, because this library is a research collection. It's not a lending library."

"It has to be," Brid said.

"It's not," he said sternly.

Brid stamped her foot, which is not something anyone should do in a library. "It says right here, it's overdue." She flipped open the book cover to show the guard the handwritten card listing the borrower's name, the date it was taken out, and the due date. The name was written in a clear cursive with little flourishes. It read, *Mr. Lyon F. Post.*

The guard pulled reading glasses from the lapel of his blazer and held the book away from him in the way grown-ups do when they read small print.

"Well, I'll be." He pulled a walkie-talkie from his coat. "Shimmy, come in," he said into the radio.

"Shimmy here," a voice answered almost immediately.

"Some kids here with an overdue book from this library."

"Can't be."

"Was due in 1937."

"You've got one slow reader there." Shimmy cracked up loudly at his own joke, while the people in line behind CJ and Brid tsked with annoyance.

"What year did we stop lending?" asked the guard, looking irritated.

"1970."

"Where've you kids been since 1970?" the guard asked, not even smiling.

"Not born?" said CJ.

The guard finally grinned, and spoke into his radio again. "They were not members of the planet Earth at that time, Mr. Shimmy. What should they do?"

A long pause followed, then Shimmy said, "Take it to the head librarian's office, third floor."

CJ and Brid soon found themselves on the third floor, face-to-face with an efficient-looking woman sitting behind a large, clean desk. Her hair was pulled into a tight bun, and she had droopy jowls that jiggled when she spoke. Her name tag read MISS CASSIDY.

"May I help you?" she said, peering at the children over pointy glasses. She rubbed her lips together, as if making sure her lipstick was covering all parts of her mouth.

"We need to return this," CJ said. He expected her to be surprised and thankful. But he didn't expect the reaction he got.

The woman flipped open the book. Thankfully, she didn't look at the inside title page, where someone had written in pen. She simply typed the title into her computer, as if this were a routine matter. When the overdue information came up on her screen, she sat there for a long minute, reading. Then she closed the book and gave the children a meaningful stare.

"Let's see," she said. "This was due on April twenty-ninth, 1937, and today is September first, 2010, so that would be three thousand eight hundred fourteen weeks when we charged two cents per week." Her fingers moved quickly over the calculator. "Your fine is seventy-six dollars and twenty-eight cents, and be happy I'm not adjusting that for inflation."

"Are you kidding me?" said Brid. "It's not ours; we're just returning it! It looks like a valuable book, and my brother thought we should bring it back. We shouldn't have to pay this!"

"So you're saying you found this? This is a rare edition, so I'm sure the police would be interested in knowing where you 'found' it," Miss Cassidy said.

CJ was dumbfounded. "Let me get this straight. We do a good deed and return something, and now we have to pay for it?"

Brid piped in, "What if we were just to take it back home, and then we could keep both the book and our money. You don't make any sense."

"Well, you could leave with the book," the woman snipped, "but then I would have to call security, who would in turn call the police. Or you could return it, pay the fine, and collect the package that was to be given to the people who returned it. Pick your poison," she added, snapping her gum and punching some keys on her computer.

"Package of what?" asked CJ.

The woman didn't look up from her screen as she replied. "When Mr. Post borrowed this book seventy-three years ago, he left something behind at the checkout counter. According to our records—which are impeccable—he left word that the package should be given to whoever returned the book, whether he or someone else. His wife was very generous to this library, so we couldn't just ignore his simple request. Now that you are returning the book, I guess you are entitled to the package—if, that is, the fines are paid up." She pushed up her glasses and waited.

CJ said, "Ah, we need a minute here." He motioned to his sister to step into the hallway.

"She is just trying to get our money," said Brid.

"Either that, or she is playing some game with us."

"We don't have that sort of cash anyway," said Brid.

CJ looked at the floor.

"Do we?" Brid asked.

"Mom gave me ninety dollars today to buy two sets of Saint James's school uniform."

"What if you bought only one uniform?"

"Hello, did you hear me say I only have ninety dollars? One uniform is forty-five dollars, and the fine is seventy-six dollars and twenty-eight cents."

Brid was silent.

"Brid, did you bring some money?"

"C'mon, I have to get my uniform, too!"

"You are so busted. Give it up. We'll both just have one uniform," CJ said.

"And we'll both be doing laundry every night," Brid replied.

They grinned at each other and returned to the woman at the desk.

"Good thing you came back. I'd hate to have to call security," she said.

"Aren't you curious where we found this book?" Brid asked.

"Not at all," she said, though the kids didn't believe

her. How strange it was that they were about to fork over so much money for someone to take a rare book off their hands.

Miss Cassidy took their cash and disappeared into another office. Ten, then twenty minutes ticked by, and the children wondered if they had been duped.

Just as Brid was about to go looking for her, the woman returned, holding a package the size of a large book. It was wrapped in yellowed paper and red-and-white string, the type a bakery wraps its boxes in. She looked reluctant to give it to the children.

"Listen, kids, I'm not looking to make any friends here, but there is something you two should know. Something fishy is going on with the Post estate. An elderly man has been here many times over the years requesting this, and believe me, I'd much prefer to give it to a gentleman than you two. But he never had the book, and these instructions are crystal clear," she said, nodding at her computer screen. "No *Treasure Island*, no package." She shrugged.

"Who else knows about the package?" CJ asked.

"How should I know?" Miss Cassidy said snippily. "Just some old guy, says he is a relative of the Post family. It's possible that someone working here let it slip that this package was here. I have to say, something about giving this to you children doesn't seem right either." She sniffed. "What's going on here?"

"We don't know," said Brid. "We really don't know."

CHAPTER 5

Sitting on the steps of the magnificent library, Brid held the package to her chest. Something felt sinister in the air, and everyone around her suddenly seemed suspicious. The guy selling hot dogs was looking around too much. A construction crew taking a lunch break acted like spies in a movie.

Brid said, "Patrick was the one who found the book. Let's go home and open the package there so he can see it."

"Are you kidding me? Since when do you care so much about Pat's feelings?" CJ said. "Nobody is looking at us. Let's open it now."

"CJ, something is telling me to go home," Brid said ominously.

"Nobody is watching, and nobody is thinking about

some fraidy-cat nine-year-old and her package. Open it!"

"I'm not afraid," Brid said through clenched teeth. "I'm cautious. Can we at least go somewhere discreet?" She walked over to the north end of the stairs, at the base of a giant cement urn above the lion statues. She sat down and gingerly began pulling back the brown paper, which was glued down. "It looks like a seventy-year-old loaf of bread from the bakery," she joked nervously.

"Yeah, that we paid seventy-six dollars and twenty-eight cents for!" CJ said, feeling a little guilty about making his sister do something against her will. "Look how yellow the glue marks are."

"Probably from before the days of Scotch tape," Brid muttered.

"Actually, Scotch tape came along in 1930, so I'm not sure why Mr. Post didn't use it," said CJ.

"Only you and Mr. Scotch would know that."

"Actually the guy who invented Scotch tape was named Richard Drew. Can you open that thing a little faster?"

Brid was never really surprised about the facts CJ had in his brain. She sometimes thought it was like having a computer follow her around.

"Brid, pick up the pace!"

Irritated by her bossy brother, Brid pulled what seemed to be another book from the packaging, but something metal fell out, too, clanging its way down the steps. The object stopped falling when it landed near the giant pedestal that held one of the stone lions. CJ went barreling after it.

"CJ," Brid called to him. "Here's a note from Mr. Post! I mean, I think it is, and it's addressed to whoever has this package! That's us! And this letter is written on the same stationery the other note was written on."

CJ ran back up the stairs, panting and holding the metal object. "What other note? What are you talking about?"

"I'm saying there is a note inside this book that's written on the same stationery the other note was on, the note that said we should return *Treasure Island*." Brid held up a yellowed piece of paper and a slender leather-bound book. "Listen to this," she said, reading aloud.

Dear Treasure Hunters (hopefully Eloise and Julian),

Welcome to the last will and testament of Lyon Post, also known as your father. I was going to leave you your inheritance the way everyone else does, wrapped up with a bow in an office of law, but that would be boring! Think of our rather unconventional family, our life of puzzles and poetry. Think of how much we love architecture, history, New York City, and a good mystery.

So, my sweet children, instead I have left you one final treasure hunt through some of our favorite places in New York. The directions for the hunt are all at home, so this will be easy for you. I just wanted you

to have fun with it. Think of me when you visit these
magnificent structures again, and know that I wish I
were with you.

In this book you will find poems we all loved. Just go
to the places they are about and follow the instructions
at home. Revisit our favorite sites, my children, revisit
the works of Hughes, Millay, and others. Let them
lead you long after I am gone. Let them lead you to my
second greatest treasure after yourselves, and know that
I still reside inside your hearts.

With great excitement,
Mr. Lyon Post (your father)

"So," said Brid, disappointment in her voice, "we paid all that money to read poems about New York City? How boring! And who are Hughes and Millay?"

"They're poets. I guess they're some of the poets in this book," CJ said as he flipped through the pages. "But this letter says it's a puzzle that leads to his treasure."

"You mean his treasure was never found? That was seventy years ago; of course it was found." Brid's voice was rising.

"Mr. Post said these poems are about places in New York that he liked to visit with his children," said CJ, still flipping pages. The book seemed to contain just a few poems, each printed in an ornate script. "And those places will lead to his treasure. We just have to find them."

"Don't you think someone has already solved the mystery?" Brid asked.

"Maybe not. They didn't have this book, and they didn't have this," CJ said dramatically as he slowly unfolded his fingers from the metal object that had rolled down the steps. It was a large brass key. "Mr. Post's collections were famous. If someone found them, people would know about it. Honestly, Brid, I think this was never solved, and all because . . ." His voice trailed off.

"All because his kids didn't return his library book?" Brid asked.

"Maybe it's really that simple."

"That'll teach his kids to do their chores." Brid laughed. "But why would he make things so complicated when he wanted his kids to have their inheritance anyway?"

"I don't know. I guess he just wanted them to obey him or something. I mean, it makes sense now why he wouldn't want the walls of the apartments to be renovated. He obviously needed the spaces behind the walls."

"So you think the treasure is in the walls?" Brid asked. Then, changing the subject, she said, "I wonder what Eloise and Julian were like when they were our ages. And I wonder what happened to them."

"I wonder why they never returned that book."

"We don't always do what we're asked. I get that," Brid replied.

"I wonder what this key is for," CJ muttered. "You know who we need to ask, right?"

"I was thinking the same thing," Brid said.

"We've got to get to them before they go back to boarding school," said CJ.

CHAPTER 6

When they returned home, Ray, the afternoon elevator man, was on duty. His thick eyebrows grew straight across his face and touched in the middle, as if someone had drawn a hairy gray line above his eyes. Brid and CJ quickly returned to the apartment and collected Patrick, who was playing with his Legos, looking bored. Then they summoned the elevator again.

"Take us to the Williamsons, please," said Brid when Ray appeared.

"They expecting you?" is what Ray asked, but because his words all ran together, it sounded like, "Theyespecktinyou?"

The kids had started to call Ray's talk the "uniword," a sentence all pushed into one long word. So when CJ answered, "Not sure," he said, "Nahsure."

Apparently that was good enough for Ray. He rotated the round brass throttle to the right to engage the elevator gears, and they lifted off.

On the south side of the building—the fourteenth floor—Ray rotated the wheel left, pushed the sliding brass door right, and leaned on the lever to finally pull back the wooden door to reveal the Williamsons' apartment.

"Haveaniceday," came the uniword, and in an instant Ray was gone.

The Williamsons' apartment, like many others, used the space right up to the elevator door as part of their entrance. So when the elevator door opened, the Smithforks found themselves immediately in someone else's home—someone who wasn't expecting them.

This apartment was much grander than theirs. The walls were paneled in wood that smelled like oil. There were statues that seemed to belong in a museum. This was not a home where footballs were tossed around. Pat's eyes grew wide and frightened, and he motioned back toward the elevator, pointing his finger to indicate he thought they should leave before they were found out.

"Hello?" Brid called softly. She wished Ray hadn't left them, and that she could go back home and call the Williamsons properly, but it was too late for that. A small white dog came running at them with the ferocious bravery of a rottweiler. It stood about ten inches off the ground and appeared to have fur that was blown dry. It jumped at Patrick with its teeth bared, easily reaching his thighs.

"Whoa, killer!" said Pat, raising his arms and stepping backward, away from the tiny beast. It was a bad move. He bumped into a stone pedestal that held an enormous and expensive-looking stone statue. The statue fell forward. For one horrifying second, it leaned, as they all realized it was about to smash on the unforgiving stone floor.

"Watch it!" yelled CJ. He dove toward the statue, grabbing it in a bear hug and landing on his knees. All three children exhaled in relief, and the little dog stopped yapping and ran back down the hall, his poofy fur forming a halo around his head.

Just as CJ was about to say something sharp to Pat about watching his clumsy self, Pat preempted him by giggling. Brid soon joined him, as they both realized that CJ was hugging a bone-white, headless, naked woman made of stone. It was at this moment that a woman came padding down the hall toward them. She did not look pleased.

"Hello?" CJ said in a meek voice, unsure where to begin explaining.

The woman was dressed in a gray-and-white maid's uniform. Her silvery hair was constricted inside a hairnet. Her legs were thick inside her stockings, and her feet were covered in the same blue surgical booties that the Williamson children had worn to the Smithfork apartment. Brid seemed to remember Lily saying their housekeeper was named Sonia.

"Where are you going with that statue?" she hissed in an accusing voice.

CJ was trying to get off the floor while not dropping the headless naked woman. "Um, my brother fell into the pedestal when the dog came running at him, and he knocked the statue over, and I caught it."

The woman looked skeptical. Brid tried to lift the statue out of CJ's arms, but it was heavier than it looked. "A little help here?" Brid asked the maid.

"Who let you people into this home?" she asked as Pat came to the aid of Brid and CJ. It was then that the maid realized how close the statue was to being dropped, and she grabbed it. "I asked, who let you children into this home?"

"We showed ourselves in. We live on the other side of the wall. We wanted to talk to Lukas and Lily," Brid said meekly.

The woman raised eyeglasses from a chain around her neck to get a better look at the Smithforks. Brid felt raggedy and underdressed.

"Lukas and Lily came over to our house unannounced this morning. We thought it worked both ways," CJ said. "We are really sorry. We thought it would be okay."

The woman's face softened a notch. "Really, they

didn't call first?" she asked. "I'm surprised. I will speak to them about that right now."

"Wait." CJ didn't mean to get Lukas and Lily in trouble, but the maid had already turned to a small panel near the door, and pressed Lukas's name on an LED screen. The screen seemed so out of place, so cutting-edge and modern compared to the antiques, but it did the trick.

Lukas's voice emerged from the wall. *"Oui, madame?"*

Unbelievable, CJ thought, when the maid replied to this in French. They speak French, and they aren't even French. What is up with this family?

"Toute de suite," came the reply. "I'll be right there."

Soon they heard the familiar sound of padding feet, and Lukas appeared.

"What a grand surprise!" he said.

"Yes, well, we were surprised, too!" Patrick said. Lukas just looked at him quizzically.

Brid had never heard kids talk the way the Williamsons did, who weren't kidding around. "We were just hanging out at home, and we thought if you had a moment you could show us around a little. We haven't seen the servants' rooms you told us about, and we'd like to."

"Of course, that would be a real pleasure," Lukas replied. "Let me get Lily. She would love to see you again. Sonia, do you have the keys for downstairs storage?" he asked the maid. "Also, we will be needing shoes," he added. "Something casual, such as loafers, would be perfect. I'm going to take our new neighbors to see the bowels of the building."

While Brid was still wondering how someone their age could use the word *bowels* to describe the basement, Sonia went away and returned with Lily, keys, and some shoes. She placed the shoes directly in front of the elevator so that the children would take only one step in the home while wearing them.

The servants' quarters, comprised of a long, dark row of rooms, were on a dusty and deserted floor, halfway underground. Many of the rooms had padlocks on them. Brid imagined how simply the servants must have lived compared to the splendid surroundings of the people they served.

"Does anyone live down here anymore?" CJ asked.

"No," said Lukas. "It really was a different time. This hall used to be filled with drivers, cooks, nannies, butlers, and housekeepers. Now it's filled with people's belongings." At the room on the end, he held up an antique-looking key Sonia had given him, and turned it in the lock. The door made a complaining, squealing noise. "Anyway, here are the quarters for the fourteenth-floor servants. Not much to look at, but it would make a good clubhouse."

"Clubhouse," said CJ flatly, "like for a six-year-old?"

Pat gave one of his electric-blue, wide-eyed head shakes. "Cool."

Brid knew why CJ was so irritable. He had hoped to see a keyhole, a place that would accept the massive key bulging from his front pocket—the key from the library. Instead, when Lukas opened the door, they all took in the endless shelves, which were stuffed with brown boxes and piles of books with titles like *Tiffin Glass Collectors Club*, *Garden of Earth Book of Plant Life*, and *Great Homes of Chicago 1871–1929*. Brid raised an eyebrow toward CJ, wondering if he thought any of this was relevant to the treasure hinted at in the book they picked up from the library.

"It looks like they moved out in a pretty disorganized way," Brid said.

"Or really quickly," said CJ.

"Or just didn't care much about their stuff," said Brid.

"Or what if they had just already read these books and left them for the new people?" Pat added.

"Or," said Lukas, "maybe the owner passed away." His voice was so respectful and matter-of-fact that the Smith-forks immediately felt bad about their manners.

"Is that what happened?" asked Brid finally. "Did they die?"

"Not 'they,' but 'he,'" said Lukas. "You see, Mr. Post was a huge collector, a man who loved architecture, poetry, and paintings. He had a friend named J. P. Morgan. Morgan was a financier and philanthropist, and both men were known for their incredible collections."

"Collections of what?" asked Brid.

"Mr. Morgan had art, sculptures, rare manuscripts, and early children's books; Mr. Post had architectural renderings, jewelry, and poetry. The two men hosted a monthly salon of smart, fancy people to share and discuss some of their acquisitions—to show them off. It was the hot ticket of the time."

"How do you know all that?" CJ asked him.

Lukas didn't answer but continued, "You see, Post also loved puzzles. He sometimes used to send invitations to his salons in riddle form. If you couldn't solve the riddle, you didn't know where and when the salon would be held. Apparently he never went easy on anyone or just gave them the information. When he passed on, the story was that he had a will, but it was such a riddle, his heirs couldn't collect their inheritance. He died before he had a chance to leave all the clues his family needed in order to figure out where their inheritance was."

"But what about the apartment—those rules that said the walls of the apartment had to stay the same?" Brid asked.

"Yes, obviously Post didn't want anyone to mess with his original building, but that made it hard for his family to sell. Instead, they just ordered the apartment sectioned in four and had new walls put up for the next tenants, and moved out. But that was a long time ago; your apartment was empty for years. I'm sure Mr. Post's desire to maintain the apartments' original style and beauty was a sincere one. Maybe he just couldn't bear to think of his place being destroyed.

"Want to see a photo of Post?" Lukas asked.

"Sure," the kids said in unison.

Lukas went rummaging in a box before pulling something out.

"Here it is," he said, wielding a large portrait in a wooden frame. "Behold, the Post family."

CJ and Brid gasped in a most uncool and transparent way.

CHAPTER 7

The picture that Lukas held up was a photograph. It showed a woman and a man standing expressionlessly behind their daughter, who appeared to be about eight or nine. They stood in front of a massive two-story library, with floor-to-ceiling bookshelves. In the midst of the shelving was a large painting of a solemn woman with doleful eyes. One of those eyes appeared to be the same one that looked into CJ's bedroom. Logically, the other eye still lay behind the wall in fourteen south, the Williamsons' apartment. Brid wondered if that other eye contained skip-seven writing, too.

Halfway up the wall in the photograph was a very wide shelf, and propped against that shelf in the corner was a wooden ladder—a means by which someone could retrieve a book from a high shelf. That shelf had to be the narrow ledge that held the copy of *Treasure Island*.

Lukas spoke first. "The Post family must have taken down all that shelving by the time our family bought our apartment and changed the upper floors from a library to bedrooms."

Lukas continued, "This is the father and mother, and I believe their daughter's name was Eloise." He pointed to the skinny girl who wore a coat buttoned to her chin and carried a muff. Brid and CJ gave each other a knowing glance. They knew her name was Eloise.

Looking closely at the photograph, Patrick asked, "Why is she the only one dressed to go outside while her parents are dressed to be inside?"

The Williamsons looked thoughtful. "She seems like she's about to go somewhere," said Lily.

"She looks a little familiar," said Brid, to change the subject and keep Pat from talking too much. "Did she become famous later in life?"

"That's the puzzle," said Lukas. "I once had to write a biography for a homework assignment, and I chose to write about Mr. Post, her father. But their family history came to a halt when he died in 1937. The rest of the family seemed to have just disappeared."

"What do you mean?" Brid asked, thinking that 1937

was the same year the copy of *Treasure Island* had been borrowed from the library.

"Well, they were wildly rich and social. They held magnificent parties, gave a lot of money to charity, and were always in the newspaper. One summer, the father died suddenly of a heart attack, and little was written about the family ever again, except as regards his fortune. He left the apartment to his wife and to his son and daughter, with the demand about keeping the walls intact. As we know, they did that, but then they seem to have vanished. There were newspaper stories wondering what happened to their fortune, but that was about it. Mrs. Post moved down to Washington, DC, and dropped from the party scene. The story simply ended for the Post family."

"Wait," said Patrick. "They had a son, too? He's not in the picture."

"Yes, he's hardly in any pictures, and there's little mention of him anywhere. The rumor was that he died in an accident of some sort."

"Sad," Pat said simply.

Brid looked again at the thin, solemn girl. "She doesn't look very happy, and neither do her parents. So much for my mom's idea that our apartment has happy-family karma."

Lily interjected, "People didn't smile in photographs in those days, so we cannot judge happiness by that fact. They certainly didn't yell 'cheese' the way you Americans do."

Brid answered, "First of all, you're American, too, and maybe some of us like to say 'cheese.' Second, maybe Eloise was just about to step outside, but something made them all stop and take a photo."

"Maybe she was about to go on a trip without them," said Patrick.

"Maybe boarding school," Lukas said.

"No, she's too young to be going off to school alone," said Brid.

"She looks as though she is about eight," said Lily.

"Old enough," said Lukas.

"That's old enough?" asked Brid.

"We left for boarding school when we were eight. But our school takes children as young as six."

"Six-year-olds at boarding school?" said Patrick, imagining himself heading overseas alone. "No way."

"But Mr. Post loved Eloise," said Brid. "Why would he ever send her away?"

"Children at boarding school are loved very much," said Lukas. "It's just that our parents like the structure of our education."

"The class of it," added Lily.

"What do you mean by class?" said CJ, who was suddenly missing his Brooklyn school more than ever.

"In England, people of a certain rank in society mostly attend boarding school, and back when the Posts were alive, Americans with English roots often did the same."

The children were silent for a moment while CJ fingered the photo frame. "So why do you go?" he asked.

"Go?"

"To boarding school?" said CJ.

"As I told you, our parents travel so much. It's easier on everyone this way," Lukas said.

Brid and CJ looked at each other. Maybe a nanny like Maricel wasn't so bad after all.

Before they parted ways, Lukas gave the key to the servants' quarters to Brid. "We leave in the morning for England. Why don't you use these in our absence? We'll see you again at winter holiday, right?"

Brid took the key and impulsively hugged Lily, who stood with her arms stoically at her sides.

That night, Pat lay on CJ's floor with thousands of Lego pieces spread around him. Nobody could tell what he was building. It was a flat structure, with giant spikes in the air.

CJ lay on his bed with Mr. Post's book of poetry. It contained only seven poems, and he had read and reread all of them and was starting to get some ideas about how Mr. Post's treasure hunt might work, but he didn't want to tell the others yet. He looked at the seven titles, some famous and some not.

"The Weary Blues" by Langston Hughes

"Ulysses" by Alfred, Lord Tennyson
"Faint Heart in a Rail Way Train" by Thomas Hardy
"Recuerdo" by Edna St. Vincent Millay
"The New Colossus" by Emma Lazarus
"A Crowded Trolley Car" by Elinor Wylie
"Ota Benga" by anonymous

Meanwhile, Brid had taped poster board to the wall, where she was transcribing the skip-seven message from the eye behind the wall. CJ kept glancing over at it:

SEVEN CLUES ON SEVEN STRUCTURES
GET WATER FROM ABOVE TO RUPTURE.

CJ broke the quiet hum in the room. "Guys, do you know how many poems are in this book?"

"No idea," Brid remarked. "Too many?"

"Seven, probably," said Pat without looking up.

CJ laughed. "Exactly. I'm seeing a pattern here with that number seven. In his letter, Mr. Post tells Eloise and Julian to visit some sites in New York City, sites they'd visited together in the past. Then he gives them a book that has seven poems in it. The message from the eye talks about seven structures, and the message was in skip-seven code. Wouldn't it make sense if there was one clue in each poem that points us to a specific place, like a building or structure? Maybe we just need to find seven places or buildings here in New York City."

"What do we do when we find them? Look through gigantic buildings for treasure?" Pat asked. "Won't that be hard?"

"Maybe. I have a feeling we won't know what we're looking for until we see each structure," said CJ.

Brid looked up from her notes. "So, we go to a building that a poem reminds us of, then we get water from above to rupture?" she asked.

"That's what I'm not sure about," said CJ. "But I think I'm getting closer. I don't know about the first poem, but the second one is 'Ulysses.' It's a famous poem about not giving up, not surrendering."

"What building could possibly be about not giving up?" Pat said, rummaging through his Legos. "A fort?"

"Close," said CJ. "I think the answer is in the title of this poem."

"Duh," said Brid. "It's a one-word title, and there are no buildings or forts in New York called Ulysses. Right?"

"Actually," said CJ, "there is one enormous structure in the city with that name on it. He was a general."

"Like in the army?" Patrick said.

"Yes, and he became president of the United States: Ulysses S. Grant. Ever heard of Grant's Tomb? C'mon, it's one of the corniest jokes of all time. Pat, who is buried in Grant's Tomb?" asked CJ.

"Um, Grant?"

"Bingo. There must be something in Ulysses S. Grant's tomb. Mr. Post must have left something for his son and daughter there. Maybe we can find it."

"Where exactly *is* Grant's Tomb?" Brid asked.

"Not sure, but it's in Manhattan," CJ said.

"Wait," Pat said. "So we have to get something from that structure, and the structure is a tomb? Maybe we have to get a dead body out?"

"I'm not taking any bodies anywhere," Brid said matter-of-factly.

"Eeeew, it's too creepy," Pat replied.

"Then what do we do with it?" Brid asked. "Assuming Grant's Tomb is the right answer."

"Like I said, I have no idea. But maybe we'll know when we see it," said CJ.

"No idea," repeated Brid. "But we do need to start somewhere, so let's start at Grant's Tomb."

CHAPTER 8

The next afternoon, after CJ and Brid finally did buy their school uniforms, CJ plotted the trip to Grant's Tomb at 122nd Street and Riverside Drive. He printed out internet photographs of the mausoleum, thinking they could go tomorrow or the next day.

The kids were hanging out in CJ's room. Sprawled out on CJ's bed, Brid was reading Mr. Post's book of poems, taking methodical notes as she looked for clues.

"Hey, shoes off my bed!" CJ said with an English accent.

"What are you, a member of the Williamson family?" Brid joked.

Patrick was building quietly with his Legos, trying his hardest to be silent. He'd noticed the older kids let him hang around more as long as he didn't interrupt much. He liked his new life of being included; he felt like a big kid.

He was trying to build a model of Grant's Tomb with his Lego pieces. It was hard to get the rounded roof done with the square blocks, and he was getting frustrated. Patrick glanced up at Brid. He had looked at the book of Mr. Post's poems earlier when he was alone, but the words made no sense to him. They confused him and made him feel like he couldn't help solve the mystery, that he was still a little kid after all.

Now his eyes strayed to the back cover, which was brown leather with a strange inky blob smeared across the middle. The more he stared at it, the more he saw something. Finally, he just couldn't stay quiet. "Is that book about, um . . . ?"

"What?" Brid said flatly.

"I think his poem book is about dying, 'cause his book says 'death' on the back," Pat said.

"Patrick, what are you babbling about?"

"Pat," said CJ, "can we stay on topic here? We're talking about Grant's Tomb."

"Oh," said Patrick, deflated. He tried again. "That inky blob. It says something about death."

Brid lowered the book. "Why are you being so annoying right now?"

"Look at the back of the book," Patrick insisted. Brid

turned the book over. "This thing?" she asked Pat. "It's a blob of ink."

"No. You're not holding it the right way now," Pat said. He climbed onto the bed and adjusted the book, holding it at arm's length. Brid and CJ saw one long, stretched word, only recognizable to someone looking carefully at exactly the right level.

"Holy mother of a llama," CJ said softly.

"What is that word?" said Brid.

Patrick ignored them. "It's talking about death."

"No," said CJ kindly, remembering how his little brother twisted letters sometimes. "Well, almost. It doesn't say D-E-A-T-H; it says H-E-A-R-T-H."

"Hearth," Patrick said. "What does *hearth* mean?"

Brid recorded this new development in her notebook.

"In a fireplace," said CJ. "It's the open spot in a wall at the base of the chimney."

"This apartment is full of chimneys!" said Brid, getting excited. "We have three of them. I bet something is hidden in the hearths!" she shrieked.

CJ snatched the book from Brid, ignoring the little dance she and Patrick were doing. He recited the first two lines of "Ulysses":

> *"It little profits that an idle king,*
> *By this still hearth, among these barren crags . . ."*

"I get it!" shouted Brid. "It's the second time Post is leading us to a hearth! But which one?" She slammed CJ's door open and took off down the hallway.

CJ and Patrick followed her into the living room, where Brid ducked inside the enormous limestone fireplace and stood upright. "They all have tile around them, but this one has the most." Brid's voice was muffled under the massive fireplace frame.

"What's going on here?" came Maricel's shrill voice, surprising everyone. Their nanny came into the room with Carron toddling after her.

"We were looking at tiles," CJ said quickly.

"Oh, are your parents going to change the tiles?"

Maricel asked as she reached down to pick up Carron.

"No, we're just interested in, um, the tiling," CJ said. "I mean, the hearth is really nice, and we're just admiring it."

At that moment, they were mercifully interrupted by the sound of the elevator. In sauntered Bruce Smithfork, much earlier than expected. For Carron and Patrick, all else was forgotten as they attacked their father with ferocious bear hugs. It was still light outside, not a time they were used to seeing him anymore.

"What are you up to?" Bruce Smithfork asked, glancing around quizzically. "Looking for Santa?"

None of the children knew how to answer.

CHAPTER 9

Back when they lived in Brooklyn, CJ knew he could count on his father to leave his basement office at four PM and come upstairs. Mr. Smithfork would cook, throw a football around, or help the kids with homework, but he would never, ever go back to his office. Now that he worked in a midtown skyscraper, his home office seemed like a second job he had to go to. He often came home late, and then would go right into his office. Sometimes he even ate in there.

"So, Dad," said Brid, "how'd you get out of work so early?"

Their dad pushed his bushy brown hair back from his face and said, "I thought I'd come home early because school starts tomorrow."

"Dad," said Brid, "school doesn't start till September seventh, and today is just the second."

"I knew that," their dad said a little sheepishly. "Want to throw the football around?"

This grabbed Patrick's attention. "In the park?" he asked.

"Great idea!" said Brid. "But CJ and I have a lot of homework, so why don't you just take Patrick, and we'll see you back here for dinner."

CJ glared at Brid. Homework? School hadn't even started, so how could they have homework?

"Dad," said Patrick, looking outside onto Fifth Avenue. "Didn't you notice it's raining?"

"I didn't mean football in the *park*," their dad said. "I meant living room football. They don't call this a ballroom for nothing." He winked, and CJ thought he hadn't seen his dad do that in a really long time.

Three minutes later, they were passing the football around. Maricel had carried off Carron, protesting loudly, for a bath. With its twenty-foot ceilings and rectangular shape, the living room was the perfect miniature football field. CJ moved the two long couches against the walls, making end zones. Brid stuck brooms and mops deep into the cushions so they stood upright, creating goalposts. Luckily, they hadn't done much in the way of unpacking, so there was nothing breakable in the room. Even though dragging around the furniture scratched the floor, and putting dirty mops on a couch wasn't a sanitary idea, Bruce Smithfork didn't say a word.

As soon as Brid got the final handle to stay upright, Patrick yelled, "Hike!" and the game was on. The teams were Mr. Smithfork and Patrick versus CJ and Brid, and soon both sides were in a sweaty rumble. Collapsing at last onto the floor, CJ thought it was a good time to ask their dad some questions.

"Dad, do you know who lived here before us?"

"Nope. They were renters, not owners. We bought the apartment from people we never met.

"We really liked this apartment because it had so much character. It seemed like the walls had stories to tell us, stories from a different time."

Brid and CJ looked at each other as their dad stood up and moved his tie around his forehead like a sweatband. "Go long, Pat!" he yelled as he let the ball sail to his younger son.

CJ easily two-hand touched his brother to stop the play, and Pat fell hard onto the couch.

"But the original owner died a long time ago, right?" CJ said.

"That's right. He died and left the original apartment to his family, and they divided it up into four different apartments. They all came up for sale after the Great Depression, when it was hard to sell any apartment, never mind one with bizarre rules attached. The fact that not only that owner, but any owner in the future, had to agree to not wreck the walls made it a bit of a white elephant."

"A what?" asked Brid.

"An expensive possession that is a financial burden to maintain," said CJ. "It's just an expression."

Just then, Maricel came back into the living room with Carron. She looked alarmed at the football game, but Carron was grinning.

"We pay you?" Carron asked.

"Of course you can play with us," said her dad.

"She just had her bath," said Maricel. "She shouldn't get dirty now. Playtime is done for the day."

"It's just football," said Mr. Smithfork. "Living room football is very clean."

Maricel gathered her purse from the front hall. "Good night," she said with an edge to her voice, and rang the elevator button.

Boom! Brid dove for a long-shot pass and landed on the back of the couch so hard that it fell over backward. It smacked the uncovered wooden floor with a noise that echoed loudly through the apartment. Carron burst out laughing, while Patrick dove on top of Brid. Thinking this was a game she would like, Carron got on top of him.

As they lay there, spluttering and giggling, the elevator arrived for Maricel. They were surprised to see that Ray was accompanied by two women. One wore a white blouse, dark skirt, a strand of pearls, and sensible pumps. She looked around eighty years old. The other wore what CJ had started to call "the Fifth Avenue uniform," a simple gray dress with a white apron across the front. This was the dress of the helpers: the dog walkers, the nannies, the maids, the baby nurses, and the ladies hired to buy groceries. The neighborhood was filled with women wearing these clothes.

The older woman stood with her mouth open, staring at the overturned couch and Mr. Smithfork with a tie around his head. Aside from the heavy panting of the football players, there was no sound in the room.

Maricel shrugged and stepped into the elevator, leaving the two strange women with the Smithforks.

"May I help you?" asked Mr. Smithfork.

Brid stared at the older lady. She was on the shorter side, light-skinned, twinkly-eyed, and fine-boned. Something about her seemed familiar. Brid watched the woman's eyes sweep the room, taking note of the living room goalposts and the overturned couch. For a flash, Brid thought she saw a half smile.

The woman cleared her voice. "Yes, hello. I'm your downstairs neighbor, and this is my housekeeper, Annika. We were just making certain a bomb hadn't exploded up here," she said with a smile.

Annika added, "I think Madam would like to request quieter behavior. Madam's apartment has very high ceilings, so the noise you make here is amplified down-stairs."

I'll bet she has high ceilings, thought CJ. According to the floor plan of the original apartment, that floor had much more height than the Smithfork apartment. Her ceiling had to be thirty-five feet high. But before anyone could answer, a cry came from the kitchen.

"Dinner!" It was their mom.

"Oh, yes," said Mr. Smithfork, who was now awkwardly trying to remove his tie from his forehead. "Please, ladies, we are sorry about the noise. We didn't want to play outside in the rain."

"Yeah," said Brid, "we kind of take the word *ballroom* literally."

The elderly woman cracked a full smile at Brid's joke. She seemed apologetic. So, when Mrs. Smithfork yelled, "Dinner," the second time, Patrick asked, "Want to stay for dinner? My mom makes the best chocolate cake!"

"Oh, we didn't mean to interrupt anything. We just haven't heard so much life up here in a long time. I'm glad everyone is all right," she said, smoothing her hair.

"Well, at least come meet my wife," said Mr. Smith-fork, who seemed to want a second chance to make a good impression. Brid hated that he seemed to care what people thought of him these days.

Annika bent to remove her shoes. Brid said, "You can leave your shoes on, it's not that kind of house."

"Oh, okay," Annika said with relief in her voice. Without anyone showing them where to go, the two women made the two right turns that took them down the hall to the kitchen. The family padded behind them.

Brid turned to CJ and whispered, "How did they know how to get to the kitchen?"

Mrs. Smithfork didn't cook like the chefs on television: no neat little piles of matching chopped foods arrayed in colorful bits. The Smithfork kitchen had oozy liquid dripping from the stainless steel countertops. Sprinkles of herbs dusted the floor, and bits of vegetables were scattered about. Sizzling chicken parts spat grease onto the industrial-sized gas range. CJ and Brid felt a little embarrassed that their mom looked so messy in front of these prim women.

"Hi there—welcome!" Mrs. Smithfork practically shouted.

"Hello, ma'am," said Annika. "Pleasure to make your acquaintance. I work for your downstairs neighbor, Mrs. Munn," she added, gesturing toward the older woman. "And my name is Annika."

"We just came up to say hello and, I guess, welcome you to the building. I'm embarrassed we haven't brought a housewarming gift," said Mrs. Munn.

"Would you like to stay for dinner tonight?" Mrs. Smithfork said brightly.

"Oh what a lovely invitation," said the older woman. "Perhaps another time?" She seemed surprised by

Anne Smithfork's spontaneity.

"Oh, I understand," said Mrs. Smithfork as the chicken started to smoke. "We'll see you again."

"Yes, good-bye."

"Yes," said Mr. Smithfork, looking a little defeated. "And we'll keep the noise level down."

The older lady nodded and grinned and went back to the elevator, with Annika trailing behind her.

CHAPTER 10

At one the next morning, CJ's alarm clock went off. He wasn't sure why he felt this way, but he wanted to be alone when he examined the hearth in his dad's office. In a family like his, the middle of the night was the only time he could do that. He tiptoed to the office, noticing three partially filled coffee cups. It looked like his dad had spent a long night laboring over problems with his LeCube company.

Since Bruce Smithfork's screen saver was still glowing, CJ figured his father must have just left the room. CJ sat in the office chair and watched the words *DigiSpy, a division of the LeCube Company* form a swirling cyclone on the screen. This was the new spy game his dad was inventing. Every time CJ asked if he could test it out,

Bruce Smithfork would say, "Wait till it's through my testing department." CJ could feel his insides deflate when that happened. His dad seemed to forget that CJ had once been his testing department. Now Bruce Smithfork employed people who had gone to college for that stuff, experts at making people want to buy his gaming system.

As CJ leaned back in his dad's chair, he noticed a poem etched into the wall above Mr. Post's built-in desk. It read:

> *The thief left it behind:*
> *the moon at my window.*
> *—Ryokan (1758–1831)*

Wonder why he had that there? CJ thought. That Post guy was just crazy for poetry. Weird.

He glanced out the office window, looking for the moon, but it was black outside, except for the lights of the surrounding buildings. Using just his flashlight and the blue light from the computer screen, he examined the fireplace. Nothing seemed amiss or unusual. He moved his hands up and down and felt nothing. The tiles seemed to be laid evenly, the cement holding them together perfectly aligned. He tried again, this time pushing each tile just in case there was a spring behind one of them. Nothing. CJ lay down and flashed his light up the chimney, seeing only blackness and a tiny dot of night sky.

Sadly, thought CJ, this night will give way to another day, and that day is one day closer to Saint James's School. How he wished he were back in Brooklyn. He realized they might not have time to visit Grant's Tomb before school started, but who cared? He didn't care about the Post mystery anymore. He didn't care that his family was suddenly wealthy. He felt scared about his new life, this new neighborhood that came with so many rules. And that was the last thing he thought before falling asleep right there on the floor. He slept soundly with his head under the fireplace flue, his legs sticking out into the room.

It was dawn when his father came into the office. "Fall down the chimney, CJ?" he asked casually, grabbing some papers off his desk. By the time CJ could get his eyes open, Bruce Smithfork was gone. He had not even waited to hear the answer. CJ lay on the floor, dazed, rubbing his eyes while listening to his dad shut the front door, leaving to beat the rush to midtown Manhattan. There is nothing to wake up for, thought CJ, and he drifted back into a thick sleep.

The next time CJ woke, bright sunshine was everywhere. He could hear Maricel shooing Carron off the tricycle as she rode up and down the main hallway. CJ lay there figuring out what to do with his fourth-to-last

day of freedom. Maybe he would jump onto the A train, head back to his old neighborhood. He wondered if he would look different to his old friends after almost a week of living on the Upper East Side.

His mind swimming with nonsense, CJ stared up the chimney at nothing, until the nothing that he saw suddenly looked like something.

Up in the flue, about four feet from the ground, the tiles had some sort of inscription. He trained his flashlight on it, seeing numbers separated by dashes, placed in a ring. Were they dates? They were written in a circle, so how could he know where the inscription began and where it ended?

Quickly he sat up. *Smack!* He hit his head on the cold tile at the bottom opening of the fireplace.

"Agh," he said, hardly stopping as he slammed open his dad's desk to get a pen. He wrote down the numbers, keeping them in order and noting the dashes.

Just as he finished, someone pushed the office door open so forcefully that it slammed against the opposite wall. It was Maricel. "Are you allowed in here?" she asked. CJ could tell she thought he was always up to mischief.

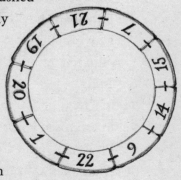

"Yes, my dad was in here with

me," CJ answered, rubbing his head.

"Okay, then." Maricel took a big breath. "Your mom is out. I put breakfast on the table for you and Brid. I'm taking Patrick and Carron to the park, and I think you should come, too."

"Park, as in playground?" CJ grimaced.

"I cannot watch you if you aren't with me, and what are you writing?" Maricel sounded exasperated as she looked at the numbers on his pad.

"Just a math problem. Can Brid and I please stay home? We won't go anywhere. We'll be good. Please?"

She looked skeptical. "I need to check with your mother."

"I used to stay home alone all the time. Really, we're used to it."

"If they stay home, then I'm staying home," Pat said. He was out of sight and his voice was muffled.

"¡Che Guevara! You see," she said, "I cannot win in this house." She threw up her arms and stormed off, taking only Carron with her, leaving CJ to stand and wonder why his Filipina nanny was speaking Spanish.

A full five minutes passed before the others came out of hiding.

"Is she gone?" asked Brid cautiously. She had been behind a closed bathroom door.

"I think so," said CJ.

Giggles came from beneath the still-overturned sofa

in the living room. CJ nodded toward the sound. "Guess Pat managed to skip the playground, too."

"Party time!" said Brid.

"No, it's clue time," CJ said dramatically.

"Really? You found something?"

CJ motioned Brid back into the office, and Patrick crawled out from under the sofa to join them. "Lie on your back, right here," CJ said as he crawled in and trained the flashlight on the exact spot.

"Whoa. Is that a secret code?" Brid asked.

"I don't know. Maybe it's from a combination lock," CJ said. "We need to check the other two hearths."

Brid took the flashlight. "So it's not really *in* the hearth, but you have to lie on the hearth to see it. Interesting." Standing upright again, she picked up her pink spiral notebook and wrote down the numbers. Then she headed down the hall toward the living room fireplace, her brothers behind her.

"I didn't see them last night, but there are numbers here, too!" she said. At about the same height in the second chimney, the tiles were laid with another circle of numbers. This circle was larger, because it had more numbers.

"Brid, hand me that paper," CJ said. Brid tossed her notebook to him. "Just tell me the numbers, and make sure you read them beginning at the twelve o'clock spot."

Though her voice sounded far away, Brid shouted the

numbers, while CJ wrote them down.

23-1-9-20-5-18-4-21-13-2

CJ stared at the numbers while Pat, seeing that their work was done in the living room, seized the chance to get to the next fireplace before them. "I'm the only one who can fit in the kitchen fireplace," he said, running down the hall, the others at his heels.

The kitchen hearth had the narrowest opening, making it hard to see inside.

Without any hesitation, Pat crawled onto the hearth, unfolded himself slowly, and stood up in the chimney.

"Pat, what's it like in there?" Brid asked, her pencil sketching the shape of the hearth.

They could hear Patrick cough. "It's dirty."

"Is there anything unusual in there? Anything you can read?"

"Nope."

"Bummer."

"Pat?"

"Uh-huh."

"You can come out now."

"When I'm done."

"When you're done with what?" said CJ.

"When I'm done seeing through the dirt. I need a rag or something to clean with."

"Seeing what through the dirt?" Brid asked impatiently.

CJ was calmer. "Pat, are you reading something?"

"Stop shaking the flashlight. I'm not reading, I'm seeing. Can you really read numbers like words, or do you just see numbers?"

CJ groaned. "Pat," he said, "you can hardly read as it is. What do you see?"

"Some very dirty numbers that I'm cleaning off with my shirt."

Brid jumped up and down, flapping her arms.

"Pat, please tell us the numbers you see," CJ said.

Pat's muffled voice read, "Twenty-two, one, fourteen, twenty, nineteen, nineteen, five, eighty-one."

"Oh no!" said CJ. "It's not what I thought."

"Not what you thought about what?" Brid asked, scribbling furiously.

"Well, at first, I thought the numbers were a substitution code, like where one is the letter *A*, two is *B*, and so forth. It's a pretty common code. But that would only work if no number was higher than twenty-six, because there are only twenty-six letters in the alphabet. Patrick saw an eighty-one, so it blows my theory. Now I don't know what the numbers mean."

Brid was quiet for a second. "Pat, before you come out," she said, "can you please give us that last number again?"

"Yup, eighty-one."

"And which digit is first in that eighty-one?"

"Duh, the one."

"So it reads *one* and then an eight?"

"Yup."

"You're a genius, Pat. C'mon out now."

"Depends."

"Depends on what?"

"Depends if you have any bubble gum for me."

CJ and Brid grinned at each other. "But how do we know he didn't jumble any of the other numbers?" CJ asked.

"Pat only turns things around at the beginning or end of a sentence," said Brid. "I bet it's the same with numbers. Let's see if it works."

Slowly, Pat pulled himself out of the hearth. He had soot on his head, which made him look like he was wearing a black cap. "How'd they ever find a grown-up as small as me to put those numbers in there?" he asked.

"Because they did it as it was being built," said CJ. "Someone put these puzzles in right from the start, in the 1920s. Mr. Post must have known for a long time he wanted to hide stuff, but the question is why?"

"Maybe he needed a place to hide his riches," Brid replied as she doodled in her notebook.

"From who?" said Pat.

"I don't know. Maybe the banks, or the government, so he wouldn't have to pay taxes?" said CJ.

"Or maybe bad guys," Patrick said.

"Maybe he was worried the good times would end, and he needed a safe place to store money and valuables. Because the good times *did* end," said Brid.

"Yes, the stock market crashed, and that started the Great Depression. Lots of people had no jobs, and some lost their homes," CJ agreed.

"Sounds a little like now," Brid said.

"A little, but much worse," said CJ. "Maybe Mr. Post thought the world was coming to an end. Maybe he didn't trust his bank, and he didn't have a backyard to bury his treasure in."

"And it's clear he didn't want anyone to just find it by accident," Brid reasoned. "CJ?" she asked as she continued to try and translate the numbers into letters.

"Yup."

"I'm definitely getting a message here."

"Do you think the answer will be in this chimney?" Pat interrupted.

"Nope," CJ said. "It's not going to be that easy. That's why I stopped carrying that big key around. No lock is suddenly going to show itself, screaming, 'Open me.' This will take some detective work."

CJ was looking over Brid's shoulder. "So it is a number-letter association," he said, smiling.

"It's not even a skip-seven," said Brid. "It's a straight substitution code. Are you ready?" she asked her brothers.

They nodded, and she began to recite three words.

CHAPTER 11

"What does that mean?" Patrick asked, looking at the three words Brid had written down, one for each of the hearths. Even if he could read them himself, they made no sense.

Tavinogus Servants Dumbwaiter

"I don't know," said Brid. "Maybe the company that installed the fireplaces did it for fun."

"Oh," said Patrick, unconvinced. "So what's fun about those words?"

"C'mon, Pat, I'm trying to figure this out!" She kept moving the letters around, her pencil scratches the only noise in the room.

Patrick was getting restless. He ripped open a bag of fried edamame chips, the only semigood thing he found in the cupboard. "So we're looking for a message?" he asked, munching loudly. CJ and Brid ignored him. Pat continued, "A message about the stupid guy in the servants' quarters?" He leaned over the notes, and sweat from his forehead began to drip onto the pages.

"Gross," said Brid, putting her notebook away. "What do you mean, a stupid guy?"

CJ laughed. "I think he means a dumb waiter. Pat, a dumbwaiter isn't a stupid guy. It's like a miniature elevator, used to bring things from one floor to another, usually from the kitchen to the dining room. I bet there used to be one in this apartment. Since one of the words is *servants*, I think we should look for it in the servants' quarters. But that first word? *Tavinogus?* Never heard of it."

Patrick kept staring at it. "But, since it's written in a circle, how do you know where the word begins and ends?"

Brid replied, "I've written down all the possibilities by moving the first letter to the back of the word until we try every possible starting point. If I move the starting place over to the *V*, then the word is *vinogusta*, whatever that is. Still, none of these words make sense to me. Look at this list!" Brid held out her paper, which read:

Tavinogus
Avinogust
Vinogusta

Inogustav
Nogustavi
Ogustavin
Gustavino
Ustavinog
Stavinogus

"I can't believe I didn't think of that," said CJ. "Let me do an internet search; maybe one of these will mean something in another language. I mean, it sort of sounds like Greek or Italian to me if you say it with an exclamation at the end. *Ustavinog* to you!"

Pat and Brid giggled. "*Nogustavi*, Patrick," Brid said. "*Nogustavi*, and you're welcome."

In their father's office, CJ typed *dumbwaiter* and *servant*, while Pat and Brid sat on either side of him, watching. "Hey, what's this?" said Pat, lightly touching the second computer. The screen came to life with the same swirling purple cyclone that CJ had seen the night before. Music blared, like something from a James Bond movie. The designs swirled into exploding fireworks, and the lights joined together to form the words:

DIGISPY, A PRODUCT OF THE LECUBE COMPANY!

As the dancing words and the music evaporated, the three Smithforks sat there in silence. The keyboard was practically begging them to hit *return*, to enter whatever fabulous world Mr. Smithfork was creating these days. They were tempted to open the game, but none had the courage.

"Now, that's interesting," said Patrick.

"Did you know Dad was working on a spy game?" Brid asked CJ.

"Dad hasn't been talking about work as much as he used to," said CJ. "I don't even know what that game does."

"Can we try it?" asked Brid.

"We should leave it alone," said CJ. "If we mess something up, he'll be mad. Let's stick to one mystery at a time."

"I thought you tested his games for him," Brid said to CJ.

"I used to," said CJ with a little catch in his voice. "Now he hires people to do it."

"Whatever."

"Whatever."

Patrick was a little relieved not to be peeking at the spy game, because he was usually the one who touched things and ended up in trouble. Now, he wanted to focus on the mystery, but neither CJ nor Brid was telling him much.

Brid and CJ knew the trick to using Pat to help them was not telling him exactly why they had him do certain things. He loved to talk and to tell secrets, and CJ and

Brid had gotten in trouble more than once when he'd told their mom something the kids were up to. But the older he got, the harder it was to fool him. Now that he had gotten information from a wall and a fireplace, he was too excited to simply go away.

"Why don't you go play basketball?" Brid said to him.

"Where? In the backyard we don't have?"

"How about the hallway? Maricel and Mom are out, so you can go crazy, and we won't tell."

"What if that old lady downstairs complains?"

"She won't," Brid said. "I have the feeling she sort of understands us."

"Oh, okay, I guess you're sick of me," Pat said, stomping out of the room. A few seconds later they could hear him pounding on the floorboards.

"He's actually been really helpful, at least more than he used to be. I almost wish we could include him," said Brid.

"Yeah, so he could blab to everyone that our house is sitting on a gold mine?" CJ snapped.

"No. He's not a baby anymore, and I think he can keep secrets. If we only give him half the information, it won't be long until he's mad, and he won't help us anymore," Brid answered.

"Whatever." CJ continued to type.

"CJ, are you nervous about school?"

"Nervous? I never get nervous. What school, anyway?"

CJ said, knowing full well what Brid was talking about. He stopped typing and closed the laptop, too agitated to continue.

"Hello? First day of a new school?"

"Who cares? It'll be fine," said CJ, as his stomach flopped. He changed the subject, talking rapidly. "You know what our problem is? Every time we have a question, it gets answered with more questions. Our list of clues grows, but not as fast as our list of questions. We know two of the words are *dumbwaiter* and *servants*. We need to find the dumbwaiter in this apartment, and my guess is it's been taken out. I'm going down into the servants' quarters to check, and besides, it's too hot in here!" With an angry slam of the desk drawer, CJ stood up and went to summon the elevator. Brid sat, puzzled and a little sad about the way her brother was acting.

Ray didn't say much as he and CJ descended to the lobby. The temperature in the elevator was oppressive. Despite that, Ray had on his full uniform: gray suit, white shirt, tie, gold brocade shoulder epaulets, cap, and white gloves. The silence felt a little uncomfortable, so CJ tried to strike up some idle chatter.

"Where is everyone?" asked CJ as they stopped in the lobby.

"This building is mostly empty during the summer," said Ray.

"But it's September."

"The whole neighborhood is empty until the night before school starts. Everyone has a summer house in the Hamptons, or they go to Europe, or out west. There are twenty-four apartments in this building, but only yours and two others are lived in this time of year."

"What about that older lady who lives beneath us? Is she new, too?"

"Whatareyoukiddinme?" Ray laughed out loud. "Yeah, about eighty years new—she moved into the building as a kid." He looked at CJ's face and added, "Don't feel bad, kid, things pick up real soon around here."

"Not sure I want it to pick up," said CJ.

"Kinda like it quiet like this, too," Ray said. "I catch up on my reading."

"So you've worked here a long time?"

"Ahhhfortyyearsorso," he said, smiling so that his giant eyebrows merged into one. "Seenalot."

"Do you know much about our apartment?"

"No. Wasemptyforsolong. After they split the original apartment into four separate ones, the Posts donated the one you're living in to a museum. Later, when the museum tried to sell it, there were no buyers. It was after the Great Depression, and some people were still in a bad way financially. Nobody really lived there. Yuz got that wall problem, too. Yaknowaboutthat, right?"

"Yes, I know. That was the rule of sale, that the walls stayed put."

"Yeah. In the last few years, all the apartments were selling for big bucks, all but those Post ones. Not too many people wanted a place with restrictions and crazy rules. So the apartment just sat until your family found it."

"Yeah. My parents didn't mind that. My mom is into restoration and stuff."

"Yeahdatsnice. Your mom's working? I never see her around."

"Yeah. Sorta, volunteer stuff, you know," said CJ, not wanting to talk about how his mother used to be around all the time, but now she always had meetings about things like furniture or buying just the right light fixture. "So you didn't know the Posts?"

"Nah, just the daughter. They were gone before my time."

"You knew the daughter?"

"Yeah, you will, too. It's too bad about her."

"What do you mean, I will, too? Is she some sort of celebrity?"

"Yeahright. She lives on the twelfth floor."

"What? Eloise Post still lives here?" CJ felt dizzy.

"Yeah, well, her life is quiet, ya know? She was tired of people asking about her family all the time, so sometimes she uses a fake name—Eloise Munn. People don't know about her or her family anymore; it's like they all vanished. Poof."

"Hard to believe she lived in all that splendor," CJ said,

thinking of the Post family photo. "And it's just her?"

"Her and that bossy maid, Annika. Lady had some bad luck in her life, never married. After her mother died, she moved back here. I guess she likes hanging around all these old memories. I can't tell you why."

"Did you ever hear rumors of the Post family treasure being left in our apartment?" CJ asked.

"DidIhear? Kid, it was all over the papers. The dad kicked off and never explained to the Post kids how to actually get their inheritance. The guy didn't trust banks anymore after the stock market crash. So he hid it himself, somewhere so safe that nobody, not even his kids, could ever get to it. Not very thoughtful, if you ask me. They took that apartment apart, found bits of clues here and there, but I think the guy was playing with people's minds."

"Yes, but he had to have left it somewhere, right? I mean, a lot of things they owned never showed up again."

"Yeahit'ssomewhere, but it ain't here. This place was under a microscope for years. Still, that guy had country houses and a place in Europe, even though those were sold by his widow. I think they all got the wrong joint, if you know what I mean."

CJ's mind was spinning. He was sure that he and Brid and Patrick had been able to get a little further in solving this mystery—because they had carried out Mr. Post's wishes. He thought of the older lady who lived below them: Was she really Eloise Post, the solemn girl in the portrait? Had she really come about the noise upstairs, or did she just want to see her old place, now that people were living there? He tried not to appear too excited, but some strange expression must have come across his face, because Ray's next comment was, "Don't worry, kid, it'll be freezing before ya know it."

CHAPTER 12

After CJ left the apartment, Brid deftly lifted the lid of her father's laptop and continued the work CJ had left unfinished. Moving each letter in turn to the back of the sequence of letters, she made new words that she could search on the internet. She learned that *Vinogusta* was a wine guide. Too modern, Brid thought, but she wrote it down anyway. She tried *ustavinog* and got the message *Do you mean ustavnog?* Brid felt her heart pounding. Did she mean *ustavnog?* She entered the alternative spelling and was led to a site for Russian newspapers. She wrote that down, too. Then she typed *gustavino*. This time she got numerous responses. The first was for a restaurant in Manhattan. Doubtful, she thought. It probably wasn't around when Mr. Post was alive. The next was a reference to a tiling system named for a builder, Rafael Guastavino. "Guastavino, whose name has sometimes been spelled Gustavino, came from Spain and made his mark on the New York City skyline," Brid read. Skyline? Buildings? Like structures?

Brid could hear Patrick, still pounding a basketball up and down the main gallery hall. She wanted to tell someone what she'd found. "CJ!" she yelled, before remembering he had gone downstairs. She thought about leaving Patrick and going to find CJ, but then thought better of it. She would have to wait.

She sat at the second computer, the one with the DigiSpy logo. She touched the desktop icon that repeated the introduction to the game. It looked spectacular. Then she noticed an icon for a DigiSpy tutorial on the desktop. There was no harm in reading through a tutorial, right? At least then she would know what her dad was up to. She looked over her shoulder, making sure she was really alone, and for once, she was.

Delicately, almost as if it were an accident, she brushed her pinky finger against the return key. The screen filled with a rainbow of graphics, a mesmerizing explosion of light and cacophonous sound. Patrick must have heard it, because the thumping of his basketball stopped, and he came running back to the office. When the explosions mellowed, the screen narrowed to focus on a boy about Brid's age, who was demonstrating what appeared to be some sort of spy game. Brid and Patrick sat watching, their mouths hanging open in awe.

However, it wasn't a game. Their dad's latest invention seemed to work like a robotic spy. It featured a simple, nozzle-shaped attachment that could be moved anywhere while feeding live footage back to the user's computer. The nozzle worked like a robot, able to slide around and film at the same time, while continually sending digital images to the home computer. As the DigiSpy's different uses were demonstrated, Brid found herself lost in thought about what could be done with such a software.

"Hey," Patrick said, "that's so cool." Brid felt surprised that he didn't say something like, "I'm going to tell Dad on you." Little Patrick was growing up, and Brid thought they could really trust him with their secret.

"Do you think Dad keeps the game attachment in this office somewhere?" Patrick asked, looking around the room.

Brid said, "Do you think that thing attaches to the computer's camera, and that's how it knows if it's going to bump into something?"

"No," Patrick replied, "I think you get the robot to move around by pressing the arrow keys on your computer."

"That's smart, Pat," said Brid. "Where do you think the robot is?"

They bent under the desk, looking for the knobby

robotic thing they'd seen in the tutorial. There was nothing like it around.

"Looks like Dad has another winner coming soon," Pat said.

"Pat, you know what I'm thinking?"

"No."

"I'm thinking we could use a DigiSpy to see what else is behind the walls of this place. No need to send you upside down behind a wall again, right?"

"I like going behind the wall. I don't mind, and besides, this thing is useless without that robot thing."

Just then, they were interrupted by the sound of footsteps, heavy ones like their dad's. "Turn it off!" said Pat. "I'll block Dad while you get that off the screen." He ran from the room while Brid frantically hit the escape key, trying to get the tutorial to stop. Why would Mr. Smithfork be home at this time of day?

The steps the children heard were heading toward the back of the apartment, near the laundry room. Pat rounded the corner at full speed, only to come face-to-face with a strange man. He was tall but stooped a little with age. He had the look of a wizened teacher, neat but not formal. His eyes were bluish gray, and his gray hair almost touched his shoulders. He had just come out of Patrick's room.

Pat gasped, thinking the man looked pale like a vampire. The man seemed equally surprised to see someone

home. They stood still, summing each other up. The man looked more lost than scary, but even so, Patrick shook with fear.

"Can I help you?" Pat asked politely, though he was uncertain how a boy should address an intruder.

The intruder seemed to think it best to get a move on. "That's okay," he said, brushing past Patrick into the laundry room, where he unlocked the back door and walked out onto the fire stairs, letting the door slam loudly behind him.

Just then Brid came running up behind Patrick. "Dad?" she asked uncertainly.

Pat shook his head. "No, Brid, it was some man. A creepy-looking man." His hands were shaking, and he sank down onto the sturdy floor.

CHAPTER 13

CJ could not believe what he had just heard. Thanks to Ray, he knew that not only was Eloise still alive, she was living just one floor below them. He wondered if she knew that Pat had gotten behind her wall through the grille opening. He wondered if she knew about *Treasure Island*.

CJ just wanted to be away from people so he could think. He stumbled down the back wooden stairs to the storage area with his mind reeling. No wonder their visitor had known where the kitchen was in their apartment. CJ wondered if Eloise thought there was treasure, her treasure, somewhere in this building, maybe even in their apartment. Was that why she still lived here? Maybe she could make sense of the seven poems in Mr. Post's book.

His mind ran through a checklist of clues and facts. They had traded *Treasure Island* for a book of seven poems and a key. They had uncovered skip writing that said to find seven structures, each related to one of seven poems. Since the poems were all about New York City, he was certain the treasure was hidden somewhere in the city— if not in this building, then in one of the structures. It had something to do with water that flows from above. Would that mean rain?

We have so many dots, thought CJ, and no way to connect them.

They needed to start somewhere, he thought as he unlocked the storage room, breathing in the stale scent of dust and old books. He started dutifully moving boxes away from the wall with no idea what he was looking for, but it felt good to be busy. If he could clear some space, he thought, he could have a real place to be alone and to think. In a few minutes, CJ saw letters on the back wall, written with elaborate strokes of a pen on the fading, yellowed paint. It appeared to be a poem, and a funny poem at that:

> *I LOVE corned beef—I never knew*
> *How good the stuff COULD taste in stew!*
> *I love it WET, I love it DRY,*
> *I love it baked and called MEAT PIE.*

The poem went on and was signed "a soldier." CJ touched the fading ink marks and wondered if that was what someone returning from war would be thinking about, the food of home.

To CJ, the poem read like Dr. Seuss, because it was funny, rhyming, silly, but with a touch of sadness behind it. He felt a little surprised to be thinking so long about the meaning of a poem. Maybe his old teacher at PS 149 was right. He'd said poetry could get under your skin and into your heart, especially if you gave a poem a chance by reading it three times. So, out of deference to the poet-soldier, CJ dutifully read about corned beef two more times.

Then he caught sight of something else on the wall. It was a seam, no wider than a fraction of an inch, running straight up to the ceiling. It was covered with paint and slightly raised. Wanting to see where the seam started, he began moving boxes off the lowest shelf. He stayed at this laborious work for a while, till he glanced at his watch. He had been downstairs for over two hours and had left Brid and Pat upstairs the whole time. He dashed up the hall, leaving the storage room open, while he went to find his brother and sister.

As Ray opened the elevator door into the Smithfork apartment, CJ could hear Brid's frantic voice. "I swear, Maricel, CJ is home. He is just hiding or something. He didn't go out and leave us alone. He would have told me if he was leaving."

Why was his sister so upset? He hadn't technically gone outside the apartment building. Was going to the basement considered leaving people home alone? He didn't think so. As he ran down the hallway, CJ rehearsed his excuse. He would just tell the truth. He had never left the building. It wasn't like he'd gone to the park or the store, right?

Maricel was seething. She didn't even let him have a chance to state his case. She pointed a finger at him and spoke in a way he had never heard her talk. "Listen, little big-man. You are not the biggest kid I have been the nanny for, and you are not the smallest. But if there is one thing you and I need to be straight on, it is that your parents trust me to take care of you, and you have to let me do that."

Maricel was standing so close to CJ that her saliva landed on his shirt. He wiped it with his hand and looked beyond her, not right at her face. "Look at me when I address you," she continued. "You are my responsibility, and you've proved to me that you cannot be trusted. From now on, I will tell you what we will be doing each day. If we are going to the playground, then you are coming to the playground, too. You will not run around free, and I am not going to get fired just because you make your own rules. Are we clear on this?" CJ wanted to scream at her, but he just stood in that grand hallway, staring at the angels stenciled on the ceilings, waiting for the avalanche of words and spit to end.

But Maricel wasn't finished yet. "Do you know that while you were out, your brother found a man in the hallway?" she screamed.

This got CJ's attention. "What?" He looked at Brid quizzically.

"It's true," Brid said, looking upset. "There was a man in the hall—we think he came out of Patrick's room. I swear, CJ, we both saw him. And then he just left, right out the back fire stairs. Ray didn't see anyone come in or out of the elevators. How is that possible? What if that man is still around here? What if he's the man the librarian said was looking for Mr. Post's poetry book? What if he knows we have it?" she finished, her voice rising to a shriek.

"Listen, guys, let's just be calm and figure out how he got in."

"We've looked everywhere! That fire door was locked. He opened it from the inside, so how did he get into our apartment in the first place?"

"Definitely a ghost," said Patrick, whose eyes were huge and round. He was actually holding one of Maricel's hands.

"Geezum, Pat, there isn't such a thing. Give that a rest."

"We'll give *you* a rest," shouted Maricel. "Just go to your room. Something terrible could have happened to these children while you were gone!"

CJ walked past all of them back to his bedroom. He slammed the door with enough force to tell everyone what he thought. In the back part of his mind, he bristled, thinking Brid was right, that the man looking for the Post book at the library had followed the children home, and he knew the book's secrets and wanted the book for himself. CJ pulled out the book, and as he began to read, the words became unfocused as wet, hot, salty tears filled his eyes.

CHAPTER 14

Hours later, CJ woke up, still wearing his clothes, his jeans sticking uncomfortably to his body. How long had he slept? Why hadn't anyone woken him for dinner? The house was completely silent, and his digital clock read 3:32 AM. Had he really just slept for twelve hours? Moonlight fell across his bed. His window was made up of many panes of glass, and the shadows from the window frames reminded CJ of bars in a jail cell. That was how CJ felt—like he lived in a jail.

He had fallen asleep still holding the book of poems. He wished they could speak. He turned on the bedside light and reread the note to the Post children from their father. Now that he knew Eloise lived below him, he felt he should just hand the whole thing over to her. The older woman had seemed perfectly nice. Technically the poetry book belonged to her—or did it?

He read, "Dear Treasure Hunters (hopefully Eloise and Julian)." That meant the Smithforks, since they had found it, right? Maybe Eloise was too old to go looking all over the city. Maybe she had lost interest after all these years. Maybe she was so angry with her father for leaving things the way he did that she wanted nothing to do with this project. Maybe.

But what if that wasn't true? The treasure would belong to her, but maybe CJ, Brid, and Pat could help her find it. Maybe the Smithforks could help solve a few of the puzzles, just to get Eloise on her way toward finding it herself. He read the salutation yet again: " . . . hopefully Eloise." Deep down, CJ knew the right thing to do. But then he had another thought: What if Eloise had no idea that any of these clues existed?

He reached down for his backpack and the list of clues. But where was his backpack? It took him a few seconds to remember that in his haste to leave the servants' quarters, he had grabbed the poetry book but left everything else downstairs. At least nobody besides the Williamson kids ever went down there, and they were in England now. His backpack was safe.

He flipped through the book. To understand where Mr. Post was coming from, CJ decided to examine the poems the way he had learned last year in English class.

He would read each poem three times. The first time he would try and have no opinion; he would just read to get a sense of the author's frame of mind. The second and third times, he would read with a little more concentration.

Because he had slept so long, he wasn't tired at all. It was quiet now, the quiet of the middle of the night. He turned to the first poem, "The Weary Blues" by Langston Hughes.

> Droning a drowsy syncopated tune,
> Rocking back and forth to a mellow croon,
>   I heard a Negro play.
> Down on Lenox Avenue the other night
> By the pale dull pallor of an old gas light
>   He did a lazy sway. . . .
>   He did a lazy sway. . . .
> To the tune o' those Weary Blues.

By the third time CJ read the poem, he could almost feel the beat in his head. He knew Lenox Avenue was a main street in Harlem, only about twenty blocks north of their apartment. Had Mr. Post taken his family there? That would be his first question for Eloise.

Maybe he should retrieve his backpack before anyone else came around. If only he didn't have to go past elevator men every time he wanted to go somewhere. Gingerly, he put his feet on the floor. He creaked down the hallway to the front door and buzzed for the elevator. It took a full five minutes for the night operator to come upstairs.

The night man was a short, older, white-haired guy. His hair was rumpled, and he seemed embarrassed as he fumbled with the circular fulcrum while putting on his white gloves. When the gears were in place and the elevator cab was in full downward motion, he began to pat his hair with his gloved hand. CJ was certain he had just woken this man up.

"Hi," said CJ, "we haven't met yet."

"Hello," came the gruff answer. This man wasn't as friendly as Ray. He seemed to have no interest in further conversation.

"What hours do you work?" asked CJ.

"Eleven PM to seven AM."

"Every night?"

"Six nights."

"When do you sleep?"

"I sleep."

"Oh, okay."

By the time they were in the lobby, the night man seemed a little more awake. He looked surprised when CJ turned and headed down into the servants' hallway.

"Where are you going?" he yelled after CJ.

"I left some stuff down here."

"Oh."

That was weird, thought CJ as he entered the storage room, realizing he didn't know the man's name. Relieved to see his backpack still there, he returned to his work of shifting boxes, moving things closer to the front of the room. So many of the artifacts seemed useless. There were dilapidated linens, so old and fragile they almost came apart in his hands, and glass vases, covered in dust. Perhaps he could introduce himself to Eloise with an offer to either return this stuff or help her sort through it.

As CJ cleared more space around the seam in the wall he'd discovered earlier, he could see that it stopped about eighteen inches from the floor. At the place where it ended, he saw the outline of a square with paint over it.

Too impatient to move anything else, CJ lay down on the wide, dusty shelf near the little square. He got a pen from his knapsack and scrambled back into position. He chipped away at the paint with the pen, until his arm ached with the effort. The next shelf, only eighteen inches above his head, greatly constricted his movement. Finally, he freed the square from the layers of paint and saw that it was made of brass. He tried pushing it.

The square didn't free right up. Instead it moved in a complaining way, stiff and uncertain. It was almost as if a spring were in there somewhere, probably rusty and creaky. CJ was eventually able to lift what seemed like a cover by wedging his fingers behind it. He could feel something roundish with pointy edges. But what was it?

He stood for a moment to let the blood circulate through his arms again. From his backpack, he drew out his cell phone. He couldn't call anyone from the basement, but when opened, it sure could provide some light.

Bending as low as he could, CJ climbed back onto the shelf and shone the bluish light from the cell phone onto the place where the square was. He found himself staring into a large brass keyhole.

"Hello?" came a voice. In his surprise, CJ dropped the cell phone. He sprang upward so fast that he slammed his head on the shelf above him.

He shimmied backward off the low shelf to see the night elevator man standing in the doorway. "Yes, what?" snapped CJ in an uncharacteristically sharp voice.

"Just thought you might need help with something."

"No, I'm, ah, I just dropped my phone behind here," CJ said.

"Need help finding it?" the guy asked.

"No, I'm, uh, moving some of this stuff."

"Uh-huh."

"You know, there's six of us in our family, so we'll be needing space down here. My mom asked me to make room for all of our things."

"Right," the guy said. His eyes kept darting around but

not settling on any one thing. "Well, your mom picks weird times of the day to send you out on chores."

"Ha!" CJ laughed stupidly and way too loudly. "Well, maybe you should go and, um, man the elevator in case someone needs to go up and down," he said.

"Yeah. I get the hint."

"What?" CJ asked, but the no-name elevator man was gone.

CJ shimmied back onto the shelf, reaching deep down for his phone and listening to his own heavy breathing in the darkest part of the night. It was a long time before he found the courage to return to the lobby and summon the elevator.

CHAPTER 15

CJ awoke to bright sunshine and the sound of his father's voice in the hallway. It took a minute before he remembered that it was Saturday, and Labor Day weekend. When he came into the kitchen for breakfast, everyone was very kind and didn't say much to him. Though he squirmed inside, remembering his humiliation yesterday at the hands of Maricel, he appreciated the space.

To CJ and Brid's surprise, they thought very little about the Post family treasure all weekend, and even the planned visit to Grant's Tomb didn't seem too important. Maricel had the weekend off, and both their parents were around for a change, even if their dad spent several hours each day in his office. Their mom helped them unpack, and CJ had to admit he liked seeing his stuff get put away. He could really see his floors, now that they were clean. They had intricate designs in the wood. His many books that had lived in piles in his Brooklyn house had ample bookshelves here. It was so easy to find stuff. He could see that only one of the walls in his bedroom was new, and the other three were the original walls of the apartment.

On Monday, they went to a barbecue in their old neighborhood in Brooklyn. They had fun, but it felt weird to hop on the subway back to the Upper East Side afterward, instead of walking down the block to the old house with the painted green floors.

The next morning, CJ stood adjusting his tie in the steamed-up bathroom mirror. He felt ridiculous in his school uniform of khaki pants, button-down shirt, tie, and blue blazer with brass buttons and a Saint James's emblem on the lapel. He looked like he worked in a bank. Brid came up behind him in a checkered tunic, a puffy-sleeved blouse, and lace-up shoes with flat heels.

"We look so dorky," she said with a grin.

"I cannot wait for this day to be over," muttered CJ. He realized he'd never told his sister about the no-name elevator operator and what he'd found in the storage room. It was too much to blurt out right then, so he decided to wait.

Mrs. Smithfork walked by, looking very different from her usual self.

"Mom, your hair turned blond!" Brid exclaimed.

"Brid, I prefer to think of it as turning back to blond, a shade I haven't enjoyed since I was about ten! Thought it would be a fun change, kind of like a disguise."

"Yeah, our uniforms are like disguises, too. Two cool kids disguised as dorks."

"Never mind that. You look great. C'mon, give me the chant: I feel good."

Brid and CJ reluctantly repeated after her, "I feel good."

"I'm going to have a great day!" their mom continued. This had been a tradition in their family ever since they were little and afraid to leave her for preschool.

"I'm going to have a great day," they both repeated in a monotone. To their surprise, the familiar words made them feel better.

"Your breakfast is on the table," their mom said. "Patrick is already there. Maricel will walk you up to Ninety-eighth Street. Your backpacks are in the front hall, and Carron and I are off to yoga class."

"Carron does yoga?" Brid asked, rolling her eyes at CJ.

"It's mommy-and-me yoga. You cannot believe how flexible that baby is!"

She brushed the back of CJ's head with her lips. "Have fun," she said, in a weird, chirpy voice that both CJ and Brid found really irritating.

With Maricel holding Patrick's hand, the three kids

headed north on Fifth Avenue, joining a parade of children wearing a multitude of uniforms. "Where did all these kids come from?" Brid asked. "These streets have been empty since we moved here."

"I guess everyone is home from their summer houses," said Maricel.

"So many different uniforms," said Patrick, "it's like we're at the Olympics."

For some reason, this made them all laugh. As they passed a kid in a tartan kilt, CJ said, "It's a sprinter from Scotland."

Next was a gaggle of girls in pale blue tunics. Brid said, "It's the gymnastics team from Finland."

Then came girls in lime-green jumpers. "Oh, it's the synchronized swimmers from Bulgaria," said CJ. Even Maricel was smiling. They kept this up until they saw a huge pack of uniformed boys about CJ's age, pulling on each other's backpacks, pretending to trip each other, and mussing each other's hair. Behind them marched a small army of women who appeared to be nannies or housekeepers, wearing the pale gray-and-white uniform of the Upper East Side. The boys were obviously from Saint James's School.

"Good luck," Brid said in a barely audible voice as CJ turned toward the wide red doors of his school. It was the first time CJ had considered that his sister could be a little nervous, too.

"Yeah, you, too. See you after school."

For some reason, this made them both feel better.

After school, CJ bolted right to his room. Nobody had spoken to him all day except in homeroom. When his homeroom teacher had introduced CJ to the class, it made him feel like a freak show. His teacher had CJ stand in front of everyone while they peppered him with questions. The teacher, Master Demeny, a bow-tied intellectual type, encouraged the class to think of the most interesting questions they could concoct, but most were pretty dull.

"Why did you move from Brooklyn?" "My dad's job."

"How many kids are in your family?" "Four."

"Do you like Saint James's?" "I've been here for half an hour."

"Do you live in the neighborhood?" "Yes."

"Why don't you try out for the soccer team?" "I did."

"What does CJ stand for?" "Cavanagh James."

"Do you play an instrument?" "Electric guitar."

"Was Brooklyn dangerous?" "Nope."

The minute the wall clock hit three PM, CJ bounded past the front doors, past Maricel waiting on the steps with the throngs of nannies and strollers, and straight home. He slammed the door of his bedroom, eager for the privacy of his own space, but Brid was already in there. She had her notebook spread before her on the floor.

"Homework?" he asked.

"Not yet. But we have to get this mystery solved before it piles on. I couldn't concentrate in school, because the treasure was all I could think about. Girls were asking me for playdates today! Playdates! I'm nine years old. Anyway, I told them I have an after-school job."

"What?" said CJ. "A job? Who would be hiring a nine-year-old?"

"I told them I worked for a detective agency."

"Brid, they're going to go home and tell their mothers, and you're going to look like a big fat liar."

"By the time they're brave enough to ask, we'll have solved this mystery, and then it won't be a lie, right?"

"Brid, there's something I have to tell you," CJ said.

"What? Are you running away from home? If you are, take me with you!"

"What? No! Do I seem that miserable?"

"Well, yes. When you disappeared on Friday, I thought for sure that you'd decided to move back to Brooklyn. I'm so glad you aren't leaving us."

"Brid, that's idiotic. I have no money and nowhere else to live. And don't you think I like my family?"

"Well, it seems like you're always mad at us, and Mom and Dad don't really talk to us anymore, so I wouldn't blame you."

"I'm not going anywhere," said CJ.

"Then what do you have to tell me?"

"On Friday while you were up in the apartment with Pat, I went back to the storage space, remember."

"Yeah, when I was taking care of Pat."

"Exactly. Don't interrupt me." He took a deep breath and told Brid about the night elevator man who didn't seem to like CJ poking around. He told her about the wall seam and the keyhole. "But that's not all," he said.

"It's not?"

"Brid, Eloise Post is not only alive, but she still lives here."

"Living in our apartment? Is she a ghost?" Brid's voice was as soft as a whisper.

"No, not a ghost. She lives in the apartment just below us. She's the lady who came up here the night we were being so noisy. She lives here." It felt good to tell his sister at last.

Brid was speechless. She didn't even reach for her pink notebook to write anything down.

"Okay, now you can speak," said CJ.

Brid's eyes were very wide, and she still didn't say a thing.

CJ said, "Are you mad I didn't take you with me to the storage room? From now on, we'll do this stuff together. Okay, Brid?"

Maybe he shouldn't have told her so much at once, he thought. "I know you want to include Patrick more, and

I think he can be a big help to us. We certainly have a lot of work to do," he continued.

But Brid didn't answer. She simply pointed behind him with terrified, enormous eyes.

"What?" CJ turned around just in time to see the figure of a man moving quickly down the hallway and darting into Patrick's bedroom.

CHAPTER 16

CJ's legs felt like they didn't belong to his body. See-ing a man running toward his little brother's bedroom, realizing Patrick could be in danger, he moved like an Olympian. He grabbed the baseball bat lying by his door and raced into the back bedroom, while Brid ran for Maricel.

"Hey, you!" yelled CJ.

He swung back the bedroom door. "You!" he yelled again. He gingerly peeked behind the door, seeing that the room looked empty and very quiet. Was the intruder in the closet? CJ kicked at the closed closet door. "Get out of there now. The police are on the way," he said, wishing it were true. His voice trembled just a little bit. He positioned Patrick's desk chair just under the door handle, effectively locking the thief in the closet, just as Brid and Maricel peeked into the room.

"He was here again?" asked Maricel. "Thank God, Patrick is at a playdate." She ran to the house phone, and Ray was in the bedroom within two minutes.

"Kids outtaderoom while I take care of this guy," said Ray, picking up CJ's bat.

"I want to stay," said CJ.

Ray was already opening the closet the tiniest crack. He looked inside, then swung the door open the entire way. Patrick didn't own a lot of clothes, and the closet was huge, so it didn't take long to realize nobody was in there.

With his heart pounding as if he had sprinted a mile, CJ checked under the bed, but he quickly saw that Pat's twenty-seven stuffed animals took up all the space. There was no way a human could fit in there. Where did he go?

Brid and Maricel came into the room.

"Are you sureyaseeing a person?" asked Ray.

"Yes," said Brid emphatically.

"I bet it's the same man Pat saw, and both times he went into this room," said CJ. "Last time he left by the fire stairs, but this time he didn't leave. He came in here."

"Yeah, butwhatI'msaying," muttered Ray, "is maybe you are seeing something that isn't real, or maybe it's real, but not dangerous."

"Like a ghost!" hollered Maricel.

"A ghost!" shrieked Brid.

"Hello?" said CJ. "Don't we all know that there isn't such a thing?" He didn't believe it was a ghost for one second.

"Wellyaknow what happened?" said Ray. "Maybe there is a ghost in this apartment. It's been such an unhappy place."

"What do you mean?" asked CJ.

Ray took a deep breath. "Well, ya know Eloise wasn't an only child."

"I think we sort of know that," said Brid, trying to remember exactly what Lukas Williamson had said about the family.

"Nah," said Ray, "she had a brother, supposed to be a nice kid. But he, um, well, he disappeared for a while. I heard he was away at some boarding school.

"By that time, his sister was already in college. They never were all together again." Ray had a faraway look in his eyes. "He just sorta disappeared, heard he went to college out West and then into the army; he didn't even show up when his mom passed away."

"You mean you were working here way back then?"

"Naw. I started in 1970. It's just that the guys who work here, we talk, yaknow? That night guy, Carlos, he was here back then."

"Yeah, that guy doesn't talk much."

"Yeah, good guy, but doesn'ttalkatall."

CJ had crawled into the closet and was looking closely at the back wall. "Look at this. It's almost like this closet has a seam. You see that slight indentation?"

Glancing at the wall, Ray said, "Honestly, kid, there's no way to go in or out of this building without getting past me or the door guy. I'd say that what you have here is either a ghost, or an overactive imagination. Neither of those things is going to hurt you."

In the background, they could hear the impatient buzzing of another tenant looking for the elevator. "Gotta go," Ray said, "but call me if you have any more problems."

As they watched him go, CJ mumbled to Brid, "It's time we include Eloise in this. We have too many questions and no answers."

Brid nodded solemnly. "Uh-huh. For a mystery that's supposed to be dead for a long time, it feels so alive."

"I bet this guy keeps coming here because he knows we are on to something. Maybe it's something he's looking for, too."

The kids looked at each other. Every day brought more questions—and still no answers.

CHAPTER 17

An hour later, Patrick was back from his playdate, and he, CJ, and Brid were descending in the elevator to the old servants' quarters. To their surprise, Maricel had made no objection when they told her where they were going, but had only told them to stay together. Abruptly, Brid turned to Ray. "We are going to clean out some things from the Post family storage area. Can you please ask Eloise to come down? She may want to keep some of these things, so we need her help." It came out of Brid's mouth so neatly and matter-of-factly that CJ thought just for an instant that she was the perfect sister.

When they got off the elevator, CJ said, "Brid, sometimes I'm very happy that you inherited brilliance from your older brother."

"I'm not sure it works that way."

"Whatever. Good idea."

The storage level seemed less sinister now than on CJ's early morning visit. Lights were on in the hall, and it smelled like cleaning fluid.

After they were inside the room and had cleared a wider path to the back wall, CJ climbed onto the low shelf again and tried to fit the large brass key into the keyhole, but he was too tall to get the key in at the right angle. Brid tried, but at last she said, "This is the right key, but something is holding it back. I think it's being held by all the layers of paint on the larger square panel."

CJ could see what she was talking about. "We need to scrape the paint off on either side. I cleared around the keyhole last night, but to open this thing we need to scrape around the seam of the entire panel."

Brid looked at her younger brother. "Pat, you're the only one who can do this. You're small enough to fit behind this shelf. Here, take this and start scraping." She gave him a wire hanger that CJ had untwisted and showed him how to scrape paint off with the sharp edge. Within minutes, Pat had a pile of paint shavings on the floor.

"Pat, get out of the way," commanded Brid. She climbed back onto the lowest shelf, key in hand. This time the key turned easily, and a large panel slid up, revealing an opening in the wall. "What the heck?"

"What is it?" Pat said.

"I can't see," complained CJ. "Is there anything in there?"

Patrick jumped into action. He squeezed behind the shelves and crawled inside. "It's a box," he said. "I'm in a metal box with a handle on the side." His voice echoed off the sides. "I'm going to try pulling this handle down." The room filled with a high-pitched sound, a bit like an electric motor, and that was the last they heard from Patrick. The paint-covered panel slid down, enclosing him inside, a weird rumbling sound could be heard, and then all was silent.

"Pat!"

Brid tried to squeeze herself behind the shelves, but she was too big. "I should get Ray, right?" she said, with panic in her voice. CJ began throwing boxes and books every which way to get closer to the panel. He crawled onto the shelf again.

"Just what, may I ask, is going on in here?" came a firm, authoritative voice.

CJ sat up, slamming his head on the shelf above him for the second time.

And there she was, Eloise Post, giving them a look that was more curious than angry. This was definitely not the way CJ had planned for them to meet. There was no time for niceties, or even a proper introduction, because they had lost Patrick.

"Our brother just disappeared back there!" CJ said. "A

panel closed; we heard a sound like a motor, and then he just disappeared."

"*Whoosh,*" Brid added, indicating the sound she heard when the panel door shut.

Eloise chuckled. "My goodness, that old thing still works?"

"Yes, this old thing still works," said CJ, not seeing anything funny.

"Wherever did you find the key for that? I misplaced mine years ago," Eloise said.

The Smithforks avoided the question. "But what is it?" Brid asked.

"Why, it's a dumbwaiter, my darling girl—a dumbwaiter for books, not for food. It's certainly not meant for little boys. I'm sure your brother is finding all sorts of nasty things in those walls. Shall we retrieve him?" Eloise asked. "Just pull that small lever in the corner downward." She motioned to CJ, who was still lying on the shelf. He reached overhead and pushed a tiny lever in the empty space where a box had been. Again, they heard the faint sound of a motor, followed by a thump when the metal box landed on the floor.

"Patrick," CJ said with relief in his voice, "get out of there."

Eloise continued, "My father used this dumbwaiter to move around the books in his library. He needed a way to bring them from storage here to our other floors."

"Is it a pulley system?" Brid asked Eloise.

"Well, the earliest dumbwaiters used pulleys, and people just pulled on the ropes to raise or lower the dumbwaiter, but this one was quite modern for its day," Eloise said rather proudly. "It has an electric motor, which explains why it was able to lift your brother's weight."

The door had slid open to reveal an empty, rectangular space.

"Patrick!" Brid said. "He's gone!"

CHAPTER 18

"Such a ridiculous place to put shelving," muttered Eloise, as she bent low to examine the space from which Patrick had vanished. "Well, children, he's bound to come out in one of the apartments on top. Don't worry yourselves. He's fine."

"Really?" said Brid incredulously. "Because I've never seen a dumbwaiter opening in our apartment."

"Remember, I said this is a book dumbwaiter, not a kitchen dumbwaiter. It runs up the south side of the building to the front of the library between that English family's apartment and the nasty man who lives below them," Eloise said.

"This is too dangerous," said CJ. "I need to go look for him."

"Trust me, it's nothing to worry about. Clearly he just got out of the dumbwaiter and went into someone's apartment. There's no way he could have gotten lost."

"I don't know, Miss Post. I think I should call my dad," Brid said.

Eloise stared at Brid. "It's interesting that you have chosen to address me by my name, when I never gave it to you." Brid and CJ looked at each other wide-eyed. They were busted. Eloise continued, "Children, if you want your parents to begin fretting, then by all means, give them a call. If you simply want your brother to come back, either go upstairs and look for him, or wait for him to come back here."

CJ and Brid didn't know what to say.

"Now, as for these ridiculous items," Eloise continued, turning toward the piles of boxes, "feel free to toss them all. I don't wish to be encumbered by them. I had assumed those English people had pitched all of it long ago."

"Well, technically the Williamsons are American," Brid said indignantly. "They just go to boarding school in England. And it's weird that you don't care about your family's stuff. Look how cute this is." She reached into a box and pulled out a carved wooden Santa face with a chipped nose.

Eloise laughed. "Ray told me you wanted me to help you sort through this, but, really, it's garbage. My family left it to be tossed long ago." With that, Eloise turned on her heel. "Nice to see you again, and if your brother comes through my wall, I'll be certain to send him down to you."

At that moment, they were interrupted by the sound of running feet.

"Hey! You're not gonna believe what I—ah!" Patrick stopped in his tracks, frozen.

"Pat!" Relief filled the room as CJ and Brid high-fived and pretended to punch him. "You're back!" said Brid.

"It's so cool!" he said. "I want to go up again."

For someone who hadn't been worried, Eloise looked very relieved. "That's quite enough for one day, young man. That dumbwaiter is older than I am, and I don't trust either one of us to work much longer." She turned to leave again.

CJ realized the opportunity to ask questions was slipping away, and he was desperate to hear what she knew of the lost Post treasure. "I think we need to talk," he said.

"Listen young man, I'm too old to start saving the planet. You can argue that my generation wrecked things around here, but please be advised we didn't know what we were doing, and now we are too old to fix it. You are on your own with that. Separating garbage? Please. Greenhouse gases, my foot," Eloise said.

"No, that's not what I want to discuss," said CJ. "I want to talk about your father and your family."

"Oh, is that what this is about?" Eloise sighed. "Another history assignment run amok? I get those every so often."

"No, it's more interesting than that. We've found some things, some clues."

She looked at him and pursed her lips. "You seem like a nice child. Let's be cordial neighbors. My father was an interesting man, but everything one could say about him has already been written and published. Any clues about his belongings have already been sought out. I'm certain you can get all the information you need from the library."

CJ tried a different approach. "You see, I really love poetry, and I'm so interested in why your family lived with poems all over the walls."

"Oh, really?" Eloise said. "Young people today don't usually take the time to know a poem. Tell me some of your favorite poets."

CJ didn't know too many poets off the top of his head. He thought of some poems he had read at his old school. "Like Longfellow and, ah, Frost."

Brid turned back a few pages in her notebook, where she had listed the poets from Mr. Post's book. "We also like Langston Hughes and Tennyson, Millay, and um, Ulysses Grant." CJ rolled his eyes at her.

"Grant the general? Don't know of any poems he wrote, but Hughes, Millay, Tennyson—that's a coincidence. They were some of my father's favorites. What exactly is your question?"

"We think there is a connection between those poets and some places in New York City. We think it has something to do with your lost inheritance."

"I don't understand."

"We think they are related. We just need to show you something."

Eloise held her fingers to her lips, almost as if she thought a ghost might be listening. "So we will meet," she said. "We will meet at the New York Public Library to study some old poetry books. It's not a lending library anymore, so we cannot take them out. I will see you there tomorrow between the hours of three thirty and five PM. I am willing to talk, but briefly. I'm an old woman with little patience left for this topic."

She pulled a silk scarf from her pocket over her head and tied it under her chin, as if she were going outside. She walked back toward the staircase, leaving piles of her past life behind her.

"She's a little cuckoo," said Patrick.

"I like her," said Brid.

"Me, too," said CJ.

"Well, I thought she was too strange to share my news with," said Patrick.

"Too strange to share your what?" Brid asked.

"My news," Patrick said. "About the words I found behind the walls."

"Pat, you found words again?"

Patrick went through an elaborate description of his journey on the dumbwaiter, how he couldn't really tell which floor he was on, how he peeked into the empty Williamson apartment through the air vents. It seemed the dumbwaiter ran in a line up the south side of the building, just as Eloise had described. He could peek out through the air ducts into all of the apartments. In one he had seen someone drinking tea in the kitchen. He had climbed out through the grille in Lily Williamson's bedroom and summoned Ray to take him from the empty Williamson apartment. "I could see the other eye in the Williamsons' apartment. And there is writing in that eye, too," he finished.

"I knew it! What did the words say?" CJ asked.

"Duh. It's probably in skip writing. You know Pat has trouble with regular reading, and you expect him to read something in skip-seven writing?" Brid said.

"You're right!" Pat said proudly, even though Brid's words sounded insulting. "That's why if you give me paper, I'll write them down for you."

"How can you write them?"

"From my arm," Pat said as he uncurled his arm. Brid and CJ saw that smeared ink marks ran up the whole length of his arm. "It's getting hard to read the letters 'cause I'm sweating," Pat said. "It was lucky I had a pen in my pocket!"

Brid opened her notebook. "Just say the letters, Pat," she said. "I'll do the writing."

"Okay." Pat took a deep breath and moved his index finger along the letters as he read: "WBZOAOLZFT-ISPUAOLPVYKLYAVNLAAOLMSVDVMNVSKLUD-HALY."

CJ was already leaning over Brid's shoulder, trying to untangle the jumble.

"Oh, and also remember," said Patrick, "that I sometimes call *D*s *B*s, and *B*s *D*s—or even *P*s."

"Right," said CJ. About ten minutes later, they had it:

PUSH THE SYMBOLS IN THEIR ORDER
TO GET THE FLOW OF GOLDEN WATER.

Brid opened CJ's clue notebook to review the message from under the other eye:

SEVEN CLUES ON SEVEN STRUCTURES
GET WATER FROM ABOVE TO RUPTURE.

Brid and CJ looked at each other without any idea what the poem meant, while Patrick wiped the sweaty ink from his arm.

CHAPTER 19

"Hard to believe these little animals got someone to write stories about them," said Brid as she, CJ, and Eloise stared at the Winnie-the-Pooh stuffed toys on the ground floor of the library. It was four o'clock on the following afternoon, and Brid and CJ had convinced Maricel that they both had homework that could only be done at the library.

"A. A. Milne wrote the Pooh stories for his son. Look how loved those animals were," Eloise said.

"Remember how Dad used to tell us stories?" Brid said to CJ. "When he wasn't so busy."

Eloise smiled. "Children, people get busy in their lives. It's just a fact, and we must try not to resent it." She turned toward the glass case holding the animals.

"They are really something, these toys. To think that they brought out someone's most creative work." Her voice sounded dreamy and wistful. "Do you know the mayor of New York City fought to keep these little creatures here? The English government wanted them back."

"But wasn't Milne English?" CJ asked.

"Yes, but he had given these toys to his American friend, and that friend donated them to this library. Inheriting things is a tricky business," Eloise said, while CJ and Brid looked knowingly at each other.

"We have something to ask you that has to do with inheritance," said CJ, getting to the point.

Eloise looked disappointed. "I told you, I'm done talking about my father. He was a very interesting man, but there is nothing else to be said. I thought we wanted to talk about poets."

"Well, we do. It's related to poetry and New York buildings, and to those clues to your inheritance, the treasure your father left you." CJ looked at her face for some sort of response, but it wasn't the reaction he expected.

"My boy, you were not alive when my father planted my inheritance in the most peculiar way possible. And you cannot have uncovered anything that isn't already known. You see, it was all over the newspapers at the time he passed away. The professional detectives my mother hired couldn't find a thing, so I don't think you will uncover anything." Eloise sighed.

"Well, those detectives never lived in the apartment, and we do," said Brid. "We're on the case all the time, and we have some theories."

"Everyone had a theory about what happened to my family's inheritance. Over the years, people came from everywhere with their ideas and their metal detectors and their infrared lights, but in the end, there was nothing there. You are being very naive if you think something will turn up in that apartment."

"But what do you think happened to the fortune? It didn't just evaporate," CJ said.

"My father was a complicated man, a man who enjoyed a good riddle, and he didn't mind making people work hard for their answers. We all knew that when the apartment was built, it included clues to a treasure hunt that he must have planned for many years. But . . ." Eloise's voice trailed off.

"But what?" Brid asked.

Eloise's eyes softened. "But he wasn't a cruel man, and he wouldn't have sent his daughter on a wild goose chase. I've come to terms with the fact that someone found everything. It hasn't been sold yet, because I would have heard about it, unless the transactions were handled in secret. For many years now, I've been trying to just forget about it. I have enough to live on."

"But how can you forget about it?" Brid asked.

"Because it's too hard to live, thinking I'm just about

to find it, and then to be continually disappointed."

"But, Eloise, we know some other things," Brid said, "things you probably don't know."

"Listen to me," she said. "I'm happy to hear your thoughts, but when you talk, please keep your voices low."

Brid and CJ had no idea why Eloise wanted their discussion to be so secret. CJ said quietly, "There's an eye behind the wall in my bedroom that is written in skip-seven writing."

"Yes, yes, I know about that. 'Seven clues on seven structures get water from above to rupture.' That was discovered years ago. The other eye reads, 'Push the symbols in their order to get the flow of golden water.' But nobody could figure out what those riddles meant." Eloise sighed.

Brid felt a little deflated. "Well, what are your theories about the clues?" she asked.

"My theory is that my father died before he could finish organizing this treasure hunt, and we are all wasting our time."

"Patrick found a book," CJ blurted out.

"Who's Patrick?" Eloise said.

"Patrick, our brother! The one who went up in the dumbwaiter yesterday."

"Oh yes, the cheeky one. Go on. What book?"

"And then we found some messages in the fireplaces,

and they have a code that reads 'Servants Dumbwaiter' and something else that's probably a name."

"Children, I'm rather confused at this point," said Eloise. "What name? Please start at the beginning."

"It spells *Guastavino*," Brid said. "And from our research, it's a popular last name in both Italy and Spain."

CJ felt better. The decision to tell Eloise more had been made for him—and by his little sister. The interest he saw cross Eloise's face proved to him that the treasure hunt had moved forward, that they really had found something Eloise had not.

"Who was Guastavino?" CJ asked.

"Guastavino and his son were tile makers and builders. They designed fireproof buildings at a time when New Yorkers were worried about fires. Back then, we had no sprinkler systems or firefighters with modern equipment. Once a building caught fire, it usually burned to the ground, along with all the buildings near it. After the Great Chicago Fire in 1871, New York was seeking more fireproof buildings, and the Guastavinos seemed to be the only men able to deliver them. In the 1920s and 1930s, they built many magnificent buildings with rounded ceilings and no wooden support beams to catch fire. Nobody else of that time could build in that manner—vaulted ceilings and no seams."

"So maybe the treasure is in a Guastavino building?" CJ asked.

"Maybe it *was*." Eloise seemed lost in thought. "But the water part throws me. I have no idea what that means, unless Guastavino built some structure that holds water."

"Like a dam? Or the reservoir in Central Park?" Brid suggested. "We need to visit some of his buildings."

"That could take a while," said Eloise, smiling. "He probably has two hundred buildings here in New York. Listen, children, you must promise not to breathe another word of this to anyone. Can I count on you?"

They both nodded their heads solemnly. CJ said, "We have more to tell you. It's about a book we returned to this library. When we did that, we were given another book, a book of poems, poems that your father liked."

"Stop," said Eloise. "This is not the place to talk freely, nor is our apartment building. It's just not safe from prying ears. Can you meet me tomorrow, same time?"

"Sure," said CJ, wondering how they would get away from Maricel for two days in a row.

"I will meet you at Belvedere Castle, at the southern side of the Great Lawn in Central Park. Do you know where that is?"

"We'll find it," said CJ.

"It's behind the Metropolitan Museum of Art, southwest. Go as high up as you can in the castle. We can speak privately there. Now, I will take my leave at once. To be continued," Eloise said.

"Okay," CJ said.

"Really, children, it's not safe to be seen with me. Be very careful, and don't share this information with anyone else."

"Okay," Brid said, watching Eloise scurry away, tying her scarf over her hair.

CJ looked at Brid. "That was weird."

"Yeah, I thought she would be happy."

"Well, she wasn't unhappy."

"No, just nervous."

"If she's nervous, should we be nervous?"

"Not sure."

"CJ?"

"Yeah?"

"I don't want you going down in the servants' quarters again without me."

CHAPTER 20

To escape Maricel's clutches the next day, CJ and Brid concocted a more elaborate plan. They told her CJ had a school project on ancient Greece, and he needed to visit the Metropolitan Museum of Art. Brid was going to help him. They planned to duck behind the massive museum and meet Eloise at Belvedere Castle.

Not surprisingly, Maricel seemed suspicious about their story, and she insisted on coming with them. But bringing Maricel also meant bringing Carron and Patrick. CJ was simply betting that Maricel would give up on following him through the museum and would eventually agree for him to meet up with her afterward. Still, it was a big risk to take. As Maricel struggled to get the bulky stroller up the enormous front steps of the museum and through the revolving doors, she showed no signs of giving up.

After just a few minutes in the museum, Carron started whining. CJ and Brid had brought notebooks and were taking very elaborate notes on the Greek statues. "You know, CJ," said Maricel, "there is a playground, the Three Bears playground, just on the side of the museum. I'm going to take Carron and Pat there, and have you meet us when you are done."

"Well, okay," CJ said, trying to sound disappointed, "but I could sure use Patrick's help, plus he's really interested in the arms and armor exhibit. Can he come with us?"

"I'm sorry," said Maricel. "If Patrick goes, then we all go." Patrick looked at CJ, knowing exactly what was going on. The other kids had briefed him the night before. Brid feared he was about to tell on them, but instead he said, "I don't want to look at any stupid knights in shining armor. I want to go to the playground."

Brid couldn't believe it. He was sacrificing himself so they could be free.

"Okay, then I guess it's just me and CJ," said Brid, a little too fake-sad.

"We'll be at the Three Bears playground on the south side of the museum," Maricel repeated. "You will meet me there in two hours, and you must be on time so I don't worry."

"I get you," CJ said, smiling at her.

"Wish we could go to the playground instead of researching the ancient Greeks," said Brid for effect.

Patrick looked uncertain, as if he were about to say something, but he reluctantly turned with Maricel and headed back out through the revolving doors and into the sunshine.

"Hurry up," said Brid, crossing to the exit doors on the north end of the hallway. "We can't be late for Eloise."

The two children bolted down the steps, slipping into the crowd outside. They ran behind the museum and up the hill that led to the Great Lawn. Ball fields were everywhere, making CJ salivate for the spring baseball season. But the surreal and magical sight of a most magnificent castle soon interrupted his thoughts. It was like something out of a fairy tale. There was even a flag on the top turret. With a sense of joy, the kids tore across the enclosed fields, running fast and free, feeling the elation of not being in a crowd and of having a terrifying and exciting secret.

The steps that led up the castle's side were crowded. There were nannies helping toddlers up the massive staircase and people taking photos. It was a human traffic jam. Why would Eloise choose such a busy place? But a funny thing happens with people. The higher they have to climb, the fewer are willing. Stair after stair, level after level, the crowds grew thinner, and the more alone Brid and CJ found themselves.

"I cannot believe a seventy-year-old lady can do this!" Brid said as she puffed and wheezed her way higher.

"Seventy? Do the math. If she was born in the nineteen twenties, she could be in her eighties."

They were to meet Eloise in the top room, which held a few small science and natural history displays. The only other people in the room were a young couple, who were speaking in German. The coast was clear. CJ and Brid heard footsteps, and then there she was, a silk scarf tied over her hair. Was it a disguise?

Eloise didn't say hello to them. She crossed the room to a corner display, something about squirrels. CJ and Brid knew instinctively not to bother her. Instead, they fixed their eyes on some papier-mâché birds hanging from the stone ceiling. Brid's heart was still pounding from climbing up all those stairs.

The German girl said something to her companion, and they turned and began to head down the steps. Eloise looked at the Smithforks and waved for them to follow her up a small staircase with a panel roof on top. There was a padlock that appeared locked but wasn't. She put her hands on the roof panel and pushed up. It sprang easily upward to reveal a few more steps. She indicated they should follow her, and they soon found themselves on the turret of Belvedere Castle, with the kingdom of Manhattan spread out below.

The scene was breathtaking, and nobody spoke for a full minute. "How did you ever find this place?" asked Brid softly.

"Everyone in New York City, everyone who is to survive in this town, needs a place like this, a place to be alone. For some it can be a bathroom with a cozy nook and a solid lock on the door, for others a rooftop filled with pigeons, but for me, it's here." Eloise looked sternly into their eyes. "And don't you dare go and tell anyone." She smiled.

"We won't," Brid said.

CJ thought of his private places: the stairwell in the back of the apartment, the servant/storage area—new places he could see himself getting used to. They might not be his old backyard, but they weren't bad.

Eloise took out a picnic blanket from her canvas bag. She spread it over the top step and stiffly lowered herself onto it. She gestured for them to sit on the concrete.

Dramatically, she untied the corners of the scarf, releasing wavy, silver-white hair. She ran her fingers through it and shook her head, and Brid thought she looked beautiful.

"Finally," she said. "I may not act excited about what you children have to say, but I appreciate your thoughts on this mystery. Please start at the beginning, and don't leave out a single detail."

Brid opened her notebook, ready to review the clues. It felt so good to be up here, in the open air, to have so much information, so many questions for which she might soon have answers, and to not worry, finally, that someone was listening.

CHAPTER 21

The afternoon passed quickly, and the sun was setting behind the Central Park trees and the West Side apartment buildings by the time CJ and Brid finished speaking. They told Eloise everything about their family, about their new apartment, and how they first learned about the mystery on moving day when they discovered the eye behind the wall. But they still had not told her everything they knew about the one most important object.

CJ unzipped his backpack and rubbed his fingers against the worn leather of Lyon Post's poetry book. "Miss Post?" he said timidly. "There is one more thing. We found a library book back behind our wall that was due in 1937, with a note asking whoever found it to return it."

Eloise nodded. "You are detectives, aren't you? I remember that old thing. I kept thinking I would get around to returning it and then I just hid it somewhere. It was one of those chores I kept thinking I'd get to. Wherever did you find it?"

"You mean you knew about it?" Brid said as she and CJ looked at each other. "Well, it was on a high shelf, behind the wall. We took it back last week, and the librarian gave us something that was waiting for many years for the person who returned the book. I believe this is yours."

Carefully, CJ placed the old, leather-bound poetry book in her hands. Eloise seemed to have no words. Lifting a finger, she opened the cracked cover to the note that lay inside. A slight wind lifted the sides of the paper, threatening to blow it away.

Slowly, she read the note her father had written to her so long ago. She kept a stoic face as she read her father's sentiments. Brid followed Eloise's eyes moving back and forth across the lines of the note at least three times. Then she turned to the next page, the page with the Langston Hughes poem, and she inhaled the way people do when they've had a great surprise. She briefly looked at the back of the book before firmly closing it. CJ and Brid didn't know why Miss Post stopped.

And, because he didn't know what to say next, CJ cleared his throat. "Our plan is this," he said. "We know we are supposed to find seven structures and push some kind of symbol on each. We think each structure is related to one of these seven poems. We think each one of these poems meant something to your family and maybe refers to someplace that you liked to go together. When we push those symbols in the order they are in Mr. Post's book, we will 'get the flow of golden water,' whatever that is."

"We think that means the treasure," Brid said.

Eloise didn't seem to be listening. Slowly, she stood up, and the children stood, too. Efficiently, she rolled up the picnic blanket and arranged it back in the canvas bag. Then she tucked the book into the bag as well. "Shouldn't you children be getting home?" she said in a low voice. "You've been gone for nearly two hours."

"We're meeting our nanny. Can we walk out together?" asked Brid, who was closing her notebook, surprised she would have nothing to write down.

"Best you go first," Eloise said, looking at them as if to say, Get a move on.

"Don't you want to tell us anything? Do you know what answers your dad is trying to give us in these poems?" CJ asked.

"Answers to what?"

"Well, obviously, you have to know what some of this means, right?"

"Why would I have to know anything?" Eloise snapped

as she tied her scarf over her head once again. "I'm an old lady who might enjoy a good story now and then, but that's about it."

"Do you mean you don't believe us?"

"I didn't say that. I do believe you have found what you said you found, and the note in this book is in both my father's handwriting and his style. I also believe you have the imagination of healthy children your age. Oh dear, I miss that active imagination."

"I can't believe this," said CJ. "Why don't you want to talk to us?"

"I love talking with you. You've been quite entertaining, but you do realize that any sane person would consider you quite off your rocker, should you go around speaking of puzzles in the wall, disappearing men in your brother's room, and poetry books left in a library for over seventy years."

"Is that it, Miss Post?" said Brid. "Do you really think we are making this all up?"

"Do you really want to know what I think?" Eloise said. "I think I see before me two very bright and lonely children. I think you miss your old life, your school, and your friends from Brooklyn very much, and your parents are too darn busy to pay attention to you right now. I think the prospect of finding treasure in an old and history-rich apartment on glamorous Fifth Avenue seems like the antidote for such loneliness. Yes, you know more than most people in the building. You know that the famous Post heiress is still living at that address under the pseudonym of Eloise Munn. Perhaps there was only one mystery to solve, and that was the location of my father's poetry book. That is probably all the treasure he meant. It's ironic really that by not doing a chore, I missed this little prize, and the walls my father had planned to erect following his death prevented me from doing that little chore. So I thank you for that. Now, I think it's time you venture back into the real world and make some new friends your own age, and really start your new life on the Upper East Side of New York City."

CJ was dismayed. "You're kidding me, right? What made you change your mind? Why won't you talk to us? There has to be more to the treasure than that book. But why is the dumbwaiter important?"

Slowly, Eloise turned back toward them and recited, "'My fairest child, I have no song to give you.'"

All three were very quiet, and a red-tailed hawk swooped low, coming within thirty feet of them.

"I know that line," said CJ. "It's from a Kingsley poem. So are you saying that you simply have nothing to tell us? That this whole thing doesn't seem plausible to you?"

"I'm saying that I love poetry, and sometimes a poem can summarize so beautifully what others cannot hear you say."

"Huh?" said Brid.

"She means a poem can say more than a rambling conversation," said CJ.

Eloise continued to recite:

> *"No lark could pipe to skies so dull and grey:*
> *Yet, ere we part, one lesson I can leave you*
> *For every day."*

CJ felt angry. "So you're going to let some dead poet speak for you? What is this supposed one lesson you are going to leave us with?"

"Young man, I cannot believe you know that poem. Charles Kingsley wrote it in the eighteen hundreds, and it's called 'A Farewell.'"

"I hate poetry," said CJ. "It's just that we read this in school, and I remember poems. They stick to my brain, and they bug me!"

Eloise continued, reciting the next verse:

> *"Be good, sweet maid, and let who will be clever;*
> *Do noble things, not dream them, all day long:*
> *And so make life, death, and that vast for-ever*
> *One grand, sweet song."*

With that, Eloise stepped down the turret steps, swung open the access door, and closed it behind her.

CJ and Brid were silent for a moment, then Brid spoke

first. "So what exactly was she saying besides good-bye?"

"The poem is saying she can't help us. That we should take action instead of just being dreamy, that we should make the most of life."

"Isn't that a little heavy?" Brid said. "I mean, it was really rude of her to leave us like that when it was her turn to share information."

"Unless," said CJ.

"Unless what?"

"Well," said CJ, "she could be plotting to use the information we just gave her to solve this mystery herself."

"That would be impossible," said Brid.

"Why?"

"Because it seems like the treasure is in our side of the apartment. Why else is that guy trying to break in? Why else are the codes just on our side?"

"How do you know they are just on our side? Remember, the other eye and its writing were in the Williamsons' apartment. And the Guastavino buildings? According to Eloise, there are over two hundred of them, and they're everywhere."

"Good point. What are your other ideas?"

"One, that she thinks we are crazy, and she wants nothing to do with us. The second idea is that she thinks we are in danger. Danger so bad that she doesn't want to risk having us involved."

Brid was silent, and when she spoke, her voice sounded

young and small. "Maybe we *should* try and be like normal kids, CJ."

"What do you mean? We are normal."

"I mean, like she told us, we should get more into school stuff, make some friends. We keep living like we'll move back to Brooklyn soon, so it's not worth the effort to meet kids our own age."

CJ replied, sounding upset, "Everyone is weird around here, with their nannies and drivers and housekeepers and playdates. They all plan to go off to boarding school when they start high school." He added, "My lab partner in science has a personal assistant."

"A what?"

"Seriously, he has a woman who just keeps the schedule for his family."

"For real?"

"Real. Like yesterday, I asked if he wanted to come over and he said that he did, and that he would tell his assistant, so she would call my nanny to figure out when we can play."

"No way." Brid broke into a grin.

"That's so snobby and weird," said CJ.

"That doesn't make him snobby or weird," said Brid. "You can't help having the family you were born into, right? It just means maybe his family is super busy."

But CJ was hardly listening. "And do you know we

have a sports day coming up, and one of the events is a drivers' race."

"What's a drivers' race?"

"A drivers' race is when everyone's chauffeurs race against each other."

"You mean like they race in their cars?"

"No, I mean like running, a footrace, one driver against another."

"No way is that true."

"Ask my lab partner when he comes over—if he comes over—if it ever fits into his schedule."

CJ smiled and Brid laughed, but there she stopped and said, "There's nobody to just hang out with."

"Yeah."

"Nobody except each other."

"I know, and I'm sick of it."

"You're sick of me?"

"A little."

"Well I'm sick of you, too!" CJ said, and suddenly both of them were laughing.

CJ put his hand out to Brid. "You know we can keep working on this ourselves, right? Even if Eloise has the book, we know what the poems are."

"I know that."

"And if we swear to not tell anyone else, *anyone*, then what is the danger, right?"

"Right."

"Shake?"

"Shake."

"Wish we had kept a copy of that book."

"Me, too."

"But we didn't."

"Nope."

Before they climbed through the panel into the top floor of the castle, they took one last look at Manhattan, its shadows, hinting at a city full of secrets.

CHAPTER 22

The days of early fall passed by, and the hot apartment turned cozy and perfect in temperature. Homework was piled on and took up an enormous amount of Brid's and CJ's time. Mrs. Smithfork heard that most kids on the Upper East Side had something called a homework helper—a college student who would come by to assist the children with their studies. Soon, the Smithforks had another new person in their lives: Charlize.

Unlike the responsible Maricel, Charlize was carefree and easygoing, a New York University student who texted her boyfriend almost continuously. In fact, she was always doing more than one thing at the same time. Even her hair couldn't seem to decide on one particular color. She was tall, with long hair that she dyed fabulous shades of blond and blonder, until it seemed white. Then she would return to some dark brown color and start all over again, bleaching, dying, making her hair a different shade of fabulous every week.

Brid liked Charlize because she French-braided Brid's hair while she quizzed her on spelling; CJ liked her because she mostly left him alone to study in the fire stairwell; and Patrick liked her because she didn't mind throwing a football back and forth while she helped him memorize math facts.

Charlize was also uninhibited enough to say things the way she saw them and to not worry what people thought of her. One Thursday night at the end of September was no different. "Why don't you kids have any friends?" she asked as Patrick hurled balls at her in the homework room. Brid sat nearby at her desk, admiring Charlize's hair, which that week hovered between chestnut and gold. "Seven plus seven."

"We have friends. Fourteen," said Patrick.

"I know *you* do," she said as she aimed at him again. "Six plus eight. It's your brother and sister I'm talking about."

"Fourteen."

"We have friends," Brid interjected. "They just live in Brooklyn."

"Geez, you're picky. You only accept friends from one borough? Six plus nine."

"Fifteen. Yeah, they say no to playdates all the time," accused Patrick.

"We're too old for playdates," said Brid, rolling her eyes at Patrick.

"So call it something else; call it hanging out with your friends," said Charlize, throwing the ball down the hall and into Patrick's room, to signal him it was time to get ready for bed. "But eventually you guys have to get a life."

CJ could hear this whole conversation from where he sat at the top of the stairwell, but he was in his private place, the place Eloise said every city person needed, and not about to join in. Since that afternoon in the castle, he was vigilant about doing his homework in the fire stairwell, a sort of indoor fire escape at the back of the apartment. He was hoping for another chance to talk to Eloise. He couldn't understand why she was so dismissive of them. As soon as they had handed her the poetry book, she had turned cold and distant. CJ needed to know why. But three weeks later, he still hadn't seen her again.

CJ thought that Charlize was wrong about one thing. They did have a life; it was just a secret one. At that moment, his thoughts were interrupted by the click of a door being unlocked. It was her door, one flight of stairs down. Should he run down and say hello? Should he sit still and make sure it was, in fact, Eloise? It was probably

Annika, her maid, taking the garbage out. He heard the door close.

Wow, he thought to himself, that garbage was thrown out in record time. But then he heard breathing, a large exhale. The person hadn't gone back in. Whoever it was was standing, listening for something. CJ didn't dare move a muscle. He looked at his homework papers spread around him. One looked as if it was about to slip off the stair below him. He stared at it, silently begging the piece of paper to hold still. And then he heard a man speak, a mysterious, gravelly voice:

"So what do you have for me?"

"I don't have anything for you," said a woman. Eloise.

"I just wish you would share with me. We should work together."

"How many years are you going to keep at this?" Eloise asked the man. "How long?"

"Eloise, I think you underestimate me. I cannot rest until I have solved this and gotten what is mine."

"How on earth can you believe it's yours?"

"I keep telling you, these two things are together. You get your inheritance, and I clear Mr. Torrio's name. When one is found, the other will be, too."

"You mean your hoodlum father's name? Why on earth do you care about him?"

"Because he wasn't a hoodlum, and I can prove that to you, once you find your inheritance. Tell me about those kids. I know they are on to something, even though they just keep finding the same old clues we found years ago."

"Those children don't know anything, and you must leave them alone."

"I wish for once you would trust me; I wish we could work together."

Bang! At the sound of something being thrown against the wall, CJ leaped to his feet. "Sorry," the man said. "I am just so frustrated!"

"Calm yourself," said Eloise. "Throwing garbage pails against the wall will get you nowhere. Whatever was here must have been taken away many years ago. Sometimes I think we have wasted our lives by staying here. I know I have, and I can't imagine why you still live here, with far less to gain than I."

CJ sucked in his breath. He wanted to run, but his legs were shivering.

"Don't you dare tangle with those children," Eloise continued. "They are innocent and don't know a thing. They thought they were just trying to help out a little old lady. You must let them be and stay out of that apartment. It's theirs now. Let it go."

CJ heard retreating footsteps and a door open and close, then complete silence. He had been right, he realized. Eloise had acted so odd when they gave her the book because she was trying to protect them. But from what?

CJ inched onto the stairs, lowering himself slowly, step by step, until he could lean forward and peek over the banister. Eloise was sitting on the lowest step with her head in her hands, and she appeared to be crying. It was the first time CJ thought she looked truly old. He wished Brid was with him. She would know what to say. He walked slowly down the steps and awkwardly put his hand on her back.

"Young man," Eloise said, lifting her head, "how dare you see me like this?" She gave him a little wink that he could see through her tears.

They both sat there for a while, saying nothing.

CJ knew now she had been trying to protect them. The man was probably the one the librarian had said was looking for the package, and he might have been the man who came into Pat's room.

"Miss Post?" he said.

"Yes, my boy?" she said, smoothing back her hair with her hands.

"Can we talk about stuff?"

"I do believe the time has come for me to be straight with you."

"Yes," he said, feeling relieved and a little nervous.

"This is quite a long story, and you know I do not like to repeat myself."

CJ felt better now that she was back to her usual, formal self.

"Do you want me to get Brid?" he asked.

"I'm not certain it's safe here, and now you know what I mean."

"Yes."

"I will meet you in our spot tomorrow at four o'clock."

CJ nodded, feeling happy and a little nervous. He was happy that the mystery was back on, that Eloise thought they had a usual spot. He was happy that Eloise was as nice as he'd thought she was, but he was nervous that he and Brid were into something more dark and dangerous than either had bargained for. He was nervous because he knew there really was a mystery in the place he now called home.

CHAPTER 23

Eloise Post was out on the castle turret by the time the Smithforks got there at exactly four the next day. She had two thick wool blankets, leather gloves, and a dark, brimmed hat pulled down on her head. The weather was much cooler than the last time they had come. Central Park looked like an artist's palette, with colorful fall leaves swirling in the cold wind. But the stone wall protected them from the breeze, and with the blankets they were perfectly warm.

When everyone was settled, Brid took out her notebook. "Please," she implored, "please begin at the very beginning."

Eloise smiled. "To really start this story, I need to set the scene. Do you know what New York City was like in the 1920s and 30s, when I was growing up?"

CJ answered, "Well, it was the biggest time of growth this city had ever seen. There was a lot of wealth and a lot of new buildings."

"We know that part," Brid said, "and it ended with the stock market crash in 1929. Many people lost their savings, and there were no jobs. That part was called the Great Depression. We studied it in school last year."

"That's all true, but I want to tell you what New York *felt* like then. I was just a baby in the twenties, so these are stories my father used to tell me as we walked around the city, looking at architecture. It was our favorite thing to do," said Eloise dreamily.

"Okay," said Brid. "Tell us what it felt like."

Eloise closed her eyes and began. "The immigrants built this town at a time when the city felt so hopeful and positive. They built the skyscrapers; they built Grand Central Terminal, the subway system, and many of the tall buildings you see along both sides of Central Park." She waved her hands, pointing toward the skyline. "The style was predominantly art deco."

"What kind of art is that?" interrupted Brid.

"It refers to an architectural and decorating style that used a lot of geometric designs, bold colors, and glass. It was a style copied from the French, and my mother loved anything French!" Eloise laughed. "The Chrysler Building and the Empire State Building were built in that time period, and they are both art deco buildings. In 1924, Calvin Coolidge was president, and by the middle of the 1920s an immigration act slowed the number of Europeans immigrating to this city. It became harder to enter the country."

"Kind of like now?" asked Brid.

"Exactly, but then an amazing thing happened: many African Americans from the South began to move up here, to bring Harlem to life."

"The Harlem Renaissance," said CJ.

"Young man, you astound me with your knowledge," said Eloise. "Yes, it was a reawakening uptown, and my father became a big fan of the music of that community.

"Meanwhile," she continued, "in our part of town lived the families of many men who had built successful businesses. There were railroad families, and oil families, even packaged-food families like mine. And because taxes were low or nonexistent, they became tremendously rich, beyond anyone's imagination. These families became very friendly with one another. There were the Fricks, the Vanderbilts, the Whitneys, my family, and about a dozen others. We all became great collectors."

"You mean like stamps?" Brid asked.

Eloise smiled. "In my family, it was mostly art, jewels, ceramics, and historical papers from other countries."

"Like legal documents?"

"Legal and religious, like ancient Bibles. People didn't

go abroad with the ease they do today, so when someone brought a tapestry home from Asia, or a golden chalice from Russia, it was really something to see and to display. My parents and their friends had enormous amounts of valuables, and collecting and showing things off was quite the rage. Have you been to the Morgan Library?" Eloise inquired. "The one on Madison Avenue?"

The children shook their heads.

"Well, you should go. It will give you an idea of what I'm talking about. My father was very good friends with J. P. Morgan's son, and often they would hold salons to discuss their travels and show off their treasures."

"We heard about those parties," said Brid excitedly. "That's why your apartment had a ballroom."

"Exactly. But there were some people the auction houses and art dealers wouldn't sell to. They didn't like people who made their money in a way that seemed suspicious or illegal. New York society never embraced the criminal element the way some cities did. Despite being rich, they were never part of the 'in' crowd, if you will. Art galleries and auction houses liked customers who they believed would eventually allow their treasures to be displayed in a museum, not some criminal's home."

"That's not so terrible," said Brid.

"Except," said Eloise, taking a deep breath.

"Except what?"

"Except that they all underestimated how ruthless

some of these bad guys could be. At first, it was little things. An art gallery window would be broken in the middle of the night, or an auction would be disrupted. Then things became worse. They began to take their revenge on people like Mr. Morgan and my father. Mr. Morgan's bank downtown was bombed, and the culprit was never found. My father's business was threatened, and then—" Eloise stopped short. "Then the most terrible thing happened."

CJ and Brid leaned forward. "Did something bad happen to your brother?" asked Brid.

Eloise sighed. "Something bad happened to my brother. After the son of Charles Lindbergh, the great aviator, was kidnapped in 1932, high-profile people worried the same thing could happen to their children. My father became crazed with worry. He hired both a nanny and a guard for me and Julian at all times. He would no longer let us go to the park to play: our bodyguard waited outside of my school to take us safely home again. We had no freedom."

"I have an idea what that feels like," said CJ.

"Finally, when we could not stand it any longer, my father sent me to boarding school under the alias Eloise Munn. I was older than Julian, you see, and my parents never felt I was in any real danger at all, but my brother was so young. He was only five years old when my father simply took him away one weekend and came home without him." Eloise's voice caught. "My father told us that Julian had gone to live with friends, but the newspapers said little Julian had been kidnapped. They said the reason my father hadn't called the police was because he was negotiating with the kidnappers on his own. But the true story, at least the story my father told me at the time, was that he left Julian in a place where he would be safe."

"So where is your brother now?" CJ asked, remembering the photograph of the young Eloise and her parents.

"Oh dear, I seem to be able to do nothing except tell you children bad news," she said. "Well, after my father died, Julian went away to boarding school, and then to college, and he never came home after that."

"So he never really moved back to 2 East 92nd Street?"

"Yes, and worse, he never wanted to see me again. I think he was jealous that I got to live with our family, and he didn't. The whole thing just broke my mother's heart."

Dusk was coming quickly to Central Park, and the cool air ran a chill up Brid's back. "Where is Julian now?" she repeated.

"I'm not certain, children. Many years after I last saw him, after my mother died, I hired a detective to find him. I know he lived on Long Island on a horse farm. But when I went to the address that the detective found, I was told that Julian had died in a riding accident. Even though my father had said that the family he'd left Julian with, the Torrios, were his friends, I still wondered if Torrio had a role in his disappearance when my father was still alive, if there had been some sort of kidnapping after all, as all the newspapers had claimed."

"And your parents?" asked Brid.

"It's very hard to recover from so much loss. They were unwilling to discuss Julian very much in my presence, and remember that I was in boarding school and rarely home. My father died of a heart attack in 1937, and it seemed he did so in the middle of writing his very complicated will."

"You mean the will that described your and Julian's inheritance?" Brid asked.

"The very one. You see, my mother had her own income, so he left all his artifacts and treasures to Julian and me, but he didn't trust banks to hold them. Instead of leaving them in a bank vault, he hid everything. He had always hinted at one last, grand treasure hunt, with clues that had been created at the time the apartment was built. But he probably didn't have time to hide all the clues before his death."

"So you were left with nothing?" Brid asked.

"Not completely nothing. There was enough money for our education. I have a modest income, and my mother left the apartment I live in to me, and the apartment on the other side to Julian, even though we didn't know where he was. I moved back here after her death. By then the estate had put walls everywhere in front of the old walls to cut our huge apartment into four family-sized apartments. Since Julian never appeared to claim his inheritance, my mother's estate rented it out to a man named Joe Torrio, from the very family some suspected of causing my brother's disappearance."

"But the Torrios didn't really do that?"

"I honestly don't know—I have no way of knowing what really happened."

Brid was looking at her notes. "What about your mother's jewels?"

"Before her death, my mother donated most of her jewelry to the Smithsonian Institution in Washington, DC. In fact, her two-hundred-seventy-five-carat diamond ring that Napoléon I gave to Marie-Louise is on display there. But my parents' other priceless items—the Fabergé porcelains, the eighteenth-century gold boxes, their Russian Imperial art objects, the jewels from the Maximilian dynasty—all went missing. The list goes on and on, and nobody has ever seen any of it again."

"And this is what you think is still in the apartment?" CJ asked.

"I used to think so, and so have others. But the apartment has been picked over so many times, and nobody has found anything. Still, I just cannot make myself leave 2 East 92nd Street; I feel it's the last place where I can be close to my family. When you handed me those poems from my father, it brought my childhood back to me. He loved this city so much."

"And he loved you," Brid said simply.

"You know, there have been moments over the years when I doubted that, but after you handed me the note and book, I felt happier. Even if we never find the treasure, I feel better about how everything has turned out. To think, I didn't get this book just because I didn't return a library book."

CJ interrupted. "But why was that book behind the wall on the shelf?"

"The walls were built before I had a chance to clear everything from the shelves. I suppose some things were left behind the walls. I remember now that I came back from a trip after my father died, and everything had been covered up by the new walls."

As they thought about that, the trio watched a crow swooping to a precipice below them, picking at the remains of some unfortunate animal.

Eloise continued, "The Torrios were aware of my father's confusing will. In fact, all of New York City knew about it. It was like a pirate treasure hunt for a while, but nothing ever showed up. In time, everyone seemed to have forgotten it, except Joe Torrio and me."

"And now us," said Brid.

"Yes, and now the Smithforks," said Eloise. "I do know

that Torrio would frequently go into your apartment and the Williamsons'. The two of them are connected by our old silver room, a thin hallway that opens onto a staircase."

"Wait a minute," interrupted CJ. "Is the access from our apartment in a large closet, like in Patrick's room?"

"Yes, just push on one side of the closet where you see a seam," Eloise said matter-of-factly. "It opens to a narrow hallway."

"We finally know who our visitor is!" said Brid. "And I thought he was a ghost."

"Yes, you may wish to nail that shut," said Eloise. "He does like to snoop around, old Torrio. He may look scary, but really, he's just annoying. He keeps telling me that there is something of the treasure left for him, too, and he needs to find it. He's never held a job, you know. He says his father and grandfather left him enough money that he can afford to be a ne'er-do-well."

"A what?" Brid asked.

"An idle, worthless person," said CJ.

"But Eloise," said Brid, "even if he found the treasure, he wouldn't own it, would he?"

"That is unclear. My father meant for me and Julian to inherit it, but Julian has either passed away or disappeared, and that letter you retrieved from the New York Public Library said only 'hopefully Eloise,' meaning it was all right if someone else found it."

"Oh, no, it didn't mean that. It couldn't have," said CJ, even though, before he met Eloise, that was exactly what he thought it meant.

"You have no idea of the value of my father's estate," Eloise continued.

"It's a lot, right?" CJ said.

"Like twenty thousand dollars?" Brid asked.

Eloise smiled. "Times have changed, and these were one-of-a-kind objects: real treasure from another era. I once made a list of what I knew to be hidden. I took it to an art appraiser; he told me the low bid on such items would be several hundred million dollars."

The Smithforks gasped. Brid had thought she might be looking for a few rare books and maybe a valuable tea set and some coins, but nothing like what Miss Post described. As the sky over Central Park darkened, everything around her seemed uneasy and sinister.

"Children, after all these years and so many false starts, it is hard for me to be truly excited. I don't want to raise your hopes or mine. But I will say how much I enjoy having someone to talk to about this, someone I can trust."

"Well, we're happy to finally have someone to talk to, too!" blurted out Brid.

Eloise smiled. "We need to stay apart from each other in the building. We don't want to attract Mr. Torrio's attention. Also, keep your eyes out for poetry. My father was a great one for the obvious."

"Meaning?" said Brid.

"Meaning that if you try to really read and understand the signs around you, you may find some answers in obvious places. I wouldn't put it past my father to have done that," said Eloise.

"You mean a place lots of people walk by every day?"

"Exactly."

CHAPTER 24

It was a crisp, beautiful Saturday morning in late October, a few weeks after their conversation with Eloise. The children hadn't seen her again, nor had they made any progress on finding the treasure without her. Brid, Patrick, and CJ sat at the breakfast table, while their dad flitted past them, putting papers in bags, taking papers out of bags, and occasionally letting a swear word fly.

"What's up with Dad?" CJ asked. He eyed his bowl of cereal with curiosity rather than hunger. It was a mix of whole-grained this and that, resembling tree bark. Their mom was on a big-time healthy-eating kick, and sometimes meals were a little too interesting.

"He has to go to the office today, and he hates working

on Saturdays." Brid always had the pulse of the family firmly in her grasp.

Mr. Smithfork had two new projects at work. The first was the launch of the DigiSpy robotic toy, and the second was the opening of a new manufacturing plant in China. Their dad had explained to them that his investors wanted bigger profits, so he was being forced to move his factory from Brooklyn to China, where workers were paid less. He would be traveling to China in a couple of days, and that was making him grumpy.

Their mom stood with her back to CJ and Brid as she added green stuff to their eggs. She had heard that plankton was full of vitamins, so mixing the stuff into their eggs was a new nutritional tactic of hers. As she yelled, "Breakfast!" Bruce Smithfork bolted for the door, pretending to be late. CJ wished he could do the same.

"See you tonight!" their dad called.

"I'll save you some eggs, Dad," Brid said.

"You can save him my eggs, too," Pat moaned. "Bet he's going to get a doughnut at work, the lucky guy."

Anne ignored them. "Carron and I are off to yoga class this morning," she said cheerfully, sliding green gloop onto their plates. Upon hearing the word *yoga*, Carron slipped off her seat and bent over to touch the floor, demonstrating her downward-dog stance.

"Very nice, Carron," their mom cooed.

Saturday and Sunday were Maricel's days off, so CJ and Brid were looking forward to being left alone. Even Charlize, the homework helper, refused to come in on weekends. Anne Smithfork cleared her throat, the way she always did when she was about to say something the children didn't want to hear.

"So, children," she said. "I know you both believe you are old enough to stay home alone, but we will be out for several hours today, and Patrick doesn't want to come with me. I have hired a caregiver, and I want no complaining from either of you."

CJ's heart sank.

"Now, this woman is very nice, and if I hear stories of disrespectful behavior from either of you, there shall be a deep and severe punishment."

Brid and CJ smirked at each other. Their mother was terrible at punishments. She could never remember what the rules were supposed to be, and when they were broken she would say things like, "No electronics for the rest of the day." Five minutes later, she would be asking the punished child if he wanted to watch a movie with her.

Anne Smithfork continued, "The sitter's name is Miss Munn, and she actually lives in the building. We met her one night—remember? Ray told me she was available for some babysitting help, and voilà! It could be a perfect match."

Brid couldn't control herself. "That lady Eloise from downstairs?" she blurted out.

"Yes, she seems very sweet, but she is a bit older, and you need to respect her age."

CJ tried to look disappointed. "Mom, do we really need a babysitter?"

"She won't be in your way, but she'll be here if anything arises. Do I make myself clear?"

"Okay," said CJ and Brid, trying to contain their joy. Patrick was eating his green eggs, oblivious to what had just transpired.

Later that morning, the kids sat watching Eloise's fingers move over a photograph of a Rafael Guastavino building that CJ had printed out. It was the Great Hall at Ellis Island, where immigrants were processed as they entered the United States.

"This is such a grand room," she said thoughtfully.

"I don't get it," Patrick said.

"Guastavino must have either designed it or—"

CJ interrupted her as he read the caption.

"It says that Guastavino used an ancient form of mortar-and-tile building called the Catalan vault. He took long, flat tiles and placed them in layers held together by cement and sand. He interlocked the tiles in layers of mortar to create curved horizontal surfaces. These were then shaped into domes or vaults."

Eloise was peering at the photograph. "Yes, you see how there is no steel or wood holding the structure up? The tiles support themselves."

CJ kept reading. "It also says his buildings were fire-proof, since they were completely made of tile and stone. There was nothing that could burn."

"Do you think the treasure is hidden there in that building?" asked Brid excitedly. "Can we go to Ellis Island?"

"Not so fast, Brid. Listen to this: Guastavino was so meticulous about quality that he manufactured his own tiles. He left his mark on more than three hundred ninety structures in New York, but because he always listed himself as a contractor, or builder, rather than the architect—the person who designs something—he was never well known. That explains why his name is pretty much forgotten in this city," CJ said.

"So true," replied Eloise. "We're all forgotten."

CJ pulled out some more photos. "These are buildings he worked on," he said. "The Custom House down at Bowling Green, part of the American Museum of Natural History, the Cathedral of Saint John the Divine, the City Hall subway station, the Plaza Hotel, the St. Regis Hotel, Temple Emanu-El, Lenox Hill Hospital, the Cloisters, Saint Vincent Ferrer Church, Grand Central Terminal, Saint Bartholomew's, Grant's Tomb . . . it goes on and on."

"Stop!" said Brid. "Are we supposed to search through each of these huge buildings?"

Eloise was peering out the window, her mind apparently elsewhere. "Yes, it's too vague. Remember that part about a symbol for each structure?" she said.

"Maybe your father left something at each of these buildings?" Brid asked.

"That is unlikely, Brid. So much time has passed between when he hid his treasure and the present. Something would have shown up by now, and it would have been in the newspapers."

"What we need to do is look at each poem," said CJ. "Eloise, you need to remember which building in New York City each poem reminds you of. Then we can see if that structure is a Guastavino structure. If it is, then we look for some symbol on that structure."

"Honestly, that does seem a bit far-fetched to me," said Eloise. "But at least it gives us something to start with."

"We'll start at the beginning, at poem number one," said CJ. 'The Weary Blues,' by Langston Hughes. That means in or around Harlem, right?"

Brid looked skeptical. "Okay, and what exactly do we look for when we get to Harlem?"

"I presume we should visit any building that Guastavino built or did the tiling for," Eloise said.

"Easy enough," said CJ as he ran an internet search for Guastavino buildings in Harlem.

"Three places," he said. "There is a Public Bath House at 243 East 109th Street, and Saint Paul's Chapel at

Columbia University, on 116th and Broadway. Also, the Cathedral of Saint John the Divine at 112th and Amsterdam. But there are others, too, it seems, on Lenox Avenue, near 125th Street—"

"Get your coat!" said Brid, rising from the floor. "C'mon, Patrick!"

"Get your bus pass," added Eloise, rising from her chair.

CHAPTER 25

As the Smithforks tumbled out onto the sidewalk, they decided the bus would be too slow. Quickly, CJ ran back inside and brought out his skateboard and Brid's and Patrick's scooters. Eloise took one look at their wheels and said, "I believe I'll take another form of transportation. I'll call my driver and I'll meet you at the address of the Guastavino building on 109th Street. You'll be fine without an adult."

Watching her disappear back into the building, they all grinned, happy to be scooting along Fifth Avenue on a beautiful fall day and knowing their mom probably wouldn't have let them go out alone. "Wish she was our regular nanny. She lets us do anything!" shouted Patrick.

"This is so bumpy!" said Brid, her voice shaking from the jostling of the sidewalk cobblestones next to the park.

Patrick was falling way behind.

"Let's go inside the park," CJ said. "We can head north on the park drive. It's mostly parallel to Fifth Avenue anyway, and it will be smooth."

In the park, families and dogs were everywhere. "Whoa," said Brid, pointing to a spout of water peeking from behind a hedge. "What is that place?" She and CJ stood on tiptoe to look over a sharply cut hedge.

"Give me a lift," requested Patrick, who was just a little too short to see over the hedge. Beyond it, they could see a wonderland of fall flowers and greenery. They picked up their wheels and walked through a set of iron gates to get a better look at the spectacular, undulating garden. Little hills were accented with flowers in different colors—sunflowers and pink wildflowers—their petals pointing toward the sun. The fountain had a statue of dancers, holding hands and twirling joyously around the water.

There was a sign on the gates that read, *Conservatory Garden. No bicycles or wheeled toys*.

"I cannot believe this place is so close by," Brid said. "It reminds me of *The Secret Garden*."

"Yeah, except seven million people live around this garden, while Mary's garden was just a few people," CJ said. "This is really distracting; let's get back to the streets."

Patrick had already taken off ahead of them, determined not to be left behind.

"Maybe this should be my quiet place," said Brid, "the place Eloise says all city kids need. It seems so cozy and safe."

CJ rolled his eyes. "Okay, but eyes on the prize, please? Let's go."

Back on Fifth Avenue, they headed north to 109th Street and turned east.

The three kids felt joyous with freedom. Harlem was so different from the Smithforks' neighborhood, even though it was only seventeen blocks away. Men played dominoes on a cardboard box, while three girls jumped double Dutch. Brid looked at them longingly. She absolutely loved to jump rope.

Everyone seemed to be speaking Spanish, even though several stores had signs in their windows that read *African Braiding*. It was a mixed-up neighborhood, much like their old neighborhood in Brooklyn. About two blocks from their destination, they came across a very old brick building that read, *Ross Tile and Terrazzo Co*. This made CJ's heart pound. He made a note to do an internet search on Ross when he got back home. They passed a spectacular piece of graffiti that read *Poder a Dominca*, or "power to Dominica," with a Dominican Republic flag. Down the street they heard the sound of balls bouncing, and the shrill voices of children mixed with salsa music.

Their pace quickened.

Brid, Patrick, and CJ raced along the sidewalk, faster and faster. A few people glared at them, but the thrill of what they were about to see made them oblivious to anything else.

The farther east they went, the higher the street numbers climbed—and then, the numbers stopped. The children saw an enormous, low-slung school: PS 83, the Luis Muñoz Rivera School. The cornerstone for the school, prominently displayed, read 1964.

The Guastavino building had been demolished.

CHAPTER 26

The children sat dejectedly on a bench across the street from the school, a long, modern building with security bars in the windows and colorful murals painted on the side. When they saw a sleek sedan pull up and Eloise slowly get out of the car's backseat, they knew there was no way to soften the news for her.

"Children, we will never solve this mystery at this pace!" Eloise called out. "I have summoned some help. My driver is here to get us quickly from Guastavino structure to Guastavino structure!"

Brid looked at CJ. "Did you notice that this building is gone, Eloise?" she said. "It's a school now."

"Yes, yes, I see that," Eloise said, looking unperturbed. "As I was saying, for the rest of the day, we are going to visit the Harlem Guastavino properties, whether they are demolished or standing. Having a car and driver to get us around will speed things up immeasurably."

CJ was confused. "Eloise, aren't you upset?"

"Children, I feel certain that we will see some sort of pattern. We haven't even cracked the ice here. This is one of many properties, and I'm sure it was unimportant to my father. I have a feeling the buildings he chose for this puzzle meant something to him and to us, and this structure wasn't one of them!"

Eloise seemed positively giddy.

"I can't believe you aren't upset," said Brid.

"Upset? I haven't felt this alive in years. I haven't had anyone to talk to about this in a very long and lonely time. I thought I would never find my father's messages, that I would go to my grave without ever finding the things he left to me. I'm not sad, I'm energized!"

CJ spoke hesitantly. "I don't understand why you've suddenly gotten so happy."

Eloise replied, "As I was coming up here, I realized that Mr. Lyon Post, brilliant man that he was, would have been aware of the perils of progress. He knew that buildings and neighborhoods he adored would be transformed. No, there was never any treasure in this particular building, because my father would have thought that far too risky. I truly believe the treasure is out there somewhere, but there were never any clues in this building because it meant nothing to us and isn't related to any of the seven poems."

"Eloise, what are we supposed to tell your driver?" CJ asked. "Won't he wonder why we want to visit all these different places?"

"That's easy!" Eloise replied. "We tell him you are doing homework for a project on architecture. I'm your babysitter, and we are dragging Brid and Patrick along because that's what happens to younger siblings, right?"

They all laughed.

"Also, I trust my driver very much. I've known him since he was sixteen, and I know he can keep a secret. No, my driver is happy to drive us around for the rest of the afternoon if that suits your schedule."

"Suits our schedule?" asked CJ.

"Aren't you our babysitter?" said Brid.

"Oh, yes, I keep forgetting."

"Where should we go first?"

"Why are you people wasting time?" Pat asked impatiently. "The 'Weary Blues' poem is telling us to go to Lenox Avenue in Harlem. What's the big deal? Let's just go there!" Pat insisted.

"Yes, the first poem is about the blues, and how cool things were up there," said Brid.

"So first we'll visit Lenox Avenue and the Guastavino buildings around it," Eloise said as they headed back to the car.

"Until we see a pattern," said Brid.

"Until then," said Eloise.

The darkened windows rolled down a bit as they approached the car. The driver got out with his back to the children. He had a little cap on his head. He reached to open the car door to let the children climb in, and then turned to face them. The children realized that he was none other than Ray, the elevator man.

"Aryuzlost?" came Ray's uniword as he smiled broadly at them.

CJ noticed Ray really only spoke like that when he was nervous or excited. The more they got to know him, the less he did it. "No, we aren't lost. I'm doing an architecture project at school, and Eloise is babysitting today."

"It's a history class," corrected Brid.

"Yes, Ray," said Eloise. "I didn't bring my roller skates to keep up with these children, so we need a knight in shining horsepower."

Ray seemed happy to see them. He swiftly popped the trunk and loaded up the scooters and skateboard.

"Ray!" said Patrick. "Who's driving the elevator?"

"Hey, it's my day off," Ray said, laughing. "This is how I relax." The children all smiled at him as they piled into the backseat.

"I didn't know you worked on weekends," said Brid, keeping the conversation away from what they were doing.

"This is my weekend job: I drive Eloise around a bit, and it gets me off my feet."

"So you work every day?" asked Brid.

"Ifahmlucky," came his reply.

Eloise interrupted. "Ray, CJ needs to take a look at a building on Lenox Avenue. Do you know where that is?"

"Yes, ma'am, very close to here," he said. He slowly accelerated into traffic as Eloise turned from the front seat and gave the children the slightest wink.

CHAPTER 27

Ray drove slowly, surrounded by people and activity. The area was bustling with life, the sidewalks clogged with people selling food, books, and jewelry. As Ray headed north up Lenox Avenue, he spouted out information as if he were their tour guide. "That's the 135th Street Branch of the New York Public Library. And around the corner at the Schomburg Center you can see the work of Aaron Douglas, the father of African American art. And there was this terrific poet—Countee Cullen; some of his poetry is on the walls. You kids should check it out someday."

"Nice place," Patrick said happily. He wished the car would move faster.

Ray asked, "Know why they called this area Sugar Hill?"

"Why?" asked CJ.

"Because during the Harlem Renaissance, in the 1920s, this area was full of people with ambition, people who were striving, people looking to live the sweet life."

"Sweet like sugar?" asked Brid as she jotted this information into her pink notebook.

"Exactly," said Ray, who seemed to be enjoying himself.

"Here is number 409 Edgecombe." He turned toward Eloise, and Brid saw him give her a little wink. "A famous place."

"Whoa," said Brid, "now that's a fancy building." Compared to the low-slung buildings around it, number 409 looked regal and enormous. "Did Guastavino build that?" she asked CJ.

He shook his head no. "This is where all that blues music was coming from, this building and the one up the street—that's where all the action was. That poet Countee Cullen and that painter Aaron Douglas lived here. Also Thurgood Marshall, who became the first African American justice of the Supreme Court. This was some building."

The kids stared at the majestic three-part building, unsure what they were supposed to be looking for. "Where is that other apartment building you were telling us about, up the street?" CJ asked. It wasn't a Guastavino building, but he was still curious.

"Yeah, let me show you that one." Ray eased down the

street and brought the car to a stop in front of number 555.

"Now Lena Horne, the actress, lived here. So did Joe Louis, the boxer; Paul Robeson, a famous singer and actor; Duke Ellington; and Count Basie! Imagine walking around inside that place. Probably had to be able to paint and sing just to be the doorman."

Eloise laughed loudly; she seemed to adore Ray and his waterfall of information.

Brid wondered why Eloise was being so patient with Ray. This building was interesting, but since Guastavino had not built it, it couldn't hold a clue. "But Ray," she said as she looked at her notes, "let's go down to 522 Lenox. CJ needs to get his homework done, and that building may be important."

"This is really interesting," CJ said, thinking of Langston Hughes and his "Weary Blues." "You see, Ray, we're studying a builder, Rafael Guastavino. He and his son built a few places around here. Can we swing down Lenox to 139th and then to Grant's Tomb? Those were both places he built. Do you think we could drive over there?"

"Okay, okay, one place at a time." Ray sighed. "But you have to admit this was some neighborhood in Langston Hughes's time."

"It was in Post's time, too," Eloise said wistfully. "And yes, we admit it."

On West 139th Street, it only took a moment to see that the building listed in Brid's notebook, number 522 Lenox, was gone. A modern brick building stood in its place. CJ placed his head in his hands, wondering how they would ever find the symbol for the Hughes poem, while Brid tried to keep things upbeat.

"So, Ray," said Brid, "let's try Grant's Tomb. It should be directly toward the Hudson River, at 122nd Street and Riverside Drive."

"Why, thank you, miss," said Ray. "You kids are really different than I was as a boy. I don't remember too many class projects I got this excited about."

CJ gave Brid a look that told her to calm down. They trusted Ray, but they didn't want the news of their detective work spread all over the building, especially not to Mr. Torrio.

Brid kept her eyes wide open. She felt certain she would recognize any sort of symbol if she saw it. "I'm sure the Ulysses poem refers to Grant's Tomb, because how many guys named Ulysses were there?" she said to CJ. "I just know we will see something that will make sense to us."

Ray had crossed Broadway and was nearly to Riverside Drive, when Eloise suddenly exclaimed, "Stop the car! There's something I have to show you." They could see the magnificent dome of Grant's Tomb just across the street.

"Do we have to get sidetracked again?" Brid moaned.

"I cannot believe this is still here! I had forgotten about it entirely," said Eloise. "Oh, yes, we have to get sidetracked."

"What is still here?" Pat asked.

"It's the Amiable Child."

"What's that?"

"Amiable—it means someone who is agreeable and good natured," CJ said.

"So it's a kid who wants to please someone?" Patrick groaned. This did not sound like his type of kid at all.

They stopped on the far side of Riverside Drive at a small, gated garden. Eloise got out of the car, and the children followed, while Ray stayed inside. Directly in front of them stood an urn-shaped cement object behind iron bars. The kids suddenly realized it was a grave site.

"Are you kidding me—there's someone buried here?" Brid asked.

"Read the inscription," Eloise said. "Out loud, if you please."

Dutifully, CJ read, "Erected to the Memory of an Amiable Child, St. Claire Pollock, Died 15 July 1797 in the Fifth Year of His Age."

"This is a grave for a kid?" Brid asked.

"You see, children, this land was farm country back then," Eloise said. "This little boy fell to his death from those high rocks. When his family sold their farm, they asked that his grave never be touched. And so it wasn't. Can you imagine such a valuable piece of land not being developed? Even if a rule makes no financial sense, sometimes people will comply out of respect."

"Kind of like not touching our walls?"

"Exactly. My father liked to come sit up here," she said, motioning to the bench that looked out over the sparkling water of the Hudson River. "This was certainly a spot that meant something to my family."

All of this sad talk was making CJ want to move on. "You know, there isn't a poem that refers to this place. We have to keep thinking of the poems and the places they remind you of. If certain poems remind you of places in New York that meant something to your dad, and if Guastavino built them, those are the places your dad is directing us to with his book of poems."

Eloise put her hand on CJ's arm. "You're right!" she said brightly. "I never thought to look outside our apartment building, but now this makes so much sense to me. Maybe my father wanted to lead me back to the places we went together when Julian and I were very young," said Eloise, "when our family was still together." The children followed her eyes across to Grant's Tomb. "Shall we make our way over there?" she asked.

"Finally," said Brid, and together they walked slowly to the impressive structure, looming large and round above the magnificent Hudson River.

"Who was this guy," Patrick asked, "to get such a big gravestone?"

"The eighteenth president of the United States," said Brid.

"And the leading Union general of the Civil War," added CJ.

"And an ardent supporter of civil rights for African Americans," said Eloise. "My father loved to come over here—and to think I haven't visited since my childhood."

Soaring, sloped roofs surrounded the entire mausoleum. The children stood back and took it all in.

Then Patrick piped up, "What sort of star is it called when it's shaped like that?" He pointed to a star mounted over the the center of the entrance.

"Duh, it's called a star," Brid said.

"Well, actually, it's a general's star. Grant had several of them," said Eloise.

"So that's the clue," Pat said matter-of-factly.

"It's very difficult to say, Pat; there could be any number of symbols here," Brid said.

"Yeah, but these other symbols aren't behind the wall," said Pat.

"What?" Brid almost dropped her notebook. "Where behind the wall?"

"The part I can see some of, but can't get to," said Pat.

"When did you see that?"

"I saw it when I went up in the dumbwaiter, but it's in a tight spot, between the Williamsons' apartment and that bad guy."

"You mean Torrio?"

"I guess."

"How did you see it?"

"I could only see some of it. It's a really big wooden thing; it looks like it has puzzle pieces, like a giant jigsaw, and I remember the star."

"Why didn't you tell us?"

"Because I had all those letters on my arm, the letters from the other eye, and I thought that was the clue."

"Well, it was, but you have to tell us everything!" said CJ. "Did it look like you could push the puzzle pieces?"

"Patrick, describe it!" Brid interrupted. "Tell us exactly what it looks like."

"Well, it's brown and made out of wood, and the wood has lines in it."

"What do you mean, lines?"

"Like a drawing or an outline."

"Huh? I don't get it," CJ said.

"Pat, why don't you draw it?" said Brid.

"Nope. Can't draw. It's like a Christmas stocking lying on its side, after you take out the presents."

"So it's the shape of an empty stocking?"

"Yeah, but on its side."

"Now, Patrick, dear," said Eloise, "I really know those walls. And I know we used to have a carved wooden mural, but I am not sure I've ever seen anything like that."

"Yeah, but you can't fit in there, because it's on the inside of the wall. That's why you didn't see it. You have to look at it sideways to see it in there, and the only way you can do that is to be inside the dumbwaiter. Guess that dumbwaiter's not so dumb!"

Everyone was staring at Pat, and it was only then that CJ realized Ray had joined them and was listening to the whole conversation.

"Whoa, guess we aren't talking about a homework assignment anymore?" Ray looked a little sad, as if he had been left out or used.

"No, Ray, I'm afraid we've kept you in the dark," Eloise said.

"I'm guessing we're back to treasure hunting, Eloise?"

"Forgive me, Ray."

She turned to the children. "Ray and I have had so many false leads in the past that he made me promise just to let it go."

"What are the chances that it's at 2 East 92nd Street? Almost none, if you ask me," Ray said.

"But Ray, with all respect, this time we aren't asking you. I know you are going to laugh at me, but these kids are really on to something."

Brid turned to CJ. "Servant . . . dumbwaiter . . .

Gustavino! Are you thinking what I'm thinking?"

"You mean, maybe the symbols we need to push aren't actually on the structures? Like, maybe there is a symbol for each structure behind the wall, and that's what we push?" CJ replied.

Eloise smiled. "Maybe I need to go see that carved wooden installation before we go see any more Guastavino buildings."

"Exactly," said CJ.

"But how do we get inside the wall?" asked Brid.

"Now, children," interrupted Eloise, "I will not permit you to climb behind the wall. It's too risky. I simply won't permit it."

"I've *got* it!" shouted Brid. Dramatically, she flipped back many pages in her notebook. "This plan is flawless," she said. "We will get behind that wall."

CHAPTER 28

Normal life kept interfering with their detective work. On Monday morning, their dad left for his business trip to China. Their mom was busy trying to find a preschool for Carron and seemed preoccupied at breakfast.

That day after school, CJ had his first friend over from Saint James's. His name was Brent, and he was CJ's science lab partner. For a kid from a fancy family, he didn't act or look fancy. He had thick blond hair that shrouded his blue eyes. His shirt was mostly untucked, and his tie was pulled askew.

Brent knew a lot about different things. Even though he was rich like the other kids, he was fun to be around. Instead of a nanny like the other kids, he had a manny—a man.

Brent had asked for the playdate, and when CJ said okay, Brent had the manny set it up. He never even had to ask his parents.

"You guys want to stop in the park and shoot some hoops?" the manny asked when they left the school. So they played basketball for a while, until Brent suggested they go to CJ's house, which was just two blocks away. The manny was tall and African American. With his perfect teeth, chiseled body, and the way he was always being upbeat, he reminded CJ of a talk show host. Brent told CJ that the manny wanted to be an actor, and he sometimes left Brent in odd places while he auditioned for a movie or a play. Brent didn't mind at all.

"My dad's never home," said Brent. "So this is the next best thing, 'cause we do guy stuff, and he's really good at my homework."

CJ didn't want to ask about the manny doing the homework, because Brent was pretty capable in science lab. He also didn't want to talk to Brent about his own missing dad, as he was certain this was a temporary thing. Once Bruce Smithfork got that factory opened in China, he would resume being his old self. CJ hoped.

When the three guys got to CJ's house, the manny told Brent he would be back in an hour. They did some complicated secret handshake, then the manny turned and left.

"Where's he going?" asked CJ.

"He mostly talks to girls," Brent said. "At least that's what he tells me."

The apartment was mercifully quiet, the other kids all out with Maricel. "Wanna play some cards?" Brent asked.

"Uh, okay," said CJ, not really into it. They pulled CJ's desk to the middle of the room, and CJ was glad he had hung a poster over the grille so the eye wouldn't peek out at them. Brent took the seat facing the door. CJ shuffled, letting the cards fan his face before he dealt.

"What's with the dot writing?" Brent asked casually.

"What?" replied CJ, startled.

"The dot writing, like they used in the late eighteen hundreds. It's all around your room." Brent pointed at the poem that wrapped around the moldings.

"They're poems," said CJ. "The guy who lived here was really into poetry and had them written like that in the moldings."

"No, I mean the dots have a message. You see how certain letters have a tiny dot over them? You just put them in order and then check out what they spell. So what does that one spell?" Brent said, staring at the eastern wall.

CJ was embarrassed that he'd never even noticed the tiny dots. "I never really looked at them."

"Really? Well, let's check them out."

Brent had already pulled a piece of paper out of his backpack and was writing down the letters that had a dot above them. The dots were small, almost like a pinprick.

Still, CJ wondered how he had missed them.

While Brent wrote, CJ worried about their secret. He had to keep Brent out of the other rooms, or he'd see the poetry on the moldings there. What if he knew something about the Post family fortune?

Brent was talking. "You see, back in England, people hated paying postage to the government. So they started to mail newspapers to one another for free. They would just put a dot beneath the letters of the words they wanted to write, and that gave them a free way to communicate with others." He seemed to like the same sort of arcane information CJ liked.

"That makes no sense. If postage was expensive, how could they mail newspapers for free?"

"Because the law was that anything with a government stamp on it could be mailed for free because they paid a government tax."

CJ thought that if this kid weren't so nosy, he might actually like him. "I'm sure this isn't anything like that."

Brent read the poem. "Let's see. I think Carl Sandburg wrote this:

> *Arithmetic is where numbers fly like pigeons in and out*
> *of your head.*
> *Arithmetic tells you how many you lose or win if you*
> *know how many you had before you lost or won.*
> *Arithmetic is seven eleven all good children go to heaven—*

or five six bundle of sticks.

Arithmetic is numbers you squeeze from your head to your hand—

And there the poem stopped. CJ thought the artist had simply run out of wall.

When Brent wrote the letters with a dot under them, it looked like this:

INSILVERROOM

"Dude!" exclaimed Brent, who CJ was beginning to not like at all anymore. "What's in the silver room?"

"Oh, that!" CJ said, thinking quickly. "There used to be a silver room here, but it was covered over years ago," he said, wondering what could be in the silver room. Was there access to the wooden mural through there?

"I thought my grandmother was the only one who still had a silver room."

"Really? What does she use it for?"

"She has a lot of parties, and I guess it's an easier way to keep things organized. She does an inventory of all her silverware before and after, and she has people shining stuff all the time in there."

Both boys jumped at the buzzer. CJ ran down the hallway to answer it, closing Brid's, Carron's, and Patrick's doors on the way. He didn't want Brent snooping and finding any other messages.

He buzzed the intercom. "Hello?"

"Got a guy named Manny here, asking for someone named Brent," said Ray.

"I'll send him down."

Brent had followed CJ down the hall. "Time to go, Brent," said CJ. "Your manny guy is here."

"Dude, he can wait."

"He said it's important you meet him downstairs right away."

"So you just stay home all by yourself?" Brent asked with wide eyes. "We can wait with you."

"No, you need to leave. Now!" CJ was surprised at the sound of his voice, and he felt a little badly that Brent was getting his jacket on, grabbing his backpack, and practically running to the elevator.

"See you at school tomorrow," CJ said, with some apology in his voice.

"Yeah, whatever," came Brent's deflated reply.

As soon as he heard the door shut, CJ ran into Patrick's room. The poem on his moldings also had little marks over certain letters, but instead of dots, some words had numbers. Guessing he had to order the letters by these numbers, he quickly wrote down the poem, one he had never heard of.

I know a little cupboard,

With a teeny tiny key,
And there's a jar of Lollypops

For me, me, me.

It has a little shelf, my dear,
As dark as dark can be,
And there's a dish of Banbury Cakes
For me, me, me.

But when CJ wrote them out in the order of the numbers he got:

NIPAMEHTHSUP

What is that supposed to mean? thought CJ. He wished he hadn't kicked Brent out quite so quickly. His thoughts were interrupted by a ruckus at the front door as Maricel came home with the other three children.

Patrick came bounding into his room. "Oh, hey," he said. Patrick never seemed to mind when others used his stuff. "Wanna play with me?" he asked as he pulled out his wrestling figures.

"No, I was just writing some things down," CJ said as Patrick leaned over his shoulder.

Patrick studied the jumble of letters. "So what map do you want to push in?" he asked.

CJ looked at him, stunned.

"What are you talking about?"

"What map do you need to push in?"

"What are you saying?"

"What you just wrote about pushing the map in. What map?"

"Patrick, I have no idea what you are saying."

"I'm not saying it. You're the one who wrote it and now you won't even tell me why and you're in my room writing stuff, so you should tell me!"

CJ looked again at his paper. "Show me where you see that?"

"So easy." Patrick swept his finger right to left across the lettering. "Just read it backward. It says, 'Push the map in,' and by the way, CJ, you write with no finger spaces, which is really, really bad."

Watching Patrick, CJ thought his little brother might be smarter than any of them.

"Hey, Patrick?"

"Yup."

"That big thing you saw behind the wall, that wooden thing with lines that looked like a Christmas stocking on its side?"

"Yup."

CJ pulled his brother down the hall and pointed to the map of Manhattan he had pinned to his bedroom door. "Would you say it looks like this shape?" he asked.

"Totally."

CHAPTER 29

CJ was staring at the map on his door, lost in thought. He felt like he did when he ate large amounts of brownies, all jittery.

"Do you have the map here that you want to push?" Patrick asked again.

When CJ did not answer, Pat got distracted by his toy wrestling figures. He had no idea how important his revelation was.

CJ paced and thought about what the writing on Brid's moldings might say. He wanted to burst through her door and tell her, but she had brought a friend home from school. He would have to wait.

He went into the closet in Pat's bedroom, where Eloise had told them Torrio had gotten in. Was that the silver room the moldings had referred to? CJ pushed the back panel, and nothing happened. He pushed the sides the way Eloise told him, and silently the panel slid aside, revealing a narrow hall, dark and uninviting. CJ didn't enter. He thought about going down to Eloise's apartment to ask her about it, but he didn't want to do so unannounced. He'd learned from the Williamsons to call ahead, especially if he was entering by way of a secret panel.

He looked on the kitchen blackboard for Eloise's phone number, but the collage of messages, phone numbers, and Carron's art made finding it a daunting task. He had no idea how his mother found anything at all.

CJ decided to go to Eloise's back door by way of the fire stairs. He could do that without a doorman and an audience. He knocked, but there was no sound from within. He had brought a pen, paper, and some tape, and he began to write: "Dear Eloise, Access to map with symbols may be from silver room. Please advise." He folded the note and taped it to the door, thinking she or Annika would find it by evening. He couldn't wait to speak with her.

CJ was about to turn and bolt up the stairs again, when he heard a noise from below. It was a door, opening and closing rapidly.

Torrio? But he lived on the other side, below the Williamsons' apartment. It couldn't be him. Unless . . . did he travel between all four apartments using the fire stair-wells *and* the silver room? Did everyone leave their door to the fire stairwells unlocked?

CJ stood perfectly still. The other person in the stair-well had paused, too, because no noise came from either landing. There was a rushing sound in CJ's ears, his own blood coursing through his body, so loud that he prayed nobody else could hear it.

For a moment, it was as if these two people were almost daring each other to make the first move. CJ heard a soft ticking sound and wondered if the other person had a wristwatch on. Then CJ heard a click, and the entire stair-well was thrown into complete and utter darkness.

One full minute went by. CJ tried to adjust his eyes to the darkness but was only able to make out the banister to lead him upstairs. It stood about three feet away from him. He fixated on it, working on a plan to dash for it the moment the other person made a move upstairs.

The next thing he heard paralyzed him. The other per-son was simply walking up the stairs. Effortlessly, this person was coming closer, and CJ once again had jelly-filled legs that felt heavy and lifeless. He forced himself to reach forward for the banister, to feel his way up the stairs. He felt as if he was swimming to the top of a black and sightless pool, desperate for air at the surface. He knew there were eighteen steps between floors. He could see the faintest crack of light peeking out from his back door: the finish line, the place he needed to get to.

He let go of the banister to step onto the landing but instead, he felt his foot kick something hard, something that made him trip and fall forward, directly onto his face. His shin slammed against the firm thing again, the thing that was really the top step. He had miscounted! He hadn't run the full eighteen steps; it must have been only seventeen, and he had tripped himself.

From behind him he could hear a grunt, and before he could rise, the grunting thing tripped over him, falling hard and slamming CJ back onto the stairwell floor. Even though he couldn't see anything, CJ felt certain it was Torrio. The man groaned in CJ's ear.

"You should get Eloise to talk to me," the man said, in a low, gravelly voice. "I think you're a smart kid. You have no idea how complicated this thing is. You don't know the whole story."

CJ could hardly breathe. "Let me up," he said weakly.

"Yeah, we both need to get up." The old man's breath was pungent and smelled like coffee. He leaned on his hands, lifting himself off the floor.

"C-c-c-c-c-can't breathe," CJ said. He felt dizzy, and his mind was fuzzy. He slipped into a dark and foggy place, and that was the last thing he remembered.

CHAPTER 30

"My boy, please get up!" Something smelled bad and his throat hurt. CJ thought dreamily that it sounded like Eloise's voice, and she must have come to meet with him. He just couldn't get the energy to answer her. "Take a big sniff of this, dear, please?" she implored. He realized she was holding a jar of smelling salts.

The back door to the Smithfork apartment opened, and Brid dropped to the floor next to CJ. "What happened to you?" she asked. CJ felt her touch his forehead, and he grimaced.

Patrick's voice came next. "CJ, are you faking it?" CJ wished they would go away and let him be. His head was pounding.

Gingerly, Eloise, Brid, and Patrick got on either side of

him and helped him to sit up. Something wet ran down his forehead, and he shut his eyes.

"His forehead is bleeding!" Brid said, a touch of panic in her voice. "I need to get Mom."

"Mom isn't home," said Patrick. "It's just Maricel and Carron."

Eloise held some gauze to his forehead, and CJ met her hand with his own and pressed on the tender spot. His forehead was sticky with blood.

"Should we get Maricel?" Brid sounded a little anxious.

"No, I just fell forward in the darkness. I think I caught the edge of the top step with my head," CJ said.

Eloise looked at him skeptically. "I heard a loud noise, and when I came out here, all the lights were off, and you were lying on the ground."

"Yes, I was walking up the stairs and tripped."

"Well, let's get you inside, at the very least," Eloise said. "Does anything feel broken to you?"

"Nope," said CJ, wondering how much he should tell her. "I just feel groggy."

"I know exactly what to do for that," she said, bringing her container of smelling salts closer to his face.

A few minutes later, CJ was lying on his bed. Patrick had wandered back to his own bedroom.

"I do think you'll be fine," said Eloise, "but we would appreciate the truth. Did anyone hurt you?"

"But I told you . . ." CJ's voice trailed off. "I'm not

sure if he hurt me on purpose, or if it was an accident where we tripped over each other," he said. He took a deep breath and began to tell them what Brent had discovered and what had really happened on the staircase.

When he finished, the three of them sat in silence. Brid was looking up at his moldings. "Eloise, did you ever notice the dot writing?"

Eloise twisted her face into a half grin. "I stared at those poems on the moldings enough to see the dots, but I never paid them any mind. I always thought they were little nail heads, places where the nails were driven into the wall. I just saw a lighthearted poem about math, something to make me do my sums. Silly, right?

"Brid," she continued, "please go into your room and see if the poem on your molding has dots. If so, please copy those letters down for us."

"Right away!" Brid shouted, and took off down the hall.

Eloise stayed seated beside CJ's bed, looking thoughtful. "I thought you would be happy," CJ said.

"Happy that Torrio attacked you? It's high time we called the police on him. He's coming into your apartment, beating up children!"

"No!" said CJ. "He didn't beat me up. He was just sort of talking to me about working together. I really did trip myself up on the stairs. He even may have been trying to help me; I can't remember it so well. But this is important: we found a message about the silver room, and we need to look in there."

"But we've been through that in the past," said Eloise. "The silver room is a pathway from Pat's room to a back stair, but it's empty. I have a feeling access to the map was sealed when the walls were put up. He was either eavesdropping on you or looking for something. He refuses to believe nothing is here."

Just then Brid burst into the room, papers in her hands. "There is nothing in the other bedrooms, but I have a plan. It's time to launch Operation Mortar."

"What?" CJ said. "What is Operation Mortar?"

"It's my plan to get behind the wall to the wooden map. It's finally ready. It will take us to the next level of this mystery, if you think you're ready to go there," Brid said solemnly. "Because once Operation Mortar is launched, there is no going back."

CHAPTER 31

It seemed Brid had already gotten started. She had asked Ray to call Mr. Smithfork's office. Using his most courteous, professional voice, he had requested a DigiSpy unit be sent to their home. Once the Smithforks' home connected to the office, Ray turned into a fantastic actor who claimed his boss needed to work on DigiSpy the moment he returned from China. Ray didn't mash any words together, and the people from LeCube thought nothing of this request. The prototype arrived a couple of days later. CJ couldn't believe his sister had done all this without asking for help.

The DigiSpy was essentially a little robot with a camera. By using their computer keys, they could direct the robot to go anywhere, even tiny places behind the wall.

They practiced and soon could get clear images on the computer screen of any nook the DigiSpy pod visited in their apartment.

The third part of Operation Mortar called for Pat to go back up in the dumbwaiter with the DigiSpy. He had to stop the dumbwaiter in just the right spot under the silver room wall and make certain that the Torrio and Williamson apartments were empty before launching the pod into the spaces too small for him to crawl into. CJ would stay in the driver's seat—Mr. Smithfork's home office—with the computer. Pat would stay still in the dumbwaiter and wait to retrieve the DigiSpy pod. Once the robot had recorded the images, they would have a clear picture of the symbols Pat had seen behind the walls. CJ was increasingly sure that what they would see was a map of Manhattan, marked with symbols to push.

Project Mortar was going to be launched on Saturday. Brid had worked out a schedule:

9:00 AM: Eloise arrives to babysit.

9:15 AM: Mom leaves for baby yoga with Carron.

9:30 AM: Ray will be sitting outside the building in his car, looking as if he is awaiting his usual Saturday drive with Eloise. From that position, he can confirm that Mr. Torrio has left for his Saturday-morning walk. When the coast is clear, Patrick, Brid, and Eloise go down to storage area.

9:45 AM: Patrick enters the dumbwaiter with DigiSpy pod in front pocket of his hoodie. He must wear his headlight and carry his walkie-talkie.

9:45 AM: CJ launches DigiSpy program on Dad's computer. Brid will radio to him that Patrick is heading into the walls.

9:50 AM: Patrick activates DigiSpy pod. He and CJ communicate by walkie-talkie so CJ knows exactly when the DigiSpy is in the right spot.

10:00 AM: Using the arrow keys on his computer, CJ directs the movement of the DigiSpy. This will allow him to see the hidden wall on his computer screen.

10:05 AM: CJ prints photo of wall behind wall.

10:30 AM: Patrick retrieves DigiSpy and uses walkie-talkie to tell Brid that he is coming down in the dumbwaiter.

10:40 AM: All return to Dad's office to see photos of the hidden wall behind the wall.

That had been Brid's master plan, but this was what really happened:

When Mrs. Smithfork woke up that Saturday morning, she didn't feel well. She decided to stay home from baby yoga. She picked up the phone and, while Brid, Pat, and CJ watched helplessly, called Eloise to tell her not to come. Next, Anne proceeded to labor through the motions of making a big breakfast. Something was making her nurturing side come out, and worse, she seemed to want to talk in that heavy way.

"I miss your dad so much," she said, to nobody in particular, while making omelets for the kids. "I sometimes wonder if this China project is worth it."

Brid wished she could pour herself some cold cereal, but she didn't want to upset her mom.

"Oh, it will be worth it," CJ said.

"It makes me wonder if more really means more. Does a bigger company with bigger profits make for a happier life?" Anne Smithfork continued wistfully.

"Mom, don't get all heavy with us. He'll be home soon, and everything will be normal again," CJ answered.

"That's good, because I miss normal," their mom said. She cracked some pepper over the eggs, and the knob on top of the pepper grinder fell off and into the eggy mess. As she grabbed the top of the grinder, she upset the egg bowl, sending drippy egg whites across the counter and down the front of the cabinets.

"Darn it!" she said, in a meek, defeated voice.

"Mom," Brid said soothingly, "I think you need to go back to bed. We'll watch Carron while you take a nap."

Anne stabbed at the mess with paper towels. "You kids are so sweet. I feel like I have the flu or something."

"Really, Mom, take a nap. We'll be quiet."

As if she was sleepwalking, Anne drifted out of the room and back to bed.

"She must be really sick," said Brid. "She didn't even try to resist the offer."

An hour later, everyone except Eloise was in place. Carron was downstairs with Brid and Patrick. Pat climbed into position, DigiSpy in hand, while Carron tried to get into the dumbwaiter with him.

"Me come. Me come. Kawan come, too," Carron pleaded.

"No Kawan wit Paddy," Patrick said, imitating her. "Next time." He turned to Brid. "Let's get going," he said matter-of-factly, adjusting his headlamp.

"Pat, we haven't checked with Ray whether Mr. Torrio is in his apartment," said Brid. "We're getting a late start, so he might be back from his walk soon."

"It's not a problem," Patrick insisted. "I'll be really quiet."

"It's the DigiSpy I'm worried about. It makes a little whirring sound," Brid said.

"He's not going to hear anything behind the wall. Let's just start already."

Brid radioed up to CJ. "Rafael is ready for action," she said, using Guastavino's first name, their secret code name for the DigiSpy pod.

"Got it," CJ answered solemnly, double-clicking on the DigiSpy icon. The computer screen turned an undulating black color, and CJ worried that the DigiSpy wasn't working. He played with the lighting on the screen, but nothing helped. He radioed Brid. "Rafael's fuzzy," he reported.

"Because he's in the hoodie," Brid answered shortly.

Of course, thought CJ to himself. Of course the DigiSpy was fuzzy and dark. It was sending CJ footage of the inside of Pat's pocket.

About one minute later, CJ's screen got brighter as it became obvious that Patrick was in the right place and had taken the pod out of his pocket. When Patrick turned his headlamp toward a dark, narrow opening, CJ's screen lit up perfectly. Next, Pat turned the pod on himself. This was CJ's signal to indicate whether he could see clearly enough. He spoke into his radio. "Thumbs up, Rafael."

Patrick placed the DigiSpy on the ground. CJ touched his arrow keys, and the pod moved deeper into the space between the walls. The screen turned downright spooky, with wisps of thick cobwebs, balls of gray dust, and pipes everywhere. CJ saw some writing on the wall, and he held the DigiSpy in place to read the inscription: a heart with initials that meant nothing to him: BS

+ MB. Probably one of the original construction workers, grabbing a piece of Fifth Avenue history for himself and his love, CJ thought. Ugh.

Then CJ stopped pushing the arrow keys as something new came on the screen, something with intricate lines and pictures. He could plainly see an image of a star, a general's star like the one he had seen on Grant's Tomb! Clearly, this was one of the symbols that Mr. Post was saying needed to be pushed. The back of the wall was full of them. He realized he was looking at a huge map studded with symbols.

With his heart pounding, CJ hit his print button over and over, printing out sections of the map. The images formed a familiar shape: a map of a long, skinny island with symbols all over it. CJ felt certain that on the real map behind the wall, the symbols could be pushed. He laughed out loud. This was the missing piece: with the poems as their guide, they would be able to figure out the right seven symbols to push and solve the mystery. Once they knew the right symbols, the rest should be simple.

CJ's radio crackled and interrupted his thoughts.

"Gotta go," Pat said, not bothering to speak in code. On the screen, CJ could see what appeared to be Pat's arms reaching for the pod, but not getting close enough to grab it. Before CJ could do anything to help him, the screen went totally black. Pat seemed to have turned off

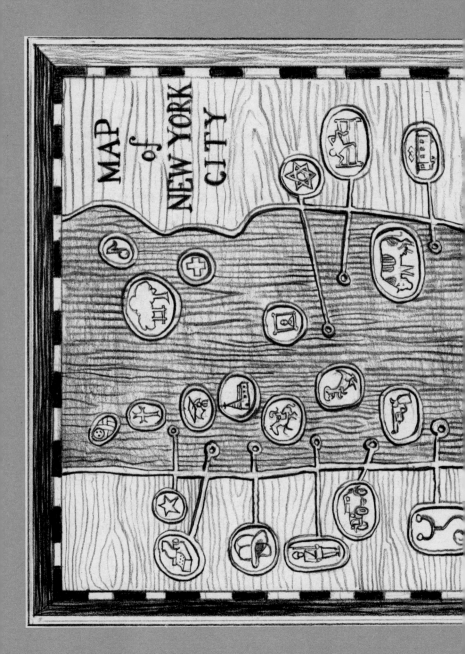

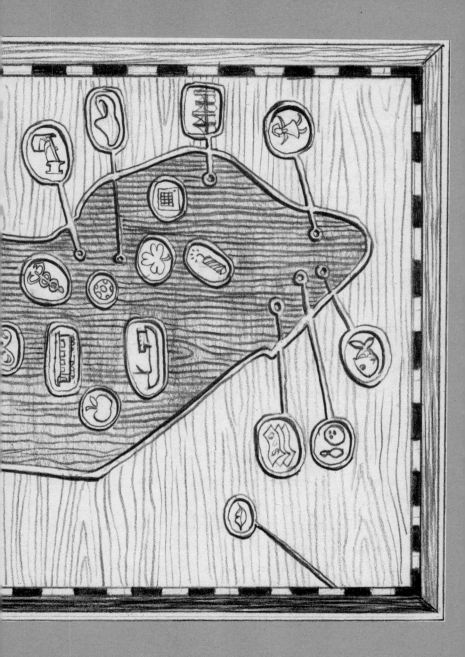

his light, and it was impossible for CJ to get an idea of which way he needed to steer the pod. He tried hitting the down key, hoping the device would simply retract back to wherever Pat was at that moment. He radioed Brid, knowing he had to say as little as possible.

"Where's Rafael?"

"Returning to earth," she said. CJ could hear Carron wailing in the background.

At that moment, Anne Smithfork shuffled into her husband's office. She sneezed. "CJ, I know Daddy doesn't want you on that computer, dear. Please don't mess anything up. Are the kids all right?"

CJ jumped up to grab the pages he'd printed. "Yeah, they're great. Brid and Pat and Carron just went down to get their scooters out of storage. They'll be right back." It felt strange to lie so easily to his mother.

"Well, please leave Daddy's stuff alone, okay? I'm going back to bed, but I called Eloise to ask her to come after all. I'm afraid I'm useless today."

"Yeah, okay," mumbled CJ, relieved that Eloise was coming and worried that they were getting in over their heads.

"CJ," Anne said exhaustedly, "I need to thank you for taking this babysitting idea so well. I know you don't need a caregiver all the time, but for now, we really need another adult around to help supervise. Thank you for being so gracious about it."

Great, CJ thought, not only do I lie to my mother, but then she thanks me for it. Ugh.

He stood and shut the door behind his mother before radioing Brid. "Any news?"

"Patrick is back." Brid paused, then said, "But Rafael has gone missing."

Chapter 32

One hour later, everyone was sitting in Mr. Smithfork's office. The printed-out map lay, pieced together, in the middle of the floor. It was enormous: about fifteen feet long and seven feet wide. Instead of street names, there were symbols that marked the many sights and secret places of Manhattan.

"I do remember seeing this in our apartment," said Eloise. "But it was on the wall in the service part of the apartment, back by the silver room. I bet it was mistakenly covered by the walls after we moved out."

"And now we have a way to get to it. But the thing is," Brid said hopefully, "Torrio didn't actually see Pat, and it's impossible that he got the pod."

"How is it impossible?" CJ asked.

"It's behind the upper half of his wall, so it'd be hard for him to reach up there. Even if he did find it, it's so small it wouldn't look meaningful to him."

"How do you know he heard anything?" CJ asked.

"I'm not sure what he heard, but his head showed up in the vent after Pat spoke on the walkie-talkie."

"What! He heard Pat speaking?" CJ said.

"How did I not think of that?" Brid said. "Of course he would hear those radios. Do you think he saw the headlamp light?" asked Brid.

"Nope. By the time he had his head up, I was able to get my light switched off," Patrick said.

"Pat, why aren't you worried?"

"Why should I be worried? Mr. Torrio heard something in the wall; so what? It could have been a mouse."

"A mouse on the thirteenth floor?"

"Yes, and a mouse that can say *Rafael*!" Pat giggled.

"What are you talking about?"

"Well, after I saw his head, Brid's voice came over the walkie-talkie asking if Rafael was okay."

"Great. I'm such a dope," said Brid.

"There was no way he knew who was in there, so who cares?" Pat answered.

"This keeps getting worse," said CJ.

"You know, he visited my room a few times, so the least I could do was go visit him, too." Pat grinned.

"Just like a friendly neighbor," Brid said skeptically.

"The thing is," Patrick said, "I had to get out of there, and I couldn't reach poor Rafael, so I left him."

"Calm down," said Brid. "Even if Torrio got back into his wall, even if he found the pod, he would think it's a toy, or something that fell behind the wall from the Williamsons' apartment. It's no big deal."

"Still," said CJ, "the faster we solve this, the better, because Rafael has to be back on Dad's desk when he comes home from China."

"Or we are so busted," said Brid.

"And how long is that?" asked Eloise.

"One week," said CJ.

"Seven days." Brid shuddered.

"Plenty of time," said Pat.

"Children, do you realize what is so mysterious?" Eloise interrupted. "Since this incredible artwork, which certainly looks like a map of Manhattan, has been located behind Mr. Torrio's walls all these years, I'd be surprised if he hasn't seen it. He has done so much investigating; how could he not have found this?"

"Oh, he probably knows it's there," said Brid. "He just has no clue what it means, since he didn't get the poetry book from the library. Even if he had gone back there and pushed some of those wooden pieces, he wouldn't know the order to push them in. Remember, we have to 'push the symbols in their order to get the flow of golden water.' Whatever golden water is."

"Well, we've got two of the symbols identified already," said Eloise.

"We do?" the kids chorused.

Eloise pointed to the map. "Look at this: the first poem is Langston Hughes's 'The Weary Blues,' where he talks about Harlem and Lenox Avenue. When I look up to Lenox Avenue on this map, I see two symbols there. One is the sun, and the other is a musical note. Even though one of the Guastavino buildings in Harlem has been demolished and we never identified a symbol that relates directly to another building in the area, that poem is about music, so clearly the right symbol to push is the musical note."

"But why couldn't the note be Carnegie Hall?" asked CJ. "You know Guastavino built that concert hall's dome."

"Well, the first poem describes Harlem, so the first symbol on the map to push must be in Harlem," said Eloise. "The poem is about music, so the symbol is the musical note. Here is what I believe my father is telling us:

"One. Find the Guastavino structure that corresponds to each poem.

"Two. Find a symbol on the map behind the wall that relates to each structure.

"Three. Push the symbols in the order of the poems in the book.

"It's that simple," Eloise finished.

"Simple?" CJ chortled. "Your father was anything but simple!"

"Well, it would have been simple if I had returned the library book when I should have and solved the mystery before the walls were closed."

"How would we ever know these things without you?" Brid said.

Eloise continued, "The next poem is 'Ulysses.' There is the general's star, over by Grant's Tomb. Clearly, that is the second symbol to push."

"And maybe he liked General Grant?" CJ asked.

"He loved General Grant and that social wife of his," Eloise answered. "We used to eat off of Grant dinner plates on patriotic holidays."

"It's so funny to hear these characters spoken of like they're still alive!" Brid said dreamily. "The third poem is about a train," she added. "It's called 'Faint Heart in a Rail Way Train.' But trains are everywhere in New York. Is this a dead end?"

The room seemed heavy in thought, and nobody spoke. Carron had lain down under her father's desk and fallen asleep.

"Great babysitter I am," Eloise said. "I forgot to put her down for a nap."

"May as well let her sleep there," CJ said practically. "Let's read this one again."

"It's not just about a train; it's more about longing for love," Eloise said. "A theme with which I used to be familiar."

"Huh?"

"I thought this was the one about the train station?" said Brid.

"Well, in theory, yes, but read it slowly, my children. It was one of my father's favorites, a Thomas Hardy poem. It's just so beautiful." Eloise had a wistful, dreamy look.

Brid decided to read the poem aloud. She cleared her throat and announced, "'Faint Heart in a Rail Way Train.' What does *faint heart* mean?"

"He just means getting faint of heart, losing the courage to do something," explained CJ.

Brid read:

> *"At nine in the morning there passed a church,*
> *At ten there passed me by the sea,*
> *At twelve a town of smoke and smirch,*
> *At two a forest of oak and birch,*
>   *And then, on a platform, she:*

> *"A radiant stranger, who saw not me,*
> *I queried, 'Get out to her do I dare?'*
> *But I kept my seat in search for a plea,*
> *And the wheels moved on. O, could it be*
>   *That I had alighted there!"*

The room was quiet, the only sounds Carron's soft snores.

"It makes me think about a big trip, like how you notice people more in a strange place," Brid began.

"Or maybe it describes the way we see things from a train?" CJ added.

"It's more a story of taking a chance, of the man wondering what would have happened if he got off the train to meet the lady," Eloise said.

"Oh," said Brid.

"Ugh," said Patrick.

"But it could mean taking a chance with anything, of being brave, not faint of heart," Eloise continued.

"Which symbol could that possibly be?" Brid said, looking at the dozens of choices on the map.

"Depends. If we think of it superficially, we look for a Guastavino property that has something to do with trains."

"So easy!" CJ cried out. "Guastavino built the Custom House downtown, right near the Bowling Green subway station. Look, there's a bowling ball symbol to show it!"

"Ha! Papa was so funny," Eloise said, her eyes sparkling. "But I don't think he cared particularly about that building. And Guastavino built many other buildings near train stations."

"So the other choices?" asked Brid.

"Didn't Guastavino also build some of the soaring

ceilings of Grand Central Station?" Eloise asked.

"He did," said CJ, "but there's no obvious symbol for that one." He checked his notes. "It's on Forty-second Street, but there's nothing on our map that looks related."

Eloise looked over his shoulder. "I'd be surprised if that wasn't notated on this map. We're missing something here, and my guess is it has to do with trains and bravery. I think we need to pay Grand Central Station a visit. We don't want to push the wrong symbol."

"Right now?" Pat asked.

"This minute," Eloise said. "We'll leave a note for your mother."

What followed was a flurry of jackets and shoes. A bag of snacks was packed, and Carron was lifted into her stroller without her even waking up.

Ray looked at them inquisitively as he swung back the elevator door. "Saturday outing? Sorry I can't drive ya today. Other guy didn't show up, so I'm back on duty."

And he winked.

CHAPTER 33

When everyone was settled on the Fifth Avenue bus heading down to Grand Central Station, CJ began to read some history of the massive train station. He had printed it off the internet and was spewing out facts he felt he needed to share with everyone. Only Eloise seemed genuinely interested.

"Do you know that about six hundred fifty thousand people pass through Grand Central Station each weekday? And the ceiling has the constellations painted on it?"

Without waiting for an answer, he added, "Franklin Delano Roosevelt used a secret passageway built below Grand Central so he could get out of his private railcar and up to his rooms at the Waldorf-Astoria Hotel without ever having to come up to street level."

"Why didn't he want to come up to the street?" asked Pat.

"Well, he was the president, and I guess all the people annoyed him," CJ answered.

"No, he was in a wheelchair, so it was hard for him to move around," Eloise said.

"His railcar is still down there, except that it's entombed forever," said CJ.

"Seems like a waste of a perfectly good railcar," Brid said.

"Oh, and the lost-and-found office at Grand Central retrieves nineteen thousand items a year. Guess what item gets lost the most?"

"Umbrellas!" said Eloise.

"Nope, coats. Two thousand of them were turned in last year."

"What about Guastavino? Does it say anything about him?" Brid asked.

"Nothing. It says the building was built in the beaux arts–style by a company called Warren and Wetmore."

"A what style?"

"Beaux arts. It just means an elaborate mix of architecture with sculpture, influenced by the Greeks and Romans. It was all the rage until 1930 or so," said Eloise.

"When that other type kicked it out?"

"Art deco? Oh, um, well, they overlapped for a bit, I guess." Eloise smiled at Brid.

"Are we sure that Guastavino built this place?" Pat chimed in.

"Typical, that man gets no credit for all his work," Eloise said. "I'm sure we can find someone there who knows."

"Here it is." CJ read, "'Rafael Guastavino graced the broad lower levels of the terminal with his famous vaults. The finest examples can be found in the Oyster Bar and Restaurant on the lower level.'"

"I'm hungry," Pat said, "hungry for some oysters."

"That can be arranged," said Eloise.

About thirty minutes later, they sat at a table in a glowing cave, full of lights that framed the arches of the vaulted ceilings. The space was enormous and filled with people sitting at tables, eating mounds of food piled on plain white plates that sat on red-checked tablecloths. All around them were tiles, beautiful soaring tiles, tessellated patterns all of the same size, laid in intricate ways.

"How exactly was Guastavino able to make this massive arched ceiling?" Brid asked. "There's no obvious frame holding it up."

"It's stronger than if there were beams surrounding it," said CJ. "He used lightweight, fireproof tiles and a lot of mortar as the glue, layering it on, shaping the tiles in exact patterns. By the day after the tiles were laid, they were so structurally sound that Guastavino could walk out on a half-finished arch hanging in midair."

"Whoa," finished Pat, who was slurping a soda while chewing on crackers. He wasn't sure he wanted to eat those slimy oysters after all.

CJ had opted for a cheeseburger. "Finish up; there is something I want to look at."

When they finished, Eloise paid their bill, essentially wiping out her babysitting proceeds. "You're the only babysitter who loses money by working," Brid noted.

"Don't worry," Eloise said. "You are paying me back in so many ways." Together they rolled Carron's stroller up a dramatic ramp.

The main floor of the station gleamed with light. The soft roar of footsteps and voices made Brid think, oddly, of beach sounds and waves.

CJ looked at his notes. "Stay here," he said. They stood in a corner, watching swarms of people walking to and from the train tracks.

"Weren't these rails built by one of those families that were friends with your dad?" Brid asked.

"Hmm, yes, the Vanderbilts," Eloise said. "I wouldn't call them friends, but definitely acquaintances."

Suddenly they were interrupted. "I am the ghost of Rafael Guastavino," came an eerie voice from the wall.

"Ahh!" Eloise yelled, while Carron, finally awake, began to giggle.

"I may be gone, but don't ever, ever forget about me and my vaults, my vaults that hide your treasure."

"Okay, this isn't funny anymore," said Brid. "That's CJ's voice, but how is he doing that?"

A few minutes later, CJ came bounding back from across the crowded room.

"Pretty cool, right? The acoustics of those vaulted, rounded ceilings allow you to talk into this corner and hear it perfectly across the crowded, noisy room. It's called the Whispering Gallery. I just read about it."

"CJ, can we stick to the program here?" said Brid. "We're looking for some symbol, something that will tell us this is the right place."

"I know, I know. Here is the part of the map we need to look at," he said, unfolding several computer print-outs. "I enlarged the area around Grand Central Station because there are a lot of symbols on the map here. A flower, a teacup, a train, and some sort of stick with a snake around it."

"Oh!" Brid said, "a caduceus. The staff with two snakes around it, like you see in a doctor's office. The Roman messenger god, Mercury, carried one, too. We learned about that in school."

"I saw that when we were walking in," Pat said. "Come outside, and I'll show you."

They filed outside again and crossed the street to see what Patrick was talking about. "There it is," Pat shouted, pointing upward at a sculpture above the huge entrance.

CJ nodded thoughtfully. "In the center . . . that would be Mercury, the god of commerce and trade and . . . crossroads."

The children could see a worker cleaning the massive statues; he was attached to the Mercury figure by his work belt.

"Crossroads, as in a place where many paths cross?" asked Brid.

"Crossroads, as in a time to make a decision?" Eloise asked.

"Crossroads are a place where one shouldn't be faint-hearted," CJ said. "Ladies and gentleman, I give you the symbol for Mercury." And he pointed on the map to their exact location at Forty-second and Park Avenue.

"So the symbol is that cad-thing?" Pat asked.

Eloise was hugging Carron. "It has to be. It's the caduceus telling me to take a chance."

"Great," said Patrick. "Next?"

CHAPTER 34

On Sunday, Eloise came upstairs without Anne requesting her, bearing a gurgling pot of chicken soup. Anne could still hardly get out of bed, except to go to the bathroom, get more water, and repetitively thank everyone for understanding her state.

CJ knew it was terrible to think this, but he felt fortunate his mother's illness was so well timed. The treasure hunters had never operated so freely and fast. For lunch, Eloise gave them baked potatoes slathered in butter. Brid knew their mother would have preferred yogurt and sprouts, but with one bite she thought she could get used to this diet.

When they were all seated, Eloise began. "The fourth poem is by Edna St. Vincent Millay." She got a fluttery voice when she spoke about the poets, which made Brid feel uncomfortable. She thought the poem sounded simple, like something Patrick would write. Why did it deserve to be famous?

"It's called 'Recuerdo,'" Eloise said, "which means 'Memory' in Spanish." Dreamily, she began to recite:

"We were very tired, we were very merry—
We had gone back and forth all night upon the ferry.
It was bare and bright, and smelled like a stable—
But we looked into a fire, we leaned across a table,
We lay on a hill-top underneath the moon;
And the whistles kept blowing, and the dawn came soon.

"We were very tired, we were very merry—
We had gone back and forth all night on the ferry;
And you ate an apple, and I ate a pear,
From a dozen of each we had bought somewhere;
And the sky went wan, and the wind came cold,
And the sun rose dripping, a bucketful of gold.

"We were very tired, we were very merry,
We had gone back and forth all night on the ferry.
We hailed, 'Good morrow, mother!' to a
    shawl-covered head,
And bought a morning paper, which neither of us read;
And she wept, 'God bless you!' for the apples and pears,
And we gave her all our money but our subway fares."

"Children, do you know how someone who lives in the moment, someone who seems to have no cares or just takes big risks, doesn't worry about being poor?"

"I guess," CJ said. "I mean, that used to be our dad."

"Well, that was what Millay was like. She went and lived with no money and no job, just so she could write her poems from her heart. She was a real bohemian."

"A what?" asked Brid.

"Someone who lives an unconventional life," said CJ. "Either that or someone who comes from Bohemia, in the Czech Republic."

Eloise continued, "She was so popular when I was young—she was what you called an 'it' girl."

"A what?" asked Brid, turning to CJ.

"A cool person, a celebrity type," he said.

"The poem is about the ferry, so I think we owe her a visit to the ferry building," said Eloise.

"You mean the ferry that gets you to Staten Island?" Brid asked.

"Yes, that's what she's talking about. There are a number of symbols right in that area of the map. Maybe one of them is related to this poem."

"And Guastavino has four creations right around it," said CJ, looking over Brid's meticulous lists. "The U.S. Custom House, the Federal Reserve Bank, the New York Stock Exchange, and the Great Hall on Ellis Island."

"But before we go down there, are we all in agreement

that this Millay poem is about the ferry?" Eloise asked.

"I guess," CJ said, while looking at the ferryboat symbol. "It just seems too easy."

"Not that easy—according to Mr. Post's map, there are three symbols in the spot where the ferry runs. There is a little ferryboat, there is a life preserver, and there is what appears to be a girl jumping. See how she looks like a cheerleader or something? So what's the meaning of this poem, and which symbol do you think is correct?" Brid asked.

"I think that it's about being joyful, right?" CJ said.

"Yes, CJ, joyful," said Eloise. "No doubt in my mind, that is the right choice."

"Eloise, can you read it again to us?" Brid asked. "Slower this time."

As Eloise began to read, the treasure hunters ate their potatoes, and felt just a little more joyful themselves.

CHAPTER 35

Before Eloise left that evening, the Smithforks had made a grave and important decision. Time was running out for them. They were certain that when their father returned from China, the missing DigiSpy pod would no longer be a funny matter, if it ever was. Bruce Smithfork didn't have much of a temper, but things like faking his identity to get the spy pod, and then losing it in the wall—along with lying to their mom about what they were doing—that was the sort of stuff that would make him angry. But they were so far into this mess that CJ couldn't think of how to ask for help from his parents, at least not until they were closer to solving everything. They needed answers, and to get them, they needed time off from school. As they shared a bag of microwave popcorn, it was Patrick who said, "I think what we need this week is another Saturday."

CJ laughed. "Except we don't have one. Dad is coming home Friday night." Without thinking, he blurted out, "Brid, we need to tell just one teeny, tiny white lie."

"And what would that lie be?" Brid asked, tossing popcorn kernels into the air and trying to catch them in her mouth.

"We need to pretend to go to school and, um, not."

Brid's mouth was full of popcorn, giving Pat a chance to speak. "It wouldn't be a terrible lie, and we can explain, right? I mean, after we find everything?"

CJ plowed ahead. "All we have to do is break into Dad's email account, which isn't hard, since he doesn't protect his password at home. Then we just email our teachers and the school nurse in the morning, telling them we're sick. Since we go to different schools, they'll never connect the dots. When they send back a confirmation email saying, 'hope he feels better' or something, we just delete that before Dad gets home. He'll never know."

"Right," said Brid uncertainly.

"What is our other option?" CJ asked. "And Eloise, we need you to come, too. We can't figure out the clue without your help."

Eloise had her head down as she attempted to wriggle Carron into her pajamas. "Agreed, children, but I do feel a bit sneaky about you skipping school."

"But it's only for one day," CJ pleaded.

Eloise was silent for a moment. "I suppose missing one day of school wouldn't be terrible. And Patrick?"

"It's too risky," CJ said, with regret in his voice. "I don't think you can come, Pat. If we are both sick from the same school at the same time, the nurse is going to catch on."

Pat hung his head. "You make me do all the hard stuff, and then you leave me out of the fun. Thanks a lot." He ran out of the room, slamming his heavy mahogany bedroom door so that nobody could see his tears.

"He'll get over it," CJ said. He sighed, then continued, "So, Brid, when Maricel drops you at school, wait in the lobby without shaking the headmistress's hand. Make sure she doesn't see you. I'll meet you and Eloise at the Eighty-sixth Street subway station at 8:07 AM. Got it?"

Both Eloise and Brid nodded.

"So, until tomorrow?" Eloise said.

"Tomorrow," they replied.

The next morning at 8:07 AM, CJ, Brid, and Eloise boarded the number four train, heading south toward the Bowling Green station. There had been only one snafu. As CJ ran to the subway station, looking up worriedly at the gray sky, a big black car with tinted windows pulled over. One of the back windows lowered, and Brent's head popped out.

"Hey! You're going the wrong way. Want a ride to

257

school?" CJ saw that the manny was driving. He gave CJ a peace sign.

"Um, no, I forgot something and I have to go home to get it," CJ lied.

Brent's face fell, and he said, "Dude, you are so going the wrong way either for your house or for school. It's okay to skip school, but don't lie to me, okay?"

CJ felt badly. "Yeah, man, sorry. I just have something I need to do today."

"Understood. Have fun," Brent said, and something in his tone made CJ feel like he really did understand.

"Yeah, sorry about lying. I just can't get caught, you know?"

"Not a problem, but you don't lie to your friends, okay?" Brent smiled.

"Got it," CJ said, feeling weirdly happy that Brent had called him a friend. He was certain his secret was safe with Brent.

The last station before Bowling Green was Wall Street. The train practically emptied, with people rushing off as soon as the brakes stopped squealing and the doors opened. It was like watching horses getting let out of a race gate.

"Those are all the people who buy and sell Dad's stock on the stock exchange," CJ said to Brid.

"Yeah, well, good thing they don't know we lost his DigiSpy pod, or his stock would go down today," she joked, but neither of them laughed. Meanwhile, Brid summoned the courage to ask Eloise something that had been bothering her.

"Eloise, what do you do during the day while we're in school?" Brid asked. As soon as she asked the question, she felt badly.

"You see, most of my childhood friends are no longer alive, or have moved away," said Eloise. "I haven't felt like part of the living world these last years. I go out and walk around, but it's hard when you feel the best times of your life have happened already."

Brid stood back, unable to think of a reply.

"But do you want to know something else?" Eloise said. "Lately, I don't feel that way," and she squeezed Brid's hand very firmly.

The train's brakes screeched loudly, and Brid was glad not to have to speak. A conductor's voice came over the intercom. "Last stop in Manhattan. Get off de train if you don wan Brookleeen."

"Guess this is our stop," said CJ, who wanted no part of the heavy conversation that Brid and Eloise had begun. They were all standing when the doors slammed back, and the warmer air of the platform hit their faces.

Eloise snapped into work mode. "Okay, I have realized we can solve two poems today. The Millay poem is about the ferry, and then we need to tackle the immigration poem, which means Ellis Island, but there are several map symbols on Ellis Island. We're lucky they're both in the same area."

They continued up the stairs to the street level, where the autumn sun hit them squarely in the eyes. The street was bustling with office workers with briefcases and trench coats, and the air was filled with the clicking noise of shoes traveling quickly on pavement. Then they saw the figure of a small boy running toward them, seeming oddly out of place, and yet familiar. It was Patrick.

Pat came running up to them, his cheeks bright red. *"Wassssssup?"* he said, laughing. "You thought you could get rid of me! I'm the one whose idea it was to skip school, so nah-nah-nah, here I am!"

"How did you beat us down here?" Brid wanted to know.

"I just crawled under the turnstile at the Ninety-sixth Street subway station and zoomed down," he said proudly.

"Patrick!" CJ was livid. "We're going to get caught now! Don't you think Saint James's will call Mom to see where you are? Didn't the headmaster see you go into the school?"

"I kept my hat pulled low when I went in, and then I went right out the kindergarten side door. They think I'm sick. You're not the only one who can write an email," Patrick retorted. "Nobody will call home."

"What sort of email did you write, Patrick?"

"It said," and Patrick put on a high, squeaky voice, "'Dear Nurse Boylan, I am sorry to say that now both boys seem to have that stomach bug. They are puking everywhere, and they won't be at school. From Patrick's father.'"

"You did not," said Brid. "You really wrote *puking* and *Patrick's father*?"

"Yeah, so what?"

"Because grown-ups don't use words like *puking*, and besides, Dad would have written *Bruce Smithfork*, not *Patrick's father*. You complete nimrod."

The Smithforks walked toward the ferry building, arguing, oblivious to the people around them.

"We are so busted! That was the stupidest email in the world! I bet all your *B*s and *D*s were in the wrong places!" Brid yelled.

"How come you're always leaving me behind?" Pat retorted.

"Because you're a baby!" CJ shouted.

Eloise had simply stopped walking. When the children realized she wasn't with them, they turned to see her standing, looking tiny, in front of the enormous ferry building. She was frozen like a statue, motionless.

Brid came running up to her. "Eloise? Is something wrong?"

"If that isn't a sign, I don't know what is." Eloise was pointing to enormous printed words high on the wall, inside the ferry building, large enough to read through the huge glass front.

Brid gasped as she looked up at the elaborate script written on the wall of the building:

WE WERE SO VERY JOLLY WE WERE SO MERRY, ALL
NIGHT WE RODE BACK AND FORTH ON THE FERRY

"But, this wouldn't have been here when your dad was alive, right?"

"No, it's just a coincidence, but to me it's a sign. Clearly, the joyful girl is the correct symbol for the fourth clue, because right now I feel like that joyful girl myself. I forgot how much my dad liked to take me here."

"Yeah, maybe we should give away apples and pears and all of our money except our subway fares." CJ grinned, his anger at Patrick momentarily forgotten. "But to who?"

"Let's walk over and get our Ellis Island tickets so we can solve poem number five, don't you think?"

A half hour later, as they boarded the boat for Ellis Island, Eloise pulled out the fifth poem.

The New Colossus

Not like the brazen giant of Greek fame,
With conquering limbs astride from land to land;

Here at our sea-washed, sunset gates shall stand
A mighty woman with a torch, whose flame
Is the imprisoned lightning, and her name
Mother of Exiles. From her beacon-hand
Glows world-wide welcome; her mild eyes command
The air-bridged harbor that twin cities frame.
"Keep, ancient lands, your storied pomp!" cries she
With silent lips. "Give me your tired, your poor,
Your huddled masses yearning to breathe free,
The wretched refuse of your teeming shore.
Send these, the homeless, tempest-tost to me,
I lift my lamp beside the golden door!"

—Emma Lazarus, 1883

"We've read that one in school, especially the part about huddled masses," CJ said as they pulled up at the dock.

"Yeah, masses of what?" Patrick asked.

"Masses of people, new immigrants, came through this island every day back in the old days. Five thousand immigrants were processed every day in the new building."

"What new building?"

"I guess this is the new building," said CJ. "The original Ellis Island building burned to the ground just five years after it opened. So the new building had to be totally fireproof."

"There was only one man for that job," Pat said, smiling.

"That's right. Rafael Guastavino built part of the new building—this one—which opened in 1900."

Brid was reading a brochure. "Do you know that forty percent of all Americans have relatives who came through here?"

"Yes, and I remember when the government tried to stem the flow of people to this country," Eloise said thoughtfully. "The rules changed to become more selective of the immigrants we accepted. Immigrants had to pass a literacy test. That happened when I was a girl."

"A literacy test?" Brid was interested.

"They had to be able to read and write in their native language to gain entrance to this country."

"I hate tests," said Patrick. "What happened if you didn't pass?"

"You got sent back to whichever country you came from."

"So what about that poem, about giving me your tired and poor and yearning to breathe free?" CJ asked.

"That poem was written in the late eighteen hundreds, but by the nineteen twenties we weren't so welcoming anymore."

"Eloise," Brid said as she unfolded a copy of the map,

"look at your father's symbols, the ones near Ellis Island. There is a suitcase."

"Too obvious."

"There is a torch."

"That could be for with the Statue of Liberty, or the fire that happened here. Too vague."

"And there are some lips," CJ noted.

"Yes, strange, isn't it? None of them feel right to me. I'm not sure what message my father was trying to convey."

Brid crossed the Great Hall and returned with several pamphlets. "We're taking a tour in five minutes," she said.

"Tour? We don't have time for a tour," CJ complained.

"The tour is free today for students and seniors, and that's what we are," she said. "Besides, we're missing something here."

They crossed the hall to join their tour group, finding out that because of the dreary weather, the Smithforks and Eloise would be the only members aside from a middle-aged couple from Ireland.

"Haven't ye any school?" the Irish lady asked Brid.

"We are working on a school project, and this is our grandmother," Brid said.

"Listen up, people," said a lanky, twenty-something tour guide wearing a green Parks Department uniform.

"As I take you on the complete step-by-step immigrant's experience of Ellis Island, we will go from the disembarkation point here in the Main Building, where an immigrant was temporarily separated from his bags and family, to the Kissing Post, where everyone was reunited."

"Kissing Post! What?" Patrick said loudly. The Irish couple chuckled.

"Kissing Post? Interesting," said CJ as he looked again at their copy of the map.

"Do you think that's the answer?" Brid asked Eloise.

"Of course," said Eloise. "It just has to be those lips! I remember my father telling me the whole story. That was the reunion area for families. There were tearful, kissing reunions, and people in that day called it the Kissing Post. How did I ever forget that?"

"Well, it has been seventy years," said CJ.

"So, it's the lips?" Brid asked again.

"Hey, mister," Patrick interrupted the tour guide. "Can we get right to the Kissing Post?"

"Uh, no," said the perplexed guide.

With that, the Smithforks and Eloise simply walked away from the group, leaving the guide looking confused. They followed Brid's map up an enormous set of steps, down a long hall, and out a back door that led to a wide patio structure.

"Oh, my goodness," Eloise said as she rubbed her fingers against the regal columns. She grabbed Patrick by the lapel of his Saint James's blazer and planted a mushy kiss on his cheek.

"So, I guess you're saying it's the lips," he said, wiping his cheek. "That has to be the next symbol on the map."

Eloise smiled and kissed him again, this time on the other cheek.

CHAPTER 36

CJ held his breath every time the phone rang that night. He was nervously anticipating the head of his school trying to get in touch with his mother and her absent children; but the phone remained silent. By nine PM he started to think they had actually gotten away with skipping school. That feeling lasted until he went to delete the emails from his father's computer.

Immediately he saw the email Patrick had sent the school. It read:

> *Dear Head Mister:*
> *I am Patrick's dad and he is sick. His broder has been puking all nite an now Pat is puking his guts out.*

He cant come back to skool till next week. From Pat-
ricks Father.

CJ's heart fell. This wasn't even close to something that the head of the school would fall for. Worse, there was a reply, not from the headmaster, but from someone called Bruce Smithfork's Mobile.

Of course, CJ thought. His father had taken a PDA with him. Of course he was able to see exactly every email coming or going from his computer, even though he was 7,500 miles away. Not only was Patrick busted, but so were Brid and CJ. CJ opened the reply email:

Dear Patrick's Daddy:

I am so sorry about the puking going on there at 2 East 92nd Street, but I hope Patrick knows he has a massive punishment coming. Hope he enjoys the next few days, because when his real father is back in town, Pat will be spending a lot of time in his room. I also saw the correspondence between Patrick's brother and sister and their schools, so I can only imagine the terrible illness overtaking your home. Please let them know they will also be confined to their bedrooms once I get back, thus ensuring a return to health. Mrs. Smithfork is sick, so I won't bother her about this matter until I come back to New York City. Your secret is safe for

about four days.
  From, Patrick's Real Daddy
  PS: Please learn how to use spell-check, Patrick.

Now what? CJ admitted to himself that it wasn't even Pat's fault. He blamed himself for trying this stupid trick. He should have known Patrick would have felt left out.

They were just so close, so incredibly close to the treasure, with five of the seven answers under their belts. They had a musical note, the general's star, the Mercury caduceus, the joyful girl, and the kissing lips. The sixth poem was about a trolley car. How hard could it be to determine where trolley lines had once run? CJ read the poem again:

A Crowded Trolley Car
by Elinor Wylie

The rain's cold grains are silver-gray
Sharp as golden sands,
A bell is clanging, people sway
Hanging by their hands.

Supple hands, or gnarled and stiff,
Snatch and catch and grope;
That face is yellow-pale, as if
The fellow swung from rope.

Dull like pebbles, sharp like knives,
Glances strike and glare,
Fingers tangle, Bluebeard's wives
Dangle by the hair.

Orchard of the strangest fruits
Hanging from the skies;
Brothers, yet insensate brutes
Who fear each others' eyes.

One man stands as free men stand
As if his soul might be
Brave, unbroken; see his hand
Nailed to an oaken tree.

This clue had to be the easiest one yet. The map contained four different locations for trolley cars, and most of them were along Third Avenue. With the help of Eloise, CJ felt certain they could solve this in one day. Then, they would only have to solve clue number seven before sending Pat back into the wall to push the correct symbols.

At that moment Brid walked into the room wearing her silky Peace and Love pajamas, and holding a fuzzy stuffed elephant.

"I've been reading that trolley car poem again," she said. "I like the part about people being brothers, but not looking into each other's eyes. I mean, on the bus or subway we are all smooshed together, but no one looks at anyone else. We all pretend the other people aren't there."

"Yeah, well, get this, too: we are about to be grounded when Dad comes home," CJ said.

"What? Right when we're making so much progress? There's no way we can stop."

"Well, it looks like we don't have to stop, at least not until Friday night. Read this." CJ pointed to the screen in front of him.

Brid studied her father's email. "Maybe we should just take the rest of the week off," she said.

"Week off from treasure hunting?" asked CJ.

"No, week off from school."

"You are crazy."

"Think about it. Once Dad comes home, and we're grounded, he'll make us tell him everything. Once we do that, it's all over."

"Not necessarily. Dad might find it really interesting," CJ said.

"Oh, really? Is that what you want, a bunch of grown-ups telling us that all the things we've been doing are too dangerous, and we need to let professionals handle it?"

"Professionals?"

"Yeah, like the police. Once Dad hears that Mr. Torrio came into our apartment, he and Mom will act like we're in danger. They'll call the police."

"You have a point," CJ said, rumpling his hair. He wished he knew what to do.

"Please, CJ, please let's just miss school for the rest of this week, get this mystery solved, and get in trouble with Dad on Saturday. We can be grounded on Sunday and back to school on Monday. By then, we won't care, because we will have done something that people haven't been able to do for seventy years."

"Scratch that—something that *grown-ups* couldn't do for seventy years."

"You see my point," said Brid.

"I don't know—we're already in trouble. I'll sleep on it. When we wake up in the morning, I'll give you my answer."

But by the next morning, the unbelievable had happened. Brid woke first, as always. Her room was so bright and cold she thought she had left her windows open. Actually, it was just bright because the morning sun reflected off the November snow. Not just any snow, but enormous, light, slippery snow, the sort that got school canceled. Could it be?

She ran to her dad's office and checked her school website. Nothing. She turned on the radio, which had started to announce school closings, but not for the Mockingbird School for Girls. Brid remembered another girl saying they rarely had snow days since most girls walked to school. She hit the refresh button on the school website. There was a new message: Mockingbird School would open three hours late. But then she heard a beautiful thing on the radio: "Sun shall give way to more clouds, and an even thicker blanket of snow will fall by afternoon. Prediction of eight to twelve inches."

There was no way the schools would open. She hit the refresh button again. *Bingo!*

"Mockingbird School for Girls shall be closed today and possibly tomorrow. Please check the website for updates." She went to the Saint James's website. "School closed today," it read.

She ran into CJ's room. "No school today!" she sang. "Blizzard today, *no school*! It's a sign from Mr. Post that we were meant to solve the mystery."

Just then Patrick walked in.

"No school today, Patrick. Yippeeeee!"

Pat's eyes grew wide. He stuck both index fingers in the air maniacally and swiveled his hips. "Oh yeah! Oh yeah! Let's go sledding in the park!"

"Are you crazy? Let's go find Marie Antoinette's necklace, or maybe a Fabergé egg, or Louis the Fifteenth's medallions!" said Brid.

"And bricks of gold!" shouted CJ.

Suddenly, Anne Smithfork stuck her head into the room. "Kids, you have a day off today, and I feel much better. Let's all go sledding in Central Park!"

The room turned uncomfortably silent.

"All this time in bed has given me a chance to think," she continued. "I miss the way we used to be—together all the time. When Daddy comes home, I'm telling him I want things to be like our old life. We don't need fancy furnishings. All that shopping and decorating takes up too much time and money. Maricel just called in sick, and we don't even really need Charlize the homework helper. I want to be the one to help with homework!"

CJ broke the silence. "No, Mom, you've been great. It just takes a while to settle into a new place. Right, guys?"

Brid and CJ looked nervously at each other, while Patrick hugged his mother. "Sure, Mom," Pat said. "We'd love to go sledding with you, but you were really sick. Today is your first day out of bed, and we like that lady from downstairs a lot. She can take us sledding."

CJ couldn't believe how smart Patrick was. It was the perfect response.

"No really, kids, I feel much better. Maybe we can just build a fire in the fireplace and read books, stay in our pajamas all day."

"Um, maybe for a little while," Brid said, not wanting to make their mom suspicious. Besides, she still looked so pale that Brid felt certain she would get tired soon, and she was right.

A few hours later, Anne was back in bed; Eloise had

come to relieve her. They all sat in Bruce Smithfork's office passing around a bag of chocolate-covered pretzels and looking at internet photos of old New York City trolleys and elevated trains. Outside, the snow had finally stopped falling, but the sky was still gray and ominous.

"Did you take the el a lot?" Brid asked Eloise, referring to the defunct elevated train lines.

"You know, children, I remember being on a trolley with my father, but it didn't look like this. I'm even starting to wonder if I have the right city in mind. When I think of a trolley, I think of San Francisco, not New York. And Guastavino never worked on any trolley system, right, CJ?"

"That's right. This clue may be harder than it looks," said CJ, as they pored over the enormous list of Guastavino buildings on the floor.

"Wait," Eloise said. "We used to take a trolley car to Queens. We usually would drive our motorcar around town, but my father would sometimes take the trolley to get to his food plant in Queens, and I would often go with him. I remember the feeling of being high up, looking over Manhattan and Queens. Oh dear, where were we?"

CJ was typing furiously, searching for clues on the internet about a trolley to Queens. "Listen to this!" he shouted. "In 1909 the Queensboro Bridge opened and transformed Queens. It once had been a rural area, and because transportation to Manhattan was difficult, Queens was mostly farmland until then."

"I've been on that bridge," said Eloise, "but there are no trolleys in this town anymore."

CJ continued. "Originally the bridge had two trolley lines to go back and forth from Manhattan to Queens, with stops in Roosevelt Island and Long Island City. Trolley service ended in 1955."

Brid was already looking at the map. "Where is the Queensboro Bridge?"

"Down at Fifty-ninth Street," Eloise replied. "We—"

CJ kept reading out loud. "And on the Manhattan side was a marketplace under the bridge, lined with Guastavino tile."

"Got it," Brid said, pointing to a trolley on the map. "Symbol number six is officially the trolley car on the Fifty-ninth Street Bridge. Can we go visit?" she asked Eloise.

Eloise looked out the window at the mounds of snow. "Of course, dears. We'll be just fine on that bus!"

CHAPTER 37

The Smithfork children and Eloise were in a café, sipping hot cocoa with big plops of whipped cream. Above them soared an expansive ceiling, a Guastavino ceiling, that looked golden in the late afternoon sunlight that poured in through the enormous glass windows. Minutes before, they had found the exact trolley spot—with the tracks still in place—on the Fifty-ninth Street Bridge. They could have walked across the bridge if it hadn't been for Carron's stroller. Eloise thought it was too far for both her and the toddler while snow was on the ground. When they spotted the Guastavino tiling under the bridge, they followed it until it led them to the side of a giant grocery store. They agreed that the trolley symbol located at Fifty-ninth Street on the map corresponded to clue number six, and they all felt smug with satisfaction and sugar.

Sitting back on their chairs, the young detectives spread the next poem and the map before them. It was time to solve the final, seventh clue. Jumpy with anticipation, Brid focused on the poem. "So what exactly does this mean?" she asked as she read the poem aloud.

"Ota Benga, by anonymous

"In this land of foremost progress—
In this Wisdom's ripest age—
We have placed him, in high honor,
In a monkey's cage!"

They couldn't agree about what that poem meant. Eloise kept thinking it sounded familiar.

"The big question," Eloise said, "is who was placed in a monkey's cage?"

"And the other question is, where do we find a monkey's cage?" Brid added.

"Duh," said Patrick, "the zoo."

"Yes, except there are two zoos: one in the Bronx and one in Central Park," Brid replied.

"But the map behind the wall is of Manhattan, not the Bronx," CJ said.

"I remember this!" Eloise said suddenly as she wiped

whipped cream off Carron's mouth. "This is the poem of outrage, the poem about Ota Benga."

"Otta whatta?" said Patrick, who was trying to eat the frosting off a cupcake with a knife and fork. Eloise had introduced the kids to a whole new way of eating, one involving lots of sugar. As long as they used proper etiquette, it didn't seem to matter to her what they were eating.

"Ota Benga. He died before I was born, but my father was greatly moved by his terrible treatment and often told me his story."

"What story?" Pat asked.

"Ota was a Pygmy, from a tribe of very short people who lived in the Congo, in Africa, where there was terrible violence and a lot of tribal warfare."

"Sort of like now?" asked CJ.

"Yes, but this story is most upsetting. I may not be getting my facts straight, but it went something like this: there was a man who was hired to go and buy Pygmies in the Congo, to bring them to some fair in the United States."

"You can't buy people!" Brid said indignantly.

"One would think," Eloise said. "Anyway, this man returned with a Pygmy he claimed to have rescued from slavery. His name was Ota Benga, and he was in his twenties and very short. He had filed his teeth into very sharp points, so he looked fierce. People came from all over to see him. But when the fair was over, nobody felt responsible for taking Mr. Benga back to his homeland. Some people at the American Museum of Natural History offered to let him live there. They even made some sort of molding, or cast, from his likeness. They have it displayed still."

"Ota Benga lived in the museum?" Pat asked.

"Not just any museum—some of the structures there were done by Guastavino, remember?" Brid said.

"Tell us more about Ota Benga," CJ said.

"He lived there for a while, but then he threw something at a rich lady, a donor to the museum, Mrs. Guggenheim, and she almost got konked on the head." Eloise laughed.

"You mean like the Guggenheim Museum near our apartment?"

"Exactly. Museums don't like it when their donors are treated badly," Eloise said.

"Did he hit her with a dinosaur bone?" Pat asked hopefully as his siblings laughed.

"After that, they needed another place for this young man to live, and in 1906, they moved him to the Bronx Zoo," Eloise finished. "Might I add that Guastavino built the domed ceilings of both the Museum of Natural History and a part of the Bronx Zoo—the elephant hall, I believe."

"You can't live at the zoo," Brid said.

"Worse than that, Ota Benga slept in a hammock in the monkey cage and was on display for the whole world to see. My father couldn't bear to see animals in cages, never mind a person."

"Did they ever release him?" Brid asked sadly.

"They did after some people protested. The poem got printed in *The New York Times*, which angered even more people about Ota's situation. After all that bad publicity, they released him, and he eventually found work in a factory down south."

"That's a pretty horrible story," said CJ, looking outside, where the snow was falling once again. "I'm surprised your dad would want to end this whole treasure hunt with such a sad poem."

"Well, it is sad, but think of the variety of these poems my father has chosen as poems with lessons. There are poems of enjoyment, poems about music and happiness, poems about how to navigate life, poems of bravery and commerce and making decisions at a crossroads."

"Eloise, it's almost like your dad was telling you how to live your life through some of his favorite poems," Brid said dreamily.

"Yes, it's a bit like that," said Eloise. "Except it took me so long to get the message, there isn't much of my life left to be lived. I should have met you children decades ago." Nobody bothered to say the obvious thing, that the Smithforks weren't alive decades ago.

Brid spoke first. "If we find this treasure, you can change how you live your life. You'll certainly have more money to do things with."

"Children!" Eloise stood up. "Have you looked outside?"

The children looked out the window, but all they could see was white.

The waitress walked over to them. "Sorry to interrupt, folks, but the storm's getting worse, and we're closing early. We're all worried about being able to get home."

"Oh my goodness, you're right!" Eloise said. "We need to be going, too. Look at this weather!"

There was a rustling of jackets being put on and a chorus of zippers being pulled up.

Brid looked down at Eloise's feet. She was wearing rubber booties. "Eloise, don't you own any snow boots?"

"And when exactly do you think I would be out in the snow? No, I don't own any snow boots," Eloise said, a hint of worry in her voice. "I guess we should just ride north on the bus, up to the nineties, and then walk across to Fifth Avenue."

Several minutes later, as they stood at the First Avenue bus stop, they realized that there was almost no traffic, and no sign of a bus. The few cars they saw were moving slowly, sliding on the snowy avenue.

CJ surveyed the deserted streets and wished he had

remembered his gloves. "We should probably head to the subway," he said. The three long blocks to the subway seemed endless. Stepping carefully down the gray, slushy steps at Lexington and Fifty-ninth Street, nobody spoke at all. The steam from the subway pushed warmer air into their faces, and they were relieved to hear the sound of a rumbling train.

As quickly as they could, they made their way onto a train just as the doors closed. For a moment they felt giddy with relief, until Brid said, "This is the downtown side. We need to go uptown." She glanced over at Eloise, who looked as if another round of going up and down subway stairs might be too much for her.

"Oh, dear children, how foolish of me to not be more careful. I'm a terrible babysitter."

"Eloise, you're my favorite babysitter," Patrick said as he leaned into her side.

"Let's get off at the next stop and switch trains," said CJ. "It's not a big deal."

The train was eerily silent, moving with the speed of a turtle. Carron had fallen asleep in her stroller. The conductor made an announcement, but nobody could understand what he was saying, because the radio was filled with static. When they finally pulled into the Fifty-first Street station, Patrick ran ahead onto the train platform while Brid stood blocking the door, waiting for Eloise and CJ to come with the stroller.

Bing bong, came the warning that the train was about to move again.

"Hurry up!" said Brid.

But the brakes of the stroller were locked. Brid instinctively released the doors so she could help, and they suddenly slammed shut.

As the train started to move, Brid realized they were the only people still in their car. "Don't worry," she said to Eloise. "We'll get off at the next stop."

"Where's Patrick?" Eloise exclaimed.

CJ ran to the window to look back at the platform, just as the door between cars opened and Pat made his way back to the group.

"Why are you guys always trying to lose me?" he asked, smiling. "I had to jump back into the next car right before the train pulled out."

Eloise clasped her hands in relief. "I'm getting too old for all this excitement."

This time the train moved much faster, whipping along past Grand Central, then past stops farther south. They passed by Twenty-third Street and Union Square without even slowing. "Are we headed to Brooklyn?" Brid asked CJ.

But then the train slowed, its brakes screeching and squealing until it simply stopped. The doors opened, but they were clearly between stations. As they sat there, looking puzzled, the lights went out, and they were thrown into a world that was almost completely black. The silence was so surprising and eerie that Pat thought it was actually hurting his ears to not hear any noise. "Umm, shouldn't we tell someone?" he asked in a soft voice.

"Tell who?" CJ snapped back.

"I don't think the train people know we are on here. Do you think they do?" Pat asked timidly.

"I think we should all just wait," Eloise said evenly. "We are safe and dry in here, and maybe we should act like Carron and doze a bit." In the shadowy light, CJ could see Eloise adjust her scarf a bit tighter around her face.

Brid was scared, but she said nothing. They sat for an extremely long time, the only sound from Patrick, who was zipping and unzipping his jacket.

After an hour had passed, CJ's heart was really thumping. Eloise had fallen asleep. There had to be a conductor, right? Using his softest voice so as not to wake Eloise and Carron, CJ said he was going to take a look around. He decided to take Patrick with him, afraid of what excitement his brother might drum up in his absence.

"We'll be back shortly," he told Brid, taking Patrick by the hand. "Just do not leave this train car." He flipped open his cell phone. It emitted the tiniest light.

"Okay," Brid said in a meek voice, feeling very alone with the sleeping bodies of Eloise and Carron. After her brothers left, she sat and thought about her lists of clues. They had everything they needed; now she could identify all the symbols Patrick would need to push on the map behind the wall, once they were safely home again.

Home. She was surprised to hear her own thoughts call Manhattan home. Yes, she didn't have any real friends yet, and the schoolwork was hard, but she was beginning to like living around so much history. She was even having some ideas about how to fix up her new bedroom, or about using the silver room as a clubhouse. And despite the coming punishment, she was happy her dad was coming home. As she comforted herself with these thoughts, she released herself into sleep, a sleep that would last for many hours.

CHAPTER 38

Brid woke to find a flashlight pointing directly in her eyes. The holder of the flashlight was an older man with heavy, tired eyes, and he was inches from her face. At first, she thought she was dreaming, but she wasn't. Joe Torrio was right in front of her—staring at her with a quizzical look on his face.

Brid shot up in her seat, ready to fight him if he moved closer. In the blackness of the subway car, he looked horrible, the wrinkles on his face deep and menacing.

"Don't take another step, Mr. Torrio," Brid said, in a voice as tough as leather.

His face softened, and he smiled. "I thought I'd never find you children." He sounded relieved, and to Brid's surprise, almost friendly. Torrio shone the light on Eloise and placed one of his hands on the side of her neck, taking her pulse. "Is she okay?" he asked Brid.

"Of course she's okay, and so is the baby," said Brid, confused by his concern. "If you don't mind, can you just let them sleep?"

"Phew. Let me sit down for a moment." The man sighed heavily as he plopped down across from Brid. He untied his boots, removed his socks, and began wringing water out of them.

"The train tracks," he said, "they're flooded everywhere. Almost the entire subway system is closed. I can't believe they didn't make you get off the train."

"Oh," Brid said. "I think they might have told people to get off; we just couldn't understand the garbled announcement."

Brid was considering how Torrio could possibly have found them underground. Suddenly she had a terrible thought, what if he had done something with—

"Your brothers!" Torrio said suddenly. "Where are they?"

"Um." Now was the moment she had to decide. Should she trust this man? "Um, they just, they'll be back in a minute," she lied, wishing that were true.

"We really need to get you kids out of here. There's some dangerous flooding up ahead."

"Who do you mean, 'we'?" Brid asked, suddenly very worried for Pat and CJ. She hoped they had followed the tracks to a station, gone aboveground, and were getting help.

"New York's Finest," he said. "The police, the fire department, and your mother—who is so worried about you, I expect she'll have the mayor down here in a few minutes."

"My mother knows we're missing?"

"Honey," he said, "you've been gone all night. It's almost dawn. Your mother asked Ray if he had seen you, and Ray asked me."

"How could you possibly know where we were?"

"Because I followed you. Not the whole way, but just to the subway station on the downtown side. That's when I left you. I walked home, and I assumed you'd gotten home, too. It wasn't until your mother asked Ray if he'd seen you, and Ray told me you were missing, that I realized you'd never come home. It was the fire department that was able to figure out where you might be, given how flooded things are from the melted snow and the fact the downtown six train was stuck here."

"How dare you follow us! That is so creepy!" Brid said indignantly.

"It is sort of creepy," Torrio admitted. "I didn't mean for things to turn out this way. I just wanted to talk to all of you. We have so much in common. We need to talk and to share information, and you never give me a chance."

"Why would we want to talk to you? You're mean, and you hurt CJ's head."

"Now, that was an accident," Torrio said. "He slipped on the stairs when the lights went out and bumped his head. When I heard you all coming, I knew he was in good hands. I left because I didn't want you to blame me. I'm sorry. I shouldn't have left." Torrio sighed.

"If you want to talk to us, why don't you just talk?" Brid asked defiantly.

"Listen, child, it's a complicated story," Mr. Torrio began. "Did you junior detectives and Eloise Post ever stop to think you've gotten this whole thing backward?"

"Got what backward?"

"The theory that Eloise's father and my father might not have really been friends. Did you ever stop to think you might not know the real story?"

"Eloise told us everything about your criminal family."

"Did you ever think Eloise was wrong?"

"Eloise doesn't lie."

"I'm not saying she lied, I'm saying maybe she doesn't know everything. And maybe the Torrios and the Posts just acted like enemies so that they could hide a secret," Torrio said.

"You mean hide the fact that they kidnapped Julian? Some people think Eloise's little brother was taken by your family. She missed having a brother for most of her life. She should hate you."

"Miss, with all due respect, I'm just saying you don't know everything."

"Oh really?" Brid said. "Everything Eloise has told me makes me believe I shouldn't even speak to you."

Torrio looked dejected, and, in spite of herself, Brid started to feel a little sad for him. "I don't know why you would choose to live at 2 East 92nd Street. You know you make Eloise very unhappy."

Torrio kept fidgeting with the flashlight, throwing bursts of light around the subway car. Brid wished Eloise would wake up.

"I need to talk to Eloise," Torrio said. "And she never lets me speak long enough to explain everything. I thought maybe you kids could convince her to just listen to me. She just thinks the Torrios are a bunch of hoodlums, and they're not. They never were."

"If people think your relatives kidnapped her brother, why would she ever even talk to you?"

Torrio began putting his boots back on. "They never actually did that," he said.

"Don't listen to this," came a well-rested and feisty voice. It was Eloise, who had only pretended to be asleep for the past minutes. Moving stiffly, she sat up and adjusted her glasses. "I've listened to your whole bunch of hooey. What a story you tell!"

"Listen, Miss Post, it's not a story. I have a letter from your father, a letter that explains everything. It explains that the Torrio and Post families were friends. If you would ever talk to me long enough, I'd like to read it to you."

Brid could tell Eloise didn't believe Mr. Torrio for a second. She clearly thought he was trying to be friends with them to beat them to the treasure. Her voice sounded like a low hiss. "My father may have had secrets, but the last person he would confide in was someone from your family. Why would he ever have given anything to you?"

"Maybe the Torrios helped him out in his time of need and were prepared to spend the rest of their lives under a cloud of suspicion to protect the Post family," Torrio replied.

"Friends with bootlegging, lawbreaking thugs? I don't think so," Eloise said. "You haven't a clue what you are talking about."

All of a sudden, Carron sat up, looking sweaty and confused in her snowsuit, her hair sticking straight up. "Baby!" she said to nobody in particular.

"I hate to interrupt," Brid said, "but can we please go find CJ and Patrick?"

"What! They aren't here?" Eloise exclaimed.

"Mr. Torrio," Brid said, "I don't know whether to believe you or not, but I do know we have no time to waste. My brothers left last night to walk along the tracks, and we haven't seen them since."

"What?" Torrio said.

"What?" Eloise echoed.

"It's true, and I'm sorry, but I didn't want to go after them and leave Eloise and Carron behind."

"No, honey, you did the right thing," Torrio said. "The firemen are in the next station down the line, so we can walk along the tracks. They cut all the electrical power, so it's safe. It's just going to be wet."

"And filthy," muttered Eloise.

Gingerly, they stepped out of the empty subway car and began sloshing their way slowly toward a distant light. Torrio carried Carron, while Eloise and Brid came behind him, holding hands.

They had trudged along for only a few minutes when they were confronted by a large fireman. He had FDNY RESCUE #2 inscribed on his helmet, and O'ROURKE written on his jacket.

"These the kids you were looking for?" O'Rourke asked Torrio.

"We're still missing two boys," Torrio answered.

The fireman said, "We're going to head down the line a little farther toward the next station, but I kinda doubt we'll find anyone there. It's the City Hall station—been closed for years."

"Well, where else could they be?" Brid asked, with panic in her voice.

"With miles of track to walk on? Could be anywhere," O'Rourke said. He added kindly, "Those boys are probably home in their beds by now. Let's get you kids up to the rig and get you home. We'll stay here and keep looking."

"*No!*" shouted Brid, louder than she had intended. Impulsively, she grabbed Torrio's flashlight and took off running into the blackness toward the next station.

"Get back here, kid," said the fireman, but he was no match for Brid's speed. He carried many pounds of equipment, tanks, a helmet, boots, and rain gear. And nobody could run like Brid, even with a backpack on. She went splashing down the tracks into a black hole of darkness, the flashlight bouncing with every step she took. She knew the mud was splattering her white snow pants, but she didn't care. She was beginning to think something terrible had happened to her brothers.

When she came to the next station, she stopped. There were danger signs between unlit brass light fixtures. Brid heard a shuffling noise and aimed her light at a family of rats, skillfully avoiding the water as they scurried across four sets of train tracks. She could see stained-glass sky-lights that were letting in faint morning glow high above. Most of the glass was broken, and she recognized the twisted metal detailing as the beaux arts style, the style Eloise had told them about.

Far ahead, Brid thought she saw a light go on and off. "CJ!" she called, listening to the echo of her voice. "Patrick," she hollered, hearing the sound carrying and bouncing, carrying and bouncing. The space reminded

her of Grand Central Terminal, with its rounded ceilings and no right angles anywhere. And then she heard a faint voice. "Brid?" She saw a little light come on, flicker, and go out, and she began to run again. "CJ!"

"Brid?"

It was her brothers—her pesky, bossy, silly brothers—and they were heading toward her. As she got closer, she saw that CJ had Pat on his back, piggyback style. She ran and caught up to them and hugged them harder than she ever knew she could.

"Where have you guys been?" she said, realizing that she was actually a bit mad at them.

CJ answered. "We had no light except my cell phone, so we must have passed the station stairs to the street. Then we got this far, and everything was chained shut. We couldn't get out of here."

"Couldn't you have used the cell phone to call Mom?"

"There's no cell service in New York City subways."

"What is this place?" Brid said, squinting as she looked around.

"We think it's an abandoned station, because we tried to walk up the stairs, but they're mostly crumbling, and the door to the street is barred. We couldn't get out of here," Patrick repeated, sounding very scared.

"We followed the tracks until we realized they were going in a circle. It's like the trains turn around here or something, so we were really walking nowhere," CJ said. "And then Pat cut his leg on something."

"Ew," Brid said, seeing dried blood on Patrick's snow pants.

"So what did you do all night?" Brid asked.

"Shivered," Pat said. And he wasn't even joking.

Brid shone her light on the white, green, and gold tiling that rose above them like the dome of an enormous church. Some skylight far above dimly lit the forgotten station, showing its giant leaded-glass windows.

"I think Guastavino built this station," Patrick said. "It's been—"

"Roger that. Here they are." Running toward them came the firefighter and a team of men, with Eloise, Carron, and Joe Torrio bringing up the rear. Helmet lights flooded the cavernous station, and Brid felt so happy to have responsibility pass on to an adult.

She heard CJ explaining, "Well, I was carrying him back, but he's so heavy, and when the tracks widened, we weren't sure which way we came from."

The firefighter, Kevin O'Rourke, swooped Patrick off CJ's back and into his own arms while another man looked at Patrick's leg. "Kid needs this cleaned out. It's pretty dank and dirty down here."

"What is this place?" asked CJ.

"City Hall station. Not many New Yorkers get to see this little gem. Been closed since 1945," said O'Rourke.

"Why did it close?" CJ said, with a shiver in his voice. Brid reached out to hold his hand, and he didn't pull it away.

"The trains got longer and wider, so the platforms in this station couldn't get everyone on and off safely. This is where the empty number six train turns from the downtown to the uptown tracks, but people hardly ever get to see it. They're all told to get off at the Brooklyn Bridge stop."

"But why isn't it open to the public just to visit? It's as beautiful as any piece of art," Brid said.

"Oh, you know, progress. People forget. They let things decay and fall apart. The guy who built this place probably thought he'd be famous or something, and here we are, and I've never even heard his name. One day it'll just fall apart, and then it'll be demolished and turned into something else."

"The guy's name was Guastavino," Patrick offered.

"Guasta-who?" the fireman said.

"Rafael Guastavino. Once you know about him, you sorta see him everywhere," Pat said.

"Oh. Well, now you've taught me something. And now I'll tell you a little-known fact. This little station used to be the spot where our city bragged about its transit system. The mayors in the first half of the nineteen hundreds liked to come down here for press conferences," O'Rourke said. "That's a good story about this station."

"Or how about this story?" his partner, named McHugh, offered. "Remember that blizzard in 2010 when some nutty kids spent the night here? Yeah, their mom was crazy with worry, but the kids stayed all night telling stories about architectural builders." With that he winked.

"Well, we'll remember," said Brid.

"I will, too." O'Rourke grinned.

"Brid, are you crying?" said CJ.

"No, I'm just, I don't know. We just need to get back to Mom," Brid said, sniffling.

"Yeah," said CJ. "We need to tell her everything."

"Dad, too," said Patrick.

"Yes," said CJ. "I think it's time everyone got to know about everything."

"Everything," said Brid. "I'm sick of secrets."

Eloise said nothing, but she nodded approvingly.

CHAPTER 39

Riding home in the front seat of a fire truck was the perfect end to Patrick's day. Because he hadn't really slept, his body told him it was night, even though he knew it was early morning. The firefighters had cut the bottom of his pant leg, cleaned his wound, bandaged it, and plopped him into the truck. He said it didn't hurt a bit, but still his mother insisted he sit in her lap.

Anne Smithfork had met them at City Hall, and she was so happy to have them safe again that CJ thought she might even forget to punish them. As the bumpy rig moved its way up Park Avenue, Carron sat on Eloise's lap going, "Choo choo." Nobody bothered to correct her with the fact that fire trucks made a much different sound.

It was magnificent to sweep through Manhattan after a blizzard. The plow had pushed the remaining mountains of snow up along the sides of every street, and it looked like they were driving through an endless white valley on an enormous red sleigh. The trees in the middle of Park Avenue had Christmas lights on them, which added to the magical shimmer.

"Torrio left the station after we were all safe," Brid said to CJ. "I just don't know what to think of him."

"It's not like he saved us," CJ said. "We would have found our way out eventually."

"True, I guess," Brid said, unconvinced.

"So let me get this straight," CJ said. "Torrio's family didn't kidnap Julian."

"So he says," snorted Eloise.

"But Mr. Post thought he did?"

"Well, that's what everyone suspected at the time," Eloise replied. "They were a suspicious family with ties to bad characters. My father had some dealings with the elder Mr. Torrio regarding his food plants."

"So, you're not certain that the Torrios took Julian?" CJ asked.

"It was so long ago, it's so hard to remember. That's what everyone else told me." Eloise looked confused. "I was only eight years old."

CJ said, "Joe Torrio told Brid he had a letter from Mr. Post that proved the Torrio family was innocent. Why wouldn't he have shown you that letter years ago?"

"That part makes no sense," Eloise admitted. "Honestly, I'm not certain what is true. I just know that Joe Torrio moved into this building a very long time ago. I always thought he was just trying to get closer to me to get closer to the treasure so he could take it for himself," Eloise said.

Anne Smithfork suddenly interrupted them. "Enough!" she said. "All I know about the man is that he was truly worried about your safety, and he knew where to look for you when you went missing." She gave Eloise a stern look. "When we get home, you must all take showers, get dressed, meet in the living room, and begin at the very beginning of this story. With this secret life, you would think you children had no parents. Things are going to change around here. Enjoy this ride; it may be the last time you are outside for a very long time." Her face contorted in that strange way it did when she was trying to be strict and realizing she was very bad at it.

Brid suddenly remembered something. "Doesn't Dad come home Friday?"

"Well, he was supposed to, but he called me yesterday and told me he'd changed his flight to come home today," Anne said. "Now I'm worried that all this snow will delay him." Suddenly, they all wanted to see him very much.

*　*　*

An hour later, after they'd said good-bye to Eloise and the firemen and had taken showers, CJ came into Brid's room. He still was wrestling with the new information.

"Creepy," CJ said, "yet cool." He lay on Brid's bed, which looked like a bed in a store, all perfectly plumped pillows and coordinated shams.

"CJ, let's walk to Torrio's apartment through the silver room and the fire stairwell on the Williamsons' side," Brid said.

But CJ didn't answer. He was quiet, deep in thought, his chest rising and falling rhythmically. It took a minute before Brid realized that CJ had fallen into a deep sleep, and that the silver room would have to wait.

Patrick and CJ slept and slept through the morning and afternoon, and the snow started to fall again. Brid felt restless as she kept going over her notes, trying to make sense of everything. Eloise came by later to check on everyone, and when she did, Anne Smithfork went to bed, too. She had been up all night worrying, and was now too tired to hear the story.

"Eloise, do you think we have all the information we need to solve the puzzle behind the wall?" Brid said as they sat in front of the living room fireplace, passing a bowl of chocolate-covered pretzels back and forth.

"Yes, I think we do."

"So maybe when the boys wake up?"

"I think we need to let your mother know what we

are up to," Eloise said.

"Is something wrong?" Brid asked.

"Not wrong, really," Eloise said, adjusting her skirt. "I'm confused about Mr. Torrio. I still don't think I believe him, but what if he's telling the truth?"

CJ came sauntering into the room, rubbing his eyes. "He is."

"How do you know?"

"It doesn't make sense that he would be living here just to hunt for some shot-in-the-dark treasure that isn't even his. There has to be something about this whole thing we're missing."

"There is only one way to find out."

"Yup. The minute Patrick wakes up, it's back behind the wall."

"With your mother's permission," said Eloise, with a funny lilt in her voice.

"Yeah, with Mom's permission," Brid repeated, just as the doorbell buzzed.

CJ rubbed his hair. "Doorbells don't buzz in New York City, unless . . ."

"The Williamsons?" asked Brid as she went bounding for the door. But it was Ray.

"Mr. Torrio left this for you," Ray said, and handed her a padded envelope. But instead of turning away, he just stood there and watched expectantly. "Wewuzworried boutya," Ray said, crinkling up his giant eyebrows. "Glad yur back."

"Who? Us? Don't worry about us, Ray," Brid said, and smiled as she opened the envelope. Inside was the DigiSpy pod. "It's from Torrio," she said. "Here's a note from him. 'Please let me know if I can be of any help.'"

"Dittoforme," Ray said. "I'll help you. We're getting kinda used to you kids, we like havin' you here, and we donwantanythingbadhappenen."

"What, are you friends with Torrio now?" Brid asked with a grin.

"Yeah, well, he was really worried about you last night. I didn't know he cared about anybody. Made me kinda change my opinionudaguy."

An hour later, CJ and Patrick were up and all set to solve the mystery. CJ had rebooted the DigiSpy, and Patrick was ready to go. Best of all, Anne Smithfork had heard every last detail, and now seemed the most excited of anyone.

Brid got Torrio's phone number from Ray and called to tell him they would be traveling behind his wall. It felt strange not to be that afraid of him. "You may want to come to my house," he said. "We can watch Pat through the vents, make sure he's safe. Come through the silver room and downstairs."

So, while CJ stayed at the computer, Patrick went down

to the dumbwaiter with his mother, and Eloise, Carron, and Brid touched one side of Patrick's closet to reveal a twenty-foot passage filled top to bottom with drawers and shelves. This was the place that used to hold the silverware, platters, and glasses for the countless guests who once frequented the ballroom. The passage led to a little staircase and Torrio's back door. Torrio stood there to greet them. "It's faster than going up and down the elevator," he said. Brid couldn't help but think how much fun she and her brothers would have with the silver room in the future.

They pushed through Torrio's back door and into a kitchen filled with books. There were books on architecture, history, and museums, and many collections of poems. Brid wondered if there was something about this building that turned people into poetry lovers. "Sorry about the mess," Torrio said. "I just haven't had visitors in a long while. I spend most of my time, uh . . ."

"Reading?" Eloise asked, softly fingering an old edition of Robert Frost's poetry. Brid looked around at the books stacked everywhere, the cheap black table, and the chipped gold-leaf paint on the walls. It had never occurred to her how lonely Torrio's life must be. Her thoughts were interrupted by a soft whirring noise coming through the grille, the sound of the dumbwaiter rising toward them.

"Patrick?" shouted Brid into her walkie-talkie. "Let's

review each section of wood you need to push on, before you actually push it."

"I know the order," Patrick said. "I think about it all the time. Wait while I put the DigiSpy down."

"Okay," Brid said. "The first poem is 'The Weary Blues' by Langston Hughes, and he's talking about Harlem." She quickly unfolded her printout of the map onto the card table. Torrio and Eloise gathered to look over her shoulder.

"Number one is around Lenox Avenue. The Guastavino building is gone, but the symbol has to be . . . ?" Eloise asked.

"The musical note," Patrick replied. "Cool."

"What's cool?" Brid said.

"The wood just kind of springs in when you push that spot," Patrick said. "And then it stays in." Upstairs, in front of his father's computer, CJ watched the wood piece easily notch into place.

"Okay, Patrick, now we head west on the map, on your left."

"I know, it's 'Ulysses,' that poem by the tennis boy," Pat yelled.

"What?" Brid sounded alarmed.

Upstairs, CJ chuckled into his walkie-talkie. "Tennyson!" he said. "Not 'tennis boy'! And the symbol is the general's star for General Ulysses S. Grant."

Patrick found the star and pushed it forward, once

again feeling the piece latch on to something.

"Third poem!" he yelled.

"The third poem is 'Faint Heart in a Rail Way Train,'" said Brid. "The symbol is the caduceus held by the Mercury statue at Grand Central Terminal."

"Yeah, about the guy who wished he had gotten off the train to meet some girl. Yuck!" Patrick said.

"Actually," interrupted Eloise, "the bigger thought is to follow your heart and take a chance every once in a while." They waited as Pat pushed the wooden shape with a caduceus on it. "The next poem is 'Recuerdo' by—"

"—Edna St. Vincent Millay," they all chorused.

Brid added, "Patrick, push the joyful girl, that's the symbol for that poem. Remember, from the Staten Island Ferry?"

There followed a long pause. CJ watched from upstairs, seeing that Patrick's arms couldn't reach that far south on the map. He had the DigiSpy directly in front of the correct spot, but he just couldn't reach it. It was too far away to his right, and too far up.

"Darnnnnn it!" came his shout.

"What's wrong?" they heard as Anne Smithfork's voice crackled over the walkie-talkie from the basement. She had been listening, mesmerized, the entire time.

"I can't reach that far," Pat said. "It's too high up."

"Is that behind the Williamsons' wall?" Brid asked.

"Can't he just take the dumbwaiter up higher?"

CJ came on the walkie-talkie. "It's too far to the side for Pat; the dumbwaiter can't go sideways. We need to get into the Williamsons' apartment. Pat, go down to the basement, then come up and meet us there," he said.

Brid was already heading out of Torrio's front door, Joe and Eloise coming behind her. She summoned the elevator, knowing exactly where they had to go.

Sonia, the maid, met them at the entrance to the Williamsons' apartment. Brid said, "Hi, remember me? I live on the other side of this wall, and I need to get into your side."

Sonia just stood there, looking at Brid's shoes.

"Oh, yeah," Brid said, and flipped them off, not bothering to untie her sneakers. To Brid's surprise, Lily appeared from behind Sonia.

"What an absolute pleasure!" Lily said, extending her hand. "We've just come home for half-term holiday! We haven't been here twenty minutes."

Impulsively, Brid hugged her, as Lukas appeared behind her.

"Listen, long story," Brid said, "but we have to get behind your wall. Probably one of your radiator grilles will do in that back bedroom." The elevator dinged again as Ray arrived, bringing up CJ, Patrick, Carron, and Anne.

"Shoes off, people!" Brid demanded. Sonia looked too stunned to protest as the parade filed past her. She picked up her neat basket of booties, but shrugged when nobody took any.

In Lily's ruffled bedroom, CJ extracted the screwdriver from his Swiss army knife and began to unscrew the grille cover. This was going to be easier than he'd expected. He slipped the cover off, and everyone took in the sight of the other eye.

"What in heaven's name?" said Anne Smithfork.

"Holy knuckle-duster!" said Lukas.

"That's nothing," said Patrick. "Look at the writing around her eyes while we finish this thing up. Just remember to skip seven places."

"What does he mean by that?" said Lily as she watched Patrick sink behind the wall, helped by CJ. They moved with the grace of people who did this every day.

"Patrick!" Anne protested.

"Don't worry, Mom, there is a shelf for him to walk around on," CJ said as he stuck his head in and handed Patrick his flashlight.

"Now, where were we?" Patrick asked, as if only a moment had passed.

Brid, CJ, Torrio, and Eloise all looked at each other and laughed.

CHAPTER 40

Below them, they could hear Patrick congratulating himself as he pushed the fourth symbol, the joyful girl, and a latching noise proved it was the correct choice. He yelled up to the open grille, "Isn't the Kissing Post next?"

He added, "I can see big lips right where Ellis Island should be."

Lukas Williamson gave a shrug. At some point in the last few minutes he had resigned himself to the fact that he and Lily would have to wait for answers to their questions.

"Got it," Patrick yelled up. "That's five down! What's next?"

"It's the trolley car, Patrick, back at the Queensboro Bridge," Brid said. "That's at Fifty-ninth Street on the East Side, so you have to go to the middle of the map."

"I know; it's where we had hot cocoa yesterday," said Pat happily.

Eloise sat down on Lily's pink and green tufted bedspread. She was feeling light-headed.

"So the seventh and last clue," Brid said as she looked at the expectant faces, "relates to Ota Benga. Remember he slept at the American Museum of Natural History?" She paused. "Did we ever decide on the symbol for that one? I don't think we did!"

"No!" said CJ. "That's what we were doing when the storm started and we had the subway sleepover and—"

"Silly!" Patrick's voice interrupted him. "It has to be a dinosaur; everyone knows that the Museum of Natural History is full of them." And without even waiting for confirmation, he pushed the last symbol.

The final block of wood latched like the others, but this time, it freed an entire portion of the map. It fell forward, completely unhinged from the inside wall, free of the enormous wooden frame that had held it for so long. It fell like a giant piece of jigsaw puzzle turned upside down. Everyone in Lily Williamson's bedroom heard a rumbling noise followed by a heavy thud.

"Patrick!" Anne Smithfork yelled. "Get up here."

"Whoa!" said Patrick.

Brid and CJ jammed their heads into the open space, but neither could see anything but Patrick's dancing flashlight beam.

"Here goes," Pat said as he thrust something upward. CJ could just about reach the thing Pat was holding over his head, but he grasped it and gingerly pulled it through the grille opening. It was a package.

The wrapping was of the same brown paper and red-and-white bakery string that *Treasure Island* had been bundled in, making Brid think that both packages were probably wrapped at the same time. Attached to the string was a key that looked like the same key that activated the dumbwaiter.

"What could that be for?" Lukas asked.

"Must be another key for the dumbwaiter," said CJ, glossing over the fact that nobody would need a dumbwaiter, had they gotten this far in the treasure hunt. He casually slipped the giant key into his pocket, and only Brid seemed to notice. All eyes were on the package.

Of course, the brown paper had a poem attached. CJ lifted it from the packaging and handed it to Eloise. She glanced at it and slowly read out loud:

> "For a Child
> by Fannie Stearns Davis
>
> "Your friends shall be the Tall Wind,
> The River and the Tree;
> The Sun that laughs and marches,
> The Swallows and the Sea.

"Your prayers shall be the murmur
Of grasses in the rain;
The song of wildwood thrushes
That makes God glad again.

"And you shall run and wander,
And you shall dream and sing
Of brave things and bright things
Beyond the swallow's wings.

"And you shall envy no man,
Nor hurt your heart with sighs,
For I will keep you simple
That God may make you wise."

When Eloise finished reading aloud, she looked around the room at the people surrounding her. "I'm not sure God has made me wise," she said, "but perhaps there is still time left for me to become wise. Let's open the package!"

CJ had just handed her the package when they all heard, "Um, a little help here?"

Patrick! They had forgotten to pull him up from behind the wall. CJ and Brid each reached down for one of Patrick's arms and carefully pulled him back into the room. "Good work," said CJ. Pat said nothing, but he beamed.

Eloise carefully unwrapped the brown paper packaging to reveal a framed oil painting about the size of a large notebook. It was a very accurate representation of the top two floors of 2 East 92nd Street, and the majestic roofline that adorned it, Eloise's childhood home.

The roof showed the unmistakable limestone balustrades that seemed to stand guard. An impressive water tower stood erect at the very top, with the faint profile of a brown ladder leading upward. The water tower reflected the late autumn sun, which had turned the front of the building a golden bronze. Though unsigned, the painting was visibly a masterpiece, certainly worth a lot of money.

Eloise looked at it, searching for the details of her home, the home that was the scene of so many parties, so much life, and so much drama. "This artist must have been perched on a neighboring rooftop." Eloise pondered. "To be able to paint the top of this building with that perspective, he had to have been on a roof."

"Such a beautiful painting," Anne Smithfork murmured. "Such a wonderful treasure left in the wall so very long ago."

Chapter 41

That night, Anne Smithfork made chicken curry and invited everyone over for dinner. The kitchen was a mess, but the dining room looked radiant. Gold candles made the room glow. The lights were dimmed, and soft music played. CJ had to admit that their mom's work had made their new surroundings look beautiful.

Eloise brought a belated housewarming gift: an entire set of china she had never used, dishes that had been her mother's. Each plate was hand-painted with a set of four children holding hands and dancing in the middle. Brid noted that the word *Sèvres* was written on the back of each plate.

Lily Williamson seemed pleased to be in the company of such fine dishes. "These were made in the late 1700s," she said, watching with horror as Anne Smithfork popped a plate in front of Carron.

"When?" Anne asked.

"Around Napoléon's time," Lukas answered.

Without any fuss, Anne moved the contents of Carron's plate onto a purple plastic plate with a dinosaur on it, and took her Sèvres plate back to the kitchen.

"You may not wish to place that in the dishwasher," Lily called after her.

Ray sat at the head of the very long dining table, his face scrunched up in laughter. Eloise sat erect at his side. Carron showed everyone how precisely she could use her fork and spoon, the result of coaching from Eloise.

Torrio had brought a few bottles of ginger ale that he dramatically poured into everyone's glass. He raised his cup and toasted everyone, including Anne Smithfork, the children, Ray, and even the Williamsons for allowing access to their apartment.

As dinner wound down, Joe Torrio stood and banged his knife on the side of his ginger ale glass. He cleared his throat. "I want to share this letter that Mr. Post wrote to Mr. Torrio."

"Right," interrupted CJ. "So this is from Eloise's dad to your dad?"

Mr. Torrio's face twisted strangely. "Something like that."

He cleared his throat.

"Dear Johnny,

"Enclosed is a small compensation for the unwavering friendship you showed through the most trying time of our lives. Money means so little in lieu of friendship, but as a token gesture, please accept this.

"When Julian was being threatened with kidnapping, there was nobody else I could turn to. You seemed to know good and bad people, but I never wavered in thinking you fell on this side of being good. Hiding Julian with your family at Knollwood all those years was brilliant, and I'm sure the only thing that kept him safe in those trying times. I know having him there as a pretend nephew was confusing, both to him and to your family, but it was the only way my son could be safe.

"I realize how difficult living with the shadow of suspicion over your family must have been, and there is no way to compensate you for that. I trust this letter will at last clear the Torrio family's good name. I also understand your wishing to wait to make this letter public, to keep your own family safe.

"For taking such good care of Julian, and for all the tales you had to tell to protect my family,

"I am gratefully yours,

"Mr. Lyon Post"

There was a long silence at the table until Ray finally said, "I don't get it."

Eloise had a dazed look on her face. "Knollwood? The place my parents went on weekend outings? My brother, Julian, was there?" She seemed agitated.

"Wait," Ray said. "Julianwasnever kidnapped?"

Mr. Torrio took over from there. "After the Lindbergh child was kidnapped, affluent families worried the same thing could happen to them. Because Mr. Post was so wealthy and so visible, he worried his son was in danger. The senior Mr. Torrio knew a lot of bad characters. He thought kidnapping threats were valid, and he came to Mr. Post to tell him that. Together they came up with a plan. They decided to pretend that Julian was kidnapped, when really the Posts sent Julian to live with the Torrio family. Both families pretended to dislike each other for the sake of Julian's safety."

Eloise looked up from her plate, misty-eyed. "I know my father was afraid to leave him with his governess after the Lindbergh kidnapping, afraid to go out at night, afraid to let him go to the park. But I can't believe he sent him away for so long."

"That doesn't make sense," Brid said. "Why weren't you at risk of being kidnapped, too?"

"Well, I'm three years older than Julian, so I wasn't as vulnerable," Eloise said wistfully. "But they did send me away."

"You mean boarding school?" Lukas said.

"Yes, boarding school with a new last name. At the

time, Julian was too young for boarding school."

Patrick still didn't understand. "So Julian wasn't kidnapped, he was given to another family to be raised?"

"That would be the Torrio family. The family some accused of kidnapping him were actually the ones who saved his life," said Mr. Torrio. "After his father's death, everyone thought it was time for him to go home, be back with his own family. But by then Julian was quite fond of the Torrios and mad at his own family. I felt abandoned. I felt Eloise was the favored child, and when they wanted me back with my real family, I didn't want to go." Torrio was looking down at his plate. "I was so foolish," he said, turning to Eloise. "I hope you can forgive me."

There was a painful silence in the room. Even Carron had stopped wriggling in her high chair.

"What?" Eloise said in a soft voice, her mouth hanging open.

"It's true. I missed so much, and I just thought it was far too late in our lives to even begin to be brother and sister again." Joe Torrio—Julian Post—rose from his seat and went over to Eloise. He bent low and put his hand out to shake hers. "May I have the pleasure of finally getting to know my sister?" he asked with great deference.

Eloise hugged him tightly, as if she wouldn't let him out of her sight again. "I thought you had died. I thought of you every day of my very, very old life." Eloise was crying hard now. "How dare you shock an old woman this way," she snorted and laughed at the same time.

The children watched as Ray blew his nose into his napkin, and Anne Smithfork rose and hugged the two Posts together.

"I was just so angry about the arrangement," Julian said. "Most children just want to be with their own family. No matter what."

"Well, it seems your parents tried to do their best for you," Anne Smithfork said. "Sometimes we parents do things we think are best for our children, but we can never be sure. No choice you have to make for another human being is ever easy."

Brid spoke up. "Like moving?"

"Yes," said Anne. "Like moving to a new home."

"Or a different job?" CJ asked.

"Yes," Anne said. "If you think that more money will provide more things for your family and make everyone's life better, you take the different job."

"Like Dad did," Pat said.

"Like we all did when we moved," Anne said.

"So are you finding it to be more to your liking?" Lukas asked politely. "Living here?"

The room went silent again. Glances were exchanged, but nobody said a word, and then a small whirring noise interrupted their thoughts—the noise of the approaching elevator. CJ was about to say yes; he just couldn't get the word out quickly enough. He was glad they were living there. And right then, the front door burst open and Mr. Smithfork yelled, "I'm home, two days early! Anything happen while I was gone?"

CHAPTER 42

In the tumble of hugs that followed, CJ got a wonderful gift from his father. Bruce Smithfork looked directly at him and winked. In that shared moment, CJ knew they wouldn't be in terrible trouble. His dad's punishments were more severe than his mom's, but only after repeat offenses. CJ had gotten the clear message never to skip school again, and he knew he wouldn't.

Joe Torrio introduced himself as Julian Post—and of course Bruce Smithfork didn't know of the surprise he had just missed. Anne placed a mound of curry in front of him on one of the historic plates.

"Nice dishes," Bruce said. "New?"

"Very nice," Lily Williamson agreed. "And quite old."

"So, start at the beginning," Bruce said as he shook out

his napkin and spread it on his lap. "Tell me everything I've missed while I was gone." He mussed Carron's hair and looked so happy to be home, while the children's mom stared proudly at him.

As the candles burned low in their holders and Carron nodded off in her high chair, Brid, CJ, and Patrick told everyone at the table about the mystery behind the walls, starting with the day they moved in. At last, Brid turned to face Julian.

"I have two questions for you," she said. "How did you know there was a package waiting at the library?"

Julian looked abashed. "My mother was a library donor," he said. "She mentioned that such a thing existed, but she didn't know what it was, and I never could get them to give it to me."

Brid remembered the librarian who was such a stickler for the rules that she'd charged them $76.28 for returning a library book that had been checked out so long ago. "Julian, what did you do before you moved in here? I mean, after you were grown up and everything."

Addressed by his real name, Julian smiled. "Well, I was in college, and then in the army, in Korea. Then I traveled for a long time. I was still pretty angry about being taken away from my family. It took me many long years to decide to move back here and look for the treasure myself. I did a lot of reading, and I wrote, too, mostly poetry."

Brid smiled back. "Maybe I'll read some of it. I think I might like poetry, now." She caught CJ's eye. "A little."

When Eloise excused herself to go to the powder room, CJ stood, too, and carried some of the dishes into the kitchen. He had an idea he wanted to speak to her about in private. Brid also rose from the table and followed CJ, her notebook in hand.

"Are you feeling okay?" Brid asked Eloise when she came out of the powder room.

"Once I've caught my breath? Why, yes, children. A whole new chapter of my life is about to begin, and it's a bit mind-boggling," she said, shaking her head.

Without a word, Brid opened her book and presented a drawing to CJ and Eloise. It was a sketch of the building's roofline. Eloise looked at the children with wonder.

"So how early in the morning do we head out to get the treasure?" Eloise said with a wry smile.

"You knew it, too!" CJ exclaimed.

"The treasure is not a painting," Eloise said. "The minute I saw that water tower, I just knew. It's the eighth poem, really. And my father must have written that one himself." She recited slowly,

> "Seven clues on seven structures
> Get water from above to rupture.
> Push the symbols in their order
> To get the flow of golden water."

Brid said, "So we found the structures, we found their symbols, we pushed them and got the painting, and the painting gave us a visual image of where the treasure is."

"Plus we have this," CJ said, holding up the key that had been attached to the newest package.

"Do we have to wait until morning?" Brid said.

"Honey, it's dark and snowy out there. It's too dangerous, and we're too tired," Eloise said, in her caretaker voice.

"Who's too tired?" CJ said. "I've been sleeping all day. Besides, in daylight, someone will see us from another building and probably call the police."

"Tomorrow," Eloise said, but this time there was a slight hesitation in her voice. "And my brother gets to come, too."

"Tonight in two hours," said Brid, so matter-of-factly that both CJ and Eloise raised their eyebrows. "And of course your brother has to come," she added.

Over the next two hours, the kitchen got cleaned, the guests left, and Mr. and Mrs. Smithfork turned in early. Carron was asleep, and Patrick was in his pajamas, playing with his plastic wrestling figures, when CJ and Brid came into his room. "Patrick, it's time. Put on warm winter clothes," said CJ.

Pat never asked where they were going. He dropped his wrestlers on the floor, and put on his jacket, snow pants, and boots, as if he were called to bravery every day.

CJ carried a lumpy duffel bag with some tools in it. Brid added a blanket and some other items, noticing CJ's snorkeling mask as she did so. She didn't even ask why he had it with him. CJ opened the door that led to the fire stairs, and silently the three children walked upstairs, single file, to the emergency door that led to the roof.

They paused there, listening to the wind. In a minute, they heard the sound they had been waiting for, the sound of Eloise's back door opening and closing, and her slow, purposeful footsteps. They could also hear Julian's heavier tread. Eloise let out a little laugh when she saw the three Smithforks and their lumpy bag. "I guess this is it," she said.

"If it isn't," Brid said, "I'm out of ideas *and* pages in my notebook."

CJ pushed open the door, knowing it wasn't alarmed, knowing that this building relied on old-fashioned, human methods for security. And that was exactly what they needed tonight.

The rooftops of Manhattan stood before them like a misshapen army. The moon was bulging and full, providing them with more light than they had expected. Several rooftops had floodlights on them, creating an eerie backdrop.

Just as in the painting, their particular water tower was enormous, taking up one quarter of the rooftop. The area under the tower was free from snow. Remaining drifts of snow piled up around it, outlining the tower and creating shelter from nosy city eyes. Brid dragged CJ's bag to the side of the tower and sat comfortably in the snow. Patrick dropped to the ground, scooping and shaping snow until he had a chair. He gestured to Eloise to sit down. Julian began to make his own chair, sweeping the snow aside with enthusiasm.

CJ walked around the tower with his flashlight, looking for an obvious entry point.

The tower reminded Brid of a silo, only wider and more golden. The long wooden ladder was nailed into place, leading to the top, probably seventy-five feet into the air.

"So does this just catch the rain and then send it down our pipes to our apartment?" Patrick asked.

"No," CJ said, "we have municipal water, city water that comes into big tanks in the basement. But in the nineteen twenties, when buildings started to be built over five stories tall, they had to figure out a way to get water to higher levels. These buildings have a pump that sends water to the roof tank, and then gravity lets it go back down again, into everyone's pipes, giving them just the right amount of water pressure when they need it."

"But Mom always complains about how the pressure is so weak in our apartment," Patrick said.

"It's not just your apartment," Eloise said. "It's all the apartments in this building. The water flow is quite dismal."

"Has it always been that way?" CJ asked.

"I can't remember," Eloise said. "I don't believe anyone has ever looked into it."

"Interesting. I wonder what is stopping the flow of water from that tank," CJ said with a grin. Holding a flashlight, he began to climb the ladder, silhouetted by the night sky. Eloise resisted the urge to tell him it was too dangerous, thinking the drifts of snow would give him a soft landing should he fall. And she was just too curious to forbid him to continue.

CJ stood at the top of the water tower, where a big funnel-shaped hole let him look inside. The funnel top was held on by little latches and easily moved aside.

"Do you need the stuff?" Brid asked.

"What stuff?" Patrick asked.

"Yup," CJ said, "I need it." He came back down and unzipped the duffel bag. "I can see a panel under the water about halfway down the inside. If I could just get to it—," he said, pulling the snorkel out of the bag. Eloise gasped.

"There is no way you are going into that tank, young man. You will kill yourself. Julian, talk some sense into this child! He is not going into that water tower!"

CJ was already taking off his jacket and snow boots and putting on water shoes. Under his jeans and shirt, he was wearing swimming trunks. "You better put on your wet suit," Brid suggested.

"I want to go in, too," Pat said.

"No way," CJ said as he adjusted his mask. "But you can stand at the top and repeat what I say to Brid and Eloise and Julian. It's really just a wooden tub with a giant ladder inside and outside. I can easily climb out. Brid, you hold on to this key."

Patrick looked very proud. He pulled his ski hat closer around his eyes. "Let's do it," he said.

"Wait, CJ," Julian interrupted. "Eloise is right. I'm sure you are a terrific swimmer, but this is just too risky. I'll bet there is some outside access to that panel. Maybe you could point out the area, and Brid and I can try and find the spot on the outside. My guess is that under these wooden shingles, there is a way to access the panel."

"Okay, but I still have to go in to find the panel spot," said CJ. "I promise I won't let go of the inside ladder. The water is warm. The water tank is insulated so it won't freeze. I have this metal piece of pipe," he said, pulling something else out of his bag. "I'll bang the inside of the tank in the right spot. You find that spot on the outside. It's not dangerous at all!" And maybe because they were too curious, both Julian and Eloise stopped protesting.

CJ and Patrick clambered to the top of the ladder. CJ sat at the top, looking at the sparkling city lights and the moon hanging low like a ripe orange, ready to be picked. Squatting, he turned on his headlamp. He waved one last time and disappeared over the edge and into the black water as Pat turned around and gave them a thumbs-up. Brid wondered if CJ had showered that evening before he climbed into everyone's drinking water.

Suddenly, the roof door opened, and Carlos, the night elevator man, shone a flashlight directly at them. "Youse got business out here?" he said.

"As a matter of fact, we do," Julian said, not missing a beat. "This young lady doesn't even know how to make a snow chair," he said, nodding toward Eloise. He pointed to the remains of Patrick's chair. "It's such a beautiful night to try making one."

Carlos stood silently for a few seconds. Brid glanced up at Patrick, standing frozen in place on the ladder. He didn't move a muscle and Carlos, thankfully, never looked skyward. He shrugged. "Sorry I didn't see you there, Mr. Torrio," he said, while looking quizzically over his shoulder as he left, letting the door close behind him.

Patrick immediately said, "Guys! CJ wants you to go to the far side of the tank, and he wants you to listen for the sound of his metal pipe clinking on the inside."

"Okay," Brid said as she and Julian were already moving to the far side of the water tower. They could hear a faint pinging sound, but it was above their heads, probably about twelve feet off the ground. Without hesitation, Brid began piling snow to make a mound, piling it higher and higher, until she could stand just opposite the pinging noise that came from within. "Quick, Eloise, grab that file from the duffel bag," she yelled.

Eloise quickly pulled out a thin metal file and handed it up to Brid, marveling at the fact that the children had thought to bring tools. Deftly, Brid slid the file under a wooden shingle and popped it off. She inhaled. "Whoa . . . that was easy."

Before her was an unmistakable, old-fashioned key-hole.

CHAPTER 43

CJ was so excited when he made it back down the ladder, he simply put his jacket and boots back on over his swim trunks. He didn't feel cold at all.

Patrick carved little steps on the enormous snow mound, making it easier to get up to the level of the keyhole. When everything was set, Brid handed Eloise the key. "It's time," she said. "It's finally time."

Eloise turned to Julian, "I think you should open it. You deserve to."

"No," said Julian, "we're all in this together. You go ahead."

Eloise nodded, and carefully climbed the snow steps. Reaching the top, she removed the glove from her right hand and pulled the key from her pocket. She paused.

What if this wasn't it? What if it just led to more clues, more poems, or, worse, to nothing?

With robotic stiffness, she jiggled the key into place. She turned it and heard a click. She twisted around to see four pairs of anxious eyes on the ground below her, watching her every move.

"It clicked," she whispered, and she turned back to the lock. She savored that moment when she felt so very, very hopeful, one last time.

Eloise could see that other beveled shingles on the water tower blocked the large door hidden behind the shingles, but when she tugged on the door, those shingles easily peeled away and fell like confetti to the snow below. The door groaned and opened. She peered inside, but had no direct light. She said nothing, and then inexplicably, Eloise turned and carefully made her way back down the snow steps. When she reached the bottom, she looked at each child and finally at Julian.

"It's in there," she said. "All this time, it was right where my brother and I lived. Where our family lived."

"Can we see it?" Pat said, jumping up and down.

"Let's start unloading it!" Brid said, not being able to contain herself any longer. "Treasures go in the bag!" she yelled.

"I think we should step inside. We should visit it, instead of unloading it, at least for tonight," Eloise said. "We need to show it a little respect." With that, she climbed back up and entered the secret treasure room inside the tank, the room left alone for seventy years, the room that took up one-quarter of the entire tank's space, causing the 1000-gallon water tank at 2 East 92nd Street to have 750 gallons of water and very low pressure for many years. The treasure room had been there, above them, the whole time.

One by one, they clambered into the secret room, lined with gold-colored tiles that glowed magnificently in the light reflected from CJ's headlamp. The children and Eloise and Julian were surrounded by cases and cases of black lacquered boxes. Brid opened one and gasped at the golf ball–sized emerald earrings, trimmed in diamonds. Eloise helped her adjust them onto her earlobes, where they shook light on the walls as Brid moved her head. "I believe Marie Antoinette wore those, my dear. Though I'm certain they are far more fetching on you!" Eloise joked.

CJ was poring over an ancient map encased in a gold frame. Rubies dotted the entire outline of the frame. Patrick was letting a mound of golden coins flow through his hands. "Do you think I could get dollars for these from that machine at the grocery store that turns your change into bills?" he asked.

Every time somebody opened a box, more dazzling pieces were revealed. Figurines, Russian dolls, and fragile, decorated eggs were uncovered. There were weapons and bejeweled daggers and bowls and an enormous emerald ring; there was a tiara that weighed as much as a brick. Julian placed it gently on Eloise's head. "I believe this belonged to Catherine the Great." Something about the room made them speak in hushed tones. The place was so large they could stand upright, or sit cozily on top of some of the bigger boxes. And that is what they did, for a long time.

"Do you notice the shape of the ceiling?" Eloise asked.

"It's a vault, isn't it?" said CJ. "It's rounded, no right angles anywhere."

"Did Guastavino build this little vault, too?" Patrick said, fingering a golden dagger that Eloise said she thought was from ancient Rome.

"I bet either he or his son did," Eloise whispered. "I have a feeling this was perhaps the last construction piece the Guastavinos built here in New York City."

"Yes, our father sure was a fan of Guastavino's work," Julian said.

"He was a fan of beauty and of space that couldn't burn—places that would last forever."

"Like his love for you," Brid said, reading an inscription on the wall.

"What?"

Brid read slowly as she kept the floodlight pointed on the wall:

> *"Here were the travelers L and M*

And the children made from them.
Our valuables many,
Our troubles were few,
But none was ever so treasured as you.
And others who come to dwell in this place,
Whose time came later to this space,
May they remember what happy could be
Before the four travelers
Then became three."

"So the travelers L and M?" asked Pat.

"Were Lyon and Margarite," replied Eloise. "My parents."

"And he's saying that even though they had tons of this fancy stuff—," Brid said.

"That you guys were his greatest treasure," CJ said, nodding to Eloise and Julian.

"And that the people who came after my family?" said Eloise.

"That would be us!" Patrick exclaimed.

"That he hopes you are happy, as happy as we were, before we went from a four-person family to three," Eloise said, wiping her eyes. Julian put his arm around her. "Do you see, Julian? Do you see how much our father missed you?"

"Well, we are happy," Brid said, "so maybe he gets his wish."

"Yes, I think you are happy," said Eloise. "And being around you has been making me so happy. I think my father was just afraid of losing the people and things he loved, so he tried to hide them from the world. But the trouble is that when you do that, you don't get to enjoy them very much, do you? I mean, he got to look at these precious jewels, and he got to go visit Julian, but he never got to really enjoy them. We never used the priceless china, wore these jewels, or got to know Julian as my brother. It was because my father was so afraid of losing everything. I think I understand that now."

"Maybe that's the bigger story here," CJ said. "Maybe all these poems were messages to you, messages about how to live your life differently than he did."

"Funny, to the outside world, our family really had everything anyone could dream of, but we didn't really have that much fun." Eloise was sniffling.

"So you want me to start wearing jewelry, Eloise?" Patrick joked, trying to cheer her up.

She smiled. "Let's figure out what we should do with the answer to one of New York City's biggest mysteries. We need to know what to say to the rest of the world when they hear about this."

"I think we need a plan," Brid said, turning to the very last page of her notebook. At the top of the page, she wrote, *What to do with priceless valuables worth millions.*

"We never did think this through. We never thought about what we would do if we actually found this stuff!" she muttered as she let some gold coins fall through her fingers back into their slick black box.

She began to make a list.

FACT OR FICTION

This book contains historical facts and figures mixed with made-up stuff. Here is a guide to help you discern the real from the unreal.

There was a family by the name of Post who began Post Cereals. Grape Nuts was the first type! The Posts had a daughter named Marjorie Merriweather Post, who married a wealthy banker named E. F. Hutton, and they had one daughter named Nadinia (Dina Merrill), who became a well-known actress. The story does not represent her or her family.

The family first lived on Fifth Avenue in New York City. In the late 1920s developers wanted to build a high-rise apartment building on the site of the Post brownstone. The family agreed on the condition that a

three-story apartment as large as their mansion be constructed for the family at the top of the building. They
maintained a separate entrance with a covered circular
driveway so nobody got wet in the rain while awaiting
a car or carriage. That entrance is at 2 East 92nd Street.

The Post apartment was the largest in New York City,
and they were famous for their lavish parties. It did
include such amenities as a ballroom, a silver room, a
gown room, butler's pantry, and servant quarters. To protect the wooden floor from scratches, Mrs. Post requested
guests to attach small feltlike bottoms to their heels,
much like the Williamsons' maid did. When they moved
out, the apartment was split into six smaller units.

It was true that some wealthy families of this era
frequently socialized with one another and were vora-
cious collectors of art, maps, jewels, Russian imperial
art, icons, textiles, Sèvres porcelains, and silver. The J. P.
Morgan family has much of their collection on display at
the Morgan Library on Madison Avenue at Thirty-sixth
Street. Much of the Post collection is in Washington,
DC, where Mrs. Post moved later in her life, at the Smithsonian Museum of Natural History. Coincidentally, this
Smithsonian building is a Guastavino structure as well,
where you can see some of Mrs. Post's treasures, including
her 275-karat diamond and turquoise necklace, originally
given by Napoléon I to his wife, Empress Marie-Louise.
Mrs. Post also donated an emerald that was first owned

by Cuauhtémoc—the last king of the Aztec Empire. In my imagination I expect that the Smithfork kids will later find out that this emerald is missing from the cache they found, hence reopening the mystery for them and taking them overseas in the next book.

The real Mrs. Post loved all things French and was later given the French Legion of Honor medal for underwriting the cost of field hospitals in France. Her gowns, which now reside at the Hillwood Museum in Washington, DC, all have a small red strip sewn on the left breast to note this honor.

The Posts were fans of Ulysses S. Grant and even had serving plates with his likeness on them. You can see them at Hillwood.

MOBSTERS

Prohibition was a time when it was illegal to make or sell alcohol, and it lasted from 1920 to 1933. Bootleggers and mobsters flourished then, including a real man named Joe Torrio. But an assassination attempt on him in 1925 encouraged him to move to Italy. The real Post family had nothing to do with mobsters or Joe Torrio.

CHARLES LINDBERGH

He was a famous aviator whose baby son was kidnapped in 1932. Many wealthy families feared copycat crimes. The real Post family never sent their child away.

The Seven Structures

Rafael Guastavino moved from Barcelona, Spain, to the United States in 1881, encouraged by demand for his fireproof and dramatic buildings. Rafael died in 1908, and his son took over his business at that time. The father-and-son team left an indelible mark on Manhattan and yet remain known only to a small community.

Because so much skilled labor was required to build out their sloped ceilings, it was expensive work, eventually replaced in leaner times by cheaper methods. Guastavino creations remain all over Manhattan, and yet he and his son are almost entirely forgotten.

Sugar Hill Building

It is true that the building at East One hundred ninth Street has been destroyed and replaced by a school. I included that neighborhood so the reader could have a feel for the richness of Harlem both in the 1920s and today and to not make the mystery too easy for the Smithfork detectives.

Numbers 409 and 555 Lenox Avenue did house famous African American residents but were not Guastavino buildings.

No Guastavino structures survive in Central Harlem. The closest surviving structures are the Cathedral of St.

John the Divine and St. Paul's Chapel, which is on the campus of Columbia University.

AMIABLE CHILD
Located quite close to Grant's Tomb. This is a true story.

GRANT'S TOMB
Ulysses S. Grant was a general under Abraham Lincoln during the Civil War. He became president of the United States in 1869 and served until 1877. He was also an early environmentalist, creating and protecting Yellowstone National Park.

Built by Guastavino in 1897, Grant's burial place is the largest mausoleum in North America. New Yorkers had great affection for both him and his wife, and that is why he chose to be buried in New York City.

GRAND CENTRAL TERMINAL
Finished in 1913, it is called a terminal and not a station because train lines end, or terminate, there. The Oyster Bar restaurant is a real place that opened on the first day the terminal did and remains popular today. The Mercury with caduceus statue is on the clock outside the building facing Park Avenue South. The whisper gallery really works. Franklin Delano Roosevelt did have a secret platform, number 61, that could get him from his train

to his hotel, the Waldorf-Astoria, without the public seeing that he was crippled by polio.

STATEN ISLAND FERRY
The Millay poem is printed on a wall inside the ferry building.

ELLIS ISLAND
Guastavino built the meeting hall after the original was destroyed by fire.

The Kissing Post is real. Once immigrants were given the green light for admission to the United States, they would proceed to the bottom of a long staircase, where people were reunited, often with relatives they hadn't seen in years. The Kissing Post got this name because of all the joyful reunions at that spot. There is no actual post.

QUEENSBORO BRIDGE
This is a real bridge built in 1909 connecting Manhattan to Queens at Fifty-ninth Street. Two trolley lines ran on the outer lanes of the bridge's lower level. Today a large grocery store and café is currently located beneath the bridge on the Manhattan side. There you can see excellent examples of Guastavino's work on the ceiling.

OTA BENGA
Ota was a real man whom a missionary took from the

Congo and brought to the United States. In 1906 he was part of a Bronx Zoo exhibit, and details about him living both there and at the Museum of Natural History are, sadly, true. It is also true that he attacked a donor to the museum, Mrs. Guggenheim, by throwing a chair at her.

SUBWAY
Most every New Yorker can attest to unintelligible, garbled, announcements on the subway and, of course, to finding themselves on the wrong train.

There is no cellular phone service in New York City subways.

FIREFIGHTER KEVIN O'ROURKE, RESCUE 2
He was a real person and cousin of mine, who sadly died trying to rescue people at the World Trade Center on September 11, 2001. Firefighter Dennis McHugh also died that day and was a childhood friend.

PS 149
The Smithforks' old elementary school is a real place; and the GKCC after-school program there will receive a percentage of the proceeds from this book. PS 149 is located in East New York, Brooklyn.

Acknowledgments

There were many collaborators and cheerleaders for this book but none as enthusiastic as my editor, Katherine Tegen. She has an ear for a good tale, an eye for architecture, and a mind open enough to hear a wacky idea through. To her the biggest thank-you.

To my mother, Kathleen Sherry, whose years as a Harlem public school teacher left her duly qualified to pinpoint what works and doesn't work for this age group. Her husband, Hugh Boylan, was tireless in his encouragement, as were Bill Klinsky and Toby Shapiro.

To my enthusiastic girls of summer who often found themselves with one or more of my own children at any given stage of this process: Nancy Hebert, Adele Malpass, Aripcy Salazar, Elizabeth Dennis, Melissa Fleming, Meng Khu Gurung, Brenda Earl, Amy Goodfriend, Katie

Shah, and, of course, Carron Sherry.

To Mr. Demeny's fifth-grade field trips, packed with information about New York, and my children's friends, who never seemed to mind me eavesdropping on the banter. You all gave me so much material. Specific thanks to the Cassidy, Hogan, Hebert, Shah, and Koepke kids, the second-grade Narnia boys, and fifth-grade tennis girls. I could listen to you talk among yourselves forever.

For artistic ideas and direction I'd like to thank Eric Clough and 212Box, Heather Bensko, Amy Ryan, Matt Klam, Sarah Salovaara, Hollie Chantiles, Roxann Couloucoundis, the Hillwood Museum, and the Smithfork Ranch.

To Laura Mandarano, in a class by herself.

And last, my greatest thanks goes to the people who inspire me the most: Cavan, Kiera, Owen, and Ella, the real Smithforks.

B EHOX RHN YTLMXK

LIST OF SOURCES CONSULTED

ON PUZZLES AND JUMBLES:

Coughlin, Dr. Heather. "Crack the Code!"
www.csustan.edu/math/Coughlin/SMC06.pdf

Stevenson, Robert Louis. *Treasure Island*. London: Cassell, 1883.

THE POST FAMILY:

Lane, Jim. "Marjorie Merriweather Post."
www.humanitiesweb.org/human.php?s=r&p=a&a=i&ID=868

Lisenbee, Kenneth. "Marjorie Merriweather Post: A Biography."
www.paulbowles.org/marjoriemerriweatherpost.html

Fisher, Frederick, et al. *Marjorie Merriweather Post's Art Collector's Personal Museum*. Washington, DC: Hillwood Museum and Gardens, 2000.

"A World Unique and Magnificent: Mrs. Marjorie Merriweather Post, Head of a Great U.S. Fortune." Photos by Alfred Eisenstaedt. New York: Time Inc.: *Life* magazine, Vol. 59, No.19, November 5, 1965.

Alpern, Andrew. *New York's Fabulous Luxury Apartments: With Original Floor Plans from the Dakota, River House, Olympic Tower and Other Great Buildings*. Mineola, NY: Dover, 1987.

New York Public Library.
www.nypl.org

Bellis, Mary. "The History of Scotch Tape." http://inventors.about.com/od/sstartinventions/a/Scotch_Tape.htm

The Morgan Library.
www.themorgan.org

THE POEMS:

Hughes, Langston (1902–1967). "The Weary Blues." *The Collected Poems of Langston Hughes*. New York: Knopf Doubleday, 1995.

Tennyson, Lord Alfred (1809–1892). "Ulysses." *Poems*. London: Edward Moxon, 1842.

Hardy, Thomas (1840–1928). "Faint Heart in a Rail Way Train." *The Complete Works of Thomas Hardy*. Oxford, England: Clarendon Press, 1995.

Millay, Edna St. Vincent (1892–1950). "Recuerdo." *The Poet and Her Book: A Biography of Edna St. Vincent Millay*. Jean Gould. New York: Dodd Mead, 1969.

Lazarus, Emma (1849–1887). *The New Colossus.* First published 1883 and engraved on Statue of Liberty plaque in 1903.

Wylie, Elinor (1885–1928). "A Crowded Trolley." *Nets to Catch the Wind.* New York: Harcourt Brace, 1921.

Bradford, Phillips Verner, and Harvey Blume. *Ota Benga: The Pygmy in the Zoo.* New York: St. Martin's Press, 1992.

The Seven Structures:
Ryokan (1758–1831). Here is the story of this haiku.
Ryokan and the Thief
Ryokan, a Zen master, lived the simplest kind of life in a little hut at the foot of a mountain. One evening a thief visited the hut, only to discover there was nothing to steal.
Ryokan returned and caught him. "You have come a long way to visit me," he told the prowler, "and you should not return empty-handed. Please take my clothes as a gift." The thief was bewildered. He took the clothes and slunk away.
Ryoken sat naked, watching the moon. "Poor fellow," he mused, "I wish I could have given him this beautiful moon."
www.poetry-chaikhana.com/R/Ryokan/thiefleftitb.htm

Bowen, A. P. "I Love Corned Beef." *The Stars and Stripes.* New York: G. P. Putnam's Sons, The Knickerbocker Press, 1919.

Kingsley, Charles (1819–1875). "A Farewell." *A Victorian Anthology,*

1837–1895. Edmund Clarence Stedman. Cambridge, MA:
Riverside Press, 1895.

Sandburg, Carl (1878–1967). "Arithmetic."

de la Mare, Walter (1873–1956). "The Cupbouard." *Peacock Pie:
A Book of Rhymes*. Whitefish, MT: Kessinger, 2004.

Davis, Fannie Stearns (1884–1966). "For a Child."

Himiak, Lauren. "General Grant National Memorial (Grant's
Tomb)." http://usparks.about.com/od/nationalmemorials/p/
General-Grant-Memorial.htm

Lewis, David Levering. *When Harlem Was in Vogue*. New York:
Penguin, 1979.

Jackson, Kenneth T. *The Encyclopedia of New York City*. New
Haven, CT: Yale University Press, 1995.

Collins, George, et al. *Guastavino Co. (1885–1962) Catalogue of
Works in Catalonia and America*. Actar/Col.legi D'Arquitectes de
Catalunya; Illustrated Edition, 2003.

Guastavino IV, Rafael. *An Architect and His Son: The Immigrant
Journey of Rafael Guastavino II and Rafael Guastavino III*.
Westminster, MD: Heritage Books, 2009.

Parrish, Michael E. *Anxious Decades: America in Prosperity and Depression, 1920–1941* (Norton Twentieth Century America series). Actar/Col.legi D'Arquitectes de Catalunya; Illustrated Edition, 2003.

Stravitz, David. *New York, Empire City: 1920–1945.* New York: Harry N. Abrams, 2004.

Elliott, Debbie. "Wondering About Water Towers." NPR Radio, United States. 2 Dec. 2006.
www.npr.org/templates/story/story.php?storyId=6567297

TO FIND MORE ON:

City Hall Subway Station
www.transitmuseumeducation.org/trc/background
or
www.nycsubway.org/perl/stations?5:979

The Lindbergh Kidnapping
www.fbi.gov/libref/historic/famcases/lindber/lindbernew.htm

Johnny Torrio
www.knowledgerush.com/kr/encyclopedia/Johnny_Torrio

Marie Antoinette
www.smithsonianmag.com/history-archaeology/biography/
marieantoinette.html

The Kissing Post
www.history.com/content/ellis-island/ellis-island-tour/kissing-post

The Schomburg Center
www.ny.com/museums/schomburg.center.for.research.in.black.
culture.html

Grand Central Terminal
http://grandcentralterminal.com/info/walkingtour.cfm
or
www.guidespot.com/guides/next_stop_grand_central

AFTER WORDS

On a rainy night in April 2010, Brid Smithfork lay in bed moving only her fingers. Flashes of lightning followed by thunderous booms did nothing to move her when she was so deep in thought. Wind whipped her curtains inward because she had left her windows open. Yet the only thing she noticed was the object she held in her hands, a sumptuous wooden box with carved symbols on the border. The border design of the box was the same as the border design on the cover of this book. If you turn back to the front cover, you will see it.

Eloise and Julian left New York City to travel the world after the mystery was solved. Before they left, they gave each of the Smithfork kids a gift. Brid was given the beautiful wooden box. Each night, as if in prayer, Brid had stared at the symbols and letters, waiting for them to mean something to her. It was CJ who realized the left-hand column was a simple backward skip-three code. When he stuck to the letters, ignoring the symbols just on that left column, he got a message that was the title of one of the poems in Mr. Post's book. Can you figure out which poem it refers to?

The other three sides of the four-sided border were the puzzle that kept Brid awake. But on that night, just as thunder seemed to shake her room apart, she finally figured it out.

Beginning at the top of the border and reading left to right, she let each circled number relate to the stanza of the poem. The number that came after that related to a word on that stanza line. So the circled number 12 meant the twelfth line of the poem; the 3, the third word in that line. And that first word was *refuse*. She continued in a clockwise order to pull the lines from the poem to get the message, a message that would make her stay up all night, shaking with excitement.

She didn't know it at the time, but that message would launch her, CJ, and Patrick into a far more dangerous mission than the one they have just completed. They have an ancient door to break down, a door that is heavily guarded. There will be a lamp they have to free, a priceless lamp capable of mystical powers. And somehow along with this future mission, they still have to go to school.